MW00469128

The Hack

Moses Yuriyvich Mikheyev

First published by Moses Yuriyvich Mikheyev in November 2022

Copyright © Moses Yuriyvich Mikheyev 2022
All rights reserved.

Thank you for buying an authorized edition of this independently produced and published work. It is thanks to people like you that artists and authors everywhere can continue producing original creative works. Without your help and support, this novel would not exist.
Thank you.

ISBN 978-0-5786847-6-5 (paperback)
ISBN 978-1-7366408-9-0 (hardback)

No part of this publication may be reproduced, stored, or transmitted in any form or by any means, electronic, mechanical, photocopying, recording, scanning, or otherwise without written permission from the publisher. It is illegal to copy this book, post it to a website, or distribute it by any other means without permission. Names, characters, businesses, places, events, and incidents are either the products of the author's imagination or used in a purely fictitious manner. Any resemblance to actual persons, living or dead, or actual events is purely coincidental.

Cover design by Iliyana of Wonderburg Creations
Edited by Michael Waitz, William McLaughlin, and Andrei Semenov
Formatted by Polgarus Studio

Dedicated to
William McLaughlin and Andrei Semenov
Cheers to good company!

"One can deceive a person out of what is true. . .and one can deceive a person into what is true. Yes, in only this way can a deluded person actually be brought into what is true—by deceiving him."

"What if everything in the world were a misunderstanding, what if laughter were really tears?"

Søren Kierkegaard

Preface

This is a story about two writers. One is published, rich, and famous; the other, unpublished, poor, and unknown.

The rich guy is me, Max McMillan. I'm the greatest hack ever. I swear I am.

On most days, I walk around the house naked and publish bestselling books every few months or whatever.

The women come and go like it's a damned whorehouse. But I'm thinking about marriage. See, there's this girl. She's got a name, but I can't remember it. I call her Cowgirl Up. It suits her well.

I don't love her because I don't think I can. I only love five people: my poor writer friend, Jack, his wife, Jane, their two kids, Lucy and Nathan, and my little sister, Star. I hate everyone else. Jane is dying from cancer. And I hate cancer.

This is my story. It's absurd and outrageous. It really is.

If you're an asshole like me, you'll really love this story. I swear you will. It's that crazy.

And if you buy this book, I just might buy myself another Corvette. (Hell, at least you know that I'm also honest.)

Damn, I hate cancer.

The Truth

Part One

Chapter One

It's a well-known fact that humans are hypocrites.

Earlier today, I was on my way to shoot myself.

I had the entire thing planned. I wasn't going to literally shoot myself, like Ernest Hemingway.

No, shotguns and mouths and pulling triggers sound too horrific to me.

I was going to take the easy way out and just swallow a bunch of Fentanyl, listening to Future of Forestry's *Slow Your Breath Down* as the angels descended to take my non-existent soul. And, for those of you paying any attention: No, I did not envision myself listening to the album version of *Slow Your Breath Down*; I was thinking of the *other* version. The piano & strings version, to be exact. (I am not the imbecile you have made me out to be.)

I wrote my suicide note and included all the rejection letters from the three hundred large, mid-size, and small publishers (in that order). In short: I was done. I was *hasta la vista, assholes!* and ready to go. Unfortunately, just as I am about to head upstairs for that final cup of coffee and what-have-you, I bump into my little sister, Star.

"Heebuz Jeebuz," I mutter under my breath. "Crap!"

I don't tell her anything about any plans of mine, or notes, or, you know, rejection letters.

"Hey," I say to her. "What's wrong?"

She's depressed.

"I had intravenous ketamine treatments a few weeks ago," she tells me.

Holy crap. That's awesome.

"How did it go?" I ask.

"Not good. I didn't feel anything."

Okay. Not so awesome.

"Did it make you feel better, Star?"

She shakes her head and gives me one of those I-Just-Told-You-It-Didn't-Do-Shit kinds of looks.

I nod. "Ah," I say. "So it's not the miracle cure we have made it out to be."

She's very depressed, and so I sit on our couch. It's this big, ugly brown piece of crap that has a lot of history.

She follows me and sits.

She tells me I'm the worst therapist in the world. And she's right.

I've yet to meet a therapist who actually knew what the hell he or she was talking about. And since I don't know shit, I consider myself an expert.

I want to pull out a cigarette and smoke it right in the damned living room, but I have to remind myself that I don't actually smoke (only on paper). So, I don't pull a cigarette out, and I don't light it, and I don't blow smoke around the room and look all handsome and intelligent and sexy and shit. I'm just good old Me. Non-smoker. Very much *non*.

Well, if this were a movie, I'd pull a cigarette out. But, alas, the only movie I've ever starred in was a low-budget porno where I was the sole actor. Basically, I just masturbated on-screen and made three-and-a-half women happy. But, even then, I'm not sure what "happy" meant to them. Maybe they weren't happy. Who knows? I sure as hell don't.

Well, enough about pornos.

My sister looks all gloomy. She's sitting there on this ugly, brown couch and the entire house smells like a Temple. Incense is burning; lavender or cinnamon (or whatever the hell it is) candles are lit.

The only person not lit is me. My sister? Probably not lit either. None of us are drinkers (but if you read my novels, then you'd assume I'm a raging alcoholic). Every writer lies about everything, including me.

So, there we are, just two sober assholes; one trying to eat Fentanyl; the other, ranting about depression and ketamine treatments.

My sister says something to me, but I ignore her. (If you recall, I'm trying to kill myself as well.)

"You're the worst therapist ever," she says. "You're so bad."

I don't know what to tell her at this point. I mean, should I confess and say, "Look, I have ten milligrams of Fentanyl in my room. Come, let's split the damn thing and go meet Jesus."

No, I don't say that.

Believe it or not, I'm actually *a good therapist.*

The bad ones are the ones who give you enough Fentanyl to kill yourself with. The good ones? They give you just enough to make it through the day. And when your tiny dose is out, you come back for more. It's called supply and demand, capitalism, American business. How else do therapists afford their luxury vehicles? Think about that next time you park your hub-capped 1991 Toyota Tercel next to the 2023 G-Wagon when you visit your therapist.

So, it's either Fentanyl confession or I pull something out of my ass and help my sister out.

Since I like to think of myself as a good person, I choose the obvious road: the one less traveled.

"Look," I tell her, "life can be dark at times. Shit happens. You have to retrain your brain. You have to find a way to be happier."

"But I tried. You think I haven't tried?" she replies. "It doesn't work."

She's pleading now.

"I understand," I say.

She pulls out a journal from a bookshelf. It's got a million pages in it.

"Look at this," she insists. "That's me writing all of the things I am grateful for. Every single day."

She pauses. Then she adds: "And I'm still depressed."

Heebuz Jeebuz. This is making me look really bad. Amateurish even. Crap, I don't journal at all. Maybe I should try journaling?

I take a deep breath (mostly to give me some time to think of a comeback, you know). "Well," I say, exhaling slowly (really slowly, actually, as this gives me, Big Brother, more time to think). "Maybe," I add. "Maybe you should . . ." I continue.

Huh. That's a tough place to be. Shit. I might not know what to say here.

"Well," I say for the third time (but who's counting?), "maybe you should try some . . . "

Some what?

My mind is racing. I mean, here I was preparing for suicide and now I'm scrambling to talk my sister out of suicide. That's an incredibly difficult thing to do. Talk about irony.

Damn.

"Maybe you should try some . . . LSD."

There. I said it. What a wonderful idea.

Her eyes light up.

There. I did it. I really did.

I can pat myself on the back now and go back to my room and kill myself. My good deed for the day is done now.

"You know," she says, her eyes shining, "I read somewhere they're using LSD for depression." .

"Yeah," I say. "That's true."

"So, when are we doing LSD?" she asks.

This isn't how things were supposed to go. I was supposed to offer her a solution and head back upstairs and off myself. But now . . .

What to do?

"Well," I begin, buying myself as much time as I can with long, extended pauses and well-placed "Wells."

"I think . . ." I continue.

I do this for a few more seconds, filling the space between us with nonsense and gibberish—

And then I realize language is so stupid, we might as well stop talking and just hug one another and use telepathy to send I-Love-Yous and—

But it's Planet E—and this place is a shithole for most of us.

So here we are. Stuck with assholes who think language and stupid words solve problems.

But—and here's the real kicker—we believe in the power of words.

Abra—freaking—cadabra.

But nothing happens. It seldom does.

Words have limitations. Words can't solve everything.

In fact, I'd argue words cannot replace basic things, like human touch. You can hug someone for four seconds (if it's a second longer, then you're a creep)—and that could change their life.

You don't need to spend a thousand hours arguing with your girlfriend about a bunch of nonsense.

It's entirely possible that all she needs is to feel loved. And feeling loved is not inherently a language-thing. It's not always a word-centric activity. You can make someone feel loved in a second, in the twinkling of an eye, without uttering so much as a word.

For someone who writes as much as I do, you'd think I love the English language. But I hate it. I really do. I think language is evil.

In fact, I think I might as well shut up.

I mean, that's what I do. I literally shut up and hug my sister.

And I let her cry.

Damn, I hate crying.

Chapter Two

Star calls me up a few days later.

I try my best not to pick up. I'm working on the next great American novel. It's called *May My Exes Rot in Texas.* It's going to be great.

I ignore her.

She calls again. I see the phone ringing, and I'm really pissed at her for ruining my one chance at getting famous.

"What?" I yell into the phone when she calls a third time.

"What's with the tone?" Star asks. "Why are you so upset? Is something wrong, Maxy?"

She says it so sweetly, my stupid heart melts.

Immediately, I forget I'm writing the next great—and further east—*East of Eden.*

"Well . . ." I clear my throat, a smile finding its way to my lips. "How are you feeling?"

"Pretty chirpy," she murmurs. "I started going to church again. And it's really helping me a lot."

I pause.

Damn. She's always been an atheist like me.

"Like . . . as in . . ." I stutter, "the Heebuz Jeebuz stuff?"

"It's not Heebuz Jeebuz," she says. "It's Jesus of Nazareth. Jesus Christ. You know, the Savior of us all. Like, literally."

"Okay," I mutter back. "But, like, it's literally a fairytale. You know, it's all just evil religion. One second, the priest or pope or whatever is asking you for ten percent and the next, he's raping your son or daughter ten minutes before service."

"They're not all like that," she says. "You can't just dismiss the entire thing. Throw the baby out with the bathwater. All the hospitals and food pantries run by Christians. It must mean something, right?"

I pause. "Well," I mutter, "you do have a point."

"So, like I said, Max, I'm just going to try this Jesus thing out and see if it works for me. I . . . you know . . . I need it," she whispers.

It's one of those I-Really-Need-You-To-Support-Me moments.

I smile because maybe Heebuz Jeebuz can't save me, but—who knows? It might work for Star.

"Okay," I mutter back. "I'll go to church with you."

"Promise?" she asks.

"Sure," I reply. "Why not? It's not like I can't defend myself if the priest tries to rape me. I'll wear three pairs of underwear and tight, skinny jeans. He wouldn't be able to pull 'em off in a million years."

She laughs. "Very funny, Max."

"How . . . how have you been?" I broach the subject cautiously, like I'm walking on sacred, eggshell ground. I can almost hear the eggshells crunching beneath my feet.

She pauses. "Good."

"No," I whisper, "like seriously. You okay? No more depression or whatever?"

"Max! I'm not trying to kill myself anymore! I just told you. I'm going to church on Sunday. And you're coming with me."

I nod. She can't see me nodding but she's a girl. You never know with girls. They can see everything. It's like they've got cameras on phones but we guys don't know about it. Phones were invented by women for a reason: to spy on men.

Really, I don't know if women invented phones, I do know women give birth to all the scientists (male, female, and in-between) who do the inventing, so it's practically the same thing.

Just yesterday, I learned a woman discovered DNA. How's that for giving birth to scientists? Her name was Rosalind Franklin. I looked her up on Google—and Google never lies (except for when it does).

Enough about Google.

"Max, you there?" Star asks.

"What?" I say.

"You've been awfully quiet," she says.

"I've been busy thinking."

"About what?" she asks.

"About DNA and women inventing phones and scientists being born of women."

"What does that have to do with anything?"

She's obviously confused.

"I don't know, Star!" I mutter. "It's my mind," I continue. "I'm the greatest novelist *from the future.*"

"I know you are," she says, casually. "You're going to be remembered."

"You really think so?"

I need to hear it from her. If I don't, I'll certainly kill myself by the end of the year.

"Yes. Of course. Why?"

"Because I . . . I have my doubts. My mind. It wanders."

"All great minds wander," she says, matter-of-factly.

"But not like this."

I'm fishing for another compliment. I'm pathetic like that.

"Max, you're going to be fine. I read that draft you sent, the one called *Loaded Diapers*—and I died laughing."

"Really?" My eyes light up. "You really read it?"

"Of course. I even gave it to a few of my friends. They loved it as well."

"You really think I have talent?" I ask. I'm being serious now. Really. Maybe I do suck. But if your little sister doesn't think so, then maybe you don't.

"No. It's wonderful," she replies. "Everyone thinks it's funny. You know, you're a very funny writer. People like to laugh."

"But the agents and publishers," I mutter, shaking my head. I feel like a total sack of crap.

"Screw the gatekeepers," she says. "Screw them all."

"That's not a Christian thing to say," I begin.

"I haven't been baptized yet."

"Oh," I mutter. "Does it matter?"

"Of course, it does. That's when you're officially in."

"So, you really want to do this Heebuz Jeebuz . . . I mean Jesus Christ stuff?" I'm trying not to be sacrilegious— "for Star," I tell myself. Who knows? Maybe Jesus will fry people like me in a pan. I do hope they serve breakfast in hell—and I hope it's not me.

"Yeah," she says.

"Okay. I'll be there for you."

"I know you will."

"Love you."

"Love you too," I say, after a moment's hesitation.

"Bye."

We hang up.

I sit down on the brown, piece of crap couch to think.

I always have trouble saying, "I Love You." It's such a deep thing for me. Love is. To love somebody means something to me. It means . . . well, everything. It means I'd drop everything and do whatever for that person. I'd throw my novel in the trash and run after them till kingdom come. Love does funny things to me. I tear up when I say it. I cry. It's weird. Love is. I never say it to girlfriends. They're just girlfriends. They're not my wife. And I'd only say such a thing to my wife.

Love is powerful. It means I'm going to go on that walk with you even if my joints are aching and I just swallowed an entire bottle of Tylenol. Pain, arthritis, heartburn, cancer—love makes you push through all of it. Not just some of it. Love makes me want to push through those things. Most days, I just want to kill myself. But when I'm in love, it's no longer just about me, about how I feel; it's about *the Other*. What does *she* want? And what could *I* do for *her* today?

So, love is serious business for people like me. I may be the greatest hack ever, but I'm also a romantic. At least I'd like to think so.

Love. Strange how something so small—just four little letters—can mean so much. It means everything. I would lay my life down for those I love. I mean it. Really. It's why I hate everyone. I can't lay my life down for the postman or the Walmart greeter (no offense to you, wonderful people). But for those I love . . . Man, I'd jump right out of an airplane without so much as batting an eye.

I only love five people. That's it. It's an odd number of people. I can count them all on one hand. The people who matter to me. Jack, Jane, Nathan, Lucy, and Star. That's it. I don't even know if I love my parents. Maybe one time I did, but they abandoned me and my little sister when we were little kids. I suppose it's why I don't like adults all that much. Something happens when you grow up. You become an asshole. On Earth, half the people I love are under ten. Children matter. Children—I can love children. It's the adults I have trouble understanding. There's something wrong with all of them.

Sometimes I think I'm the only adult who really gets it. Maybe it's because I never did grow up. I'm the only one who understands children. It's why I'm going to write a children's book one of these days. It won't have any swearing in it or vulgar scenes. It'll be just pure bliss. It'll be for kids of all ages. One of these days, I'm going to write a book that's going to be remembered. I think I'm going to call it something nice. Something not-so-funny. I'll dedicate it to Lucy and Nathan. And maybe to Star (when she was a little girl).

"Yeah," I mutter to myself, still sitting on the brown couch. "I'm going to be remembered for something."

I always give myself inspirational speeches. It helps me get through the hard times. I know something is wrong with me. That much is obvious.

Damn, I hate talking to myself.

Chapter Three

I live in a small apartment in Orange County, California. I live with my sister, Star. She's a waitress at a fancy-pants restaurant and makes a lot of money. Much more than I do. I work at McDonald's. I hate my life. She comes home from four to five hours of serving and brings several hundred dollars in tips. I come home from McDonald's and bring several cum stains on my black pants. It's not really cum—more like mayonnaise—but you can't tell the difference. At work, we like to make fun of ourselves. Self-deprecating humor helps alleviate some of that blue-collar pain.

"What'd you do today?" she asks me one night.

I don't answer.

"Everything all right?" she says, taking a seat next to me in the kitchen.

"I'm depressed," I blurt out.

"Why?" she asks.

"I hate making McChickens all day."

She stares at me for a few seconds and then says, "Well, aren't you going to send that book to agents?"

"What book?" I nearly yell. I'm so pathetic when I'm depressed.

"The funny one."

"My entire life is funny."

"Stop talking about yourself like that," she says, all serious.

I look at my hands and hang my head low. I really want to eat Fentanyl right now and just disappear into eternity like a ghost or something.

She puts a hand on my shoulder and places a chocolate chip cookie on my head.

She smiles to herself. "You look good with that cookie there."

I take the cookie from my head and place it in front of me, right on the counter. I want to laugh but I'm depressed, and I hate everyone.

She gets up from her seat and walks over to a cabinet.

"You want some hot chocolate?" she says, pulling a container out and turning the kettle on.

I don't say anything. Sometimes I don't talk when I'm depressed.

"Okay," she says, getting two cups ready. "You're really not in the mood, are you?"

I shake my head.

She casts me one of those Well-It's-Going-To-Get-Better looks and smiles. "I met a famous person today."

Now I'm interested. I'm always more interested in famous people when my own life is awful.

"Who?" I ask.

"He's a famous writer. And I told him about you."

"Really?" I ask, depression disappearing faster than the mailman from your mom's room. "Spill the beans."

"Dean Koontz."

"You met Dean Koontz?" I ask, floored.

"Yeah. He's nice. He and his wife came to the restaurant today and left me a tip. Eighty dollars. It's always eighty dollars."

"Well, what did you say?"

The kettle goes off and she begins pouring boiling water into the cups. "I told him I had an older brother who was—I mean is—an aspiring writer. And he asked for a copy of *Loaded Diapers.*"

Now I'm on the edge of my seat. I'm hanging on every word. "And?" I barely whisper.

"So, I gave it to him," she says matter-of-factly, bringing the hot chocolate over and taking a seat beside me.

I take a sip. It's hotter than hell.

"Sheesh!" I say. "It's hot."

"Ding-dong. I just made it."

"Well . . . so," I stutter. "Did you hear back from him?"

"I just gave him the book like two hours ago, Max," she says. "Give it a week or two. Once he reads it, I'm sure he'll recommend it to his agent. And a few weeks after that, you'll be famous."

She says it so confidently, it's almost like she's reporting the news—what happened earlier today—and not describing some theoretical, highly unlikely scenario.

I sit quietly for a second, sipping on my hot chocolate. I'm starting to feel better.

"So," I say after some time. "You really think I'm going to quit working at McDonald's soon?"

"You're going to *buy* that McDonald's," she says.

I'm stunned. I never thought about buying a McDonald's. But listening to her speak, I figure I need to go to the bank or something and start getting the paperwork ready.

I get up. Like, shoot straight up.

"Where you going?" Star asks, astonished.

"The bank," I say.

"Why?" she asks.

"I want to buy that McDonald's."

"Right now?" she asks.

"Yes! I want to freakin' buy it so I can order a McChicken and never make another one myself. I want the McChicken fresh. I want the lettuce cold. And I want my buns toasted two seconds before the sandwich is made!"

"Sit down, Maxy," she says. "You'll get that McDonald's. You just have to be patient."

I take a seat. "You're right," I whisper. "I'm stupid."

"You're not stupid," she says. "You're just excited. And, besides, you're a go-getter."

"Damn right I am!" I say. But not as confidently as she does. Honestly, I'm on the fence about the McDonald's purchase. What if my book sucks? What if the sales tank? What if I get sued for plagiarism, like the hack that I am?

My face must have darkened.

"What's wrong?" Star asks.

"I just thought about, like, everything."

"Well, cough it up. What's 'I thought about everything' mean?"

"Well," I begin. "I just thought . . . what if my book doesn't sell? Like, what if everybody hates me?"

"It's going to sell," she says. "You're going to be famous one day. I know that. It's a fact. I even know when. Next year."

"But you said in a few weeks," I push back.

"Well, maybe I was being generous with my timeline."

I nod. "Huh."

"Trust me on this, okay?"

"Okay," I mutter, half-heartedly.

Her face lights up. "I have a surprise for you!"

She gets up and goes into her room. I hear her digging around in there—tearing things up, throwing things around, making noise like a real woman.

She returns with a box in her hand. "Open it up," she says proudly, handing me the box.

I open the box.

Inside I find a camera. I take the camera out and play around with it.

"Cool," I say.

"You don't like it," she says. "I can tell."

"No, no," I retort. "It's fine. I just . . . what am I gonna do with a camera?"

"Record a porno," she says, laughing.

"With whom?" I say. "I don't even have a girlfriend."

"You'll have one soon."

"When I'm famous," I whisper.

"That's right," she says. "When you're famous."

"But seriously. What's it for?"

She takes the camera and places it on a tripod a few feet away.

"What are you doing?" I ask.

"We need to get you ready."

"For what?" I ask.

"For your interviews," she says.

"What interviews?"

"For when you're famous," she says. "Ding-dong."

"But what am I going to talk about?"

I have so much doubt, anxiety, and so many sweat glands. My

God! My palms are drenched just thinking about cameras, interviews, and babes coming up to me with their tits exposed, begging me to sign them.

"I don't think I can be famous," I say. I say it so confidently, and with so much feeling, that I'm starting to believe I'm already famous.

"Stop being a drama queen," she mutters. "You'll be famous for *Loaded Diapers* and that's a fact. Shut up and listen to me."

I nod. "But what happens if . . . you know, I screw up? What happens if I stutter on *The Tonight Show* or something? What if they see me—like, really see me? What if my beard starts growing, right on the show and . . . and pimples just grow on my face?"

"You're not going to stutter on anything. A N Y T H I N G." She spells the word out for me. "Ding-dong." She laughs under her breath. "Idiot."

I'm dumbfounded.

I sit stunned in silence for a few minutes as she turns on the camera and gets the angles right.

"Okay," she says once she's done. "Let's pretend you're on CNN or Fox News."

"What if I'm on *Oprah* instead?" I ask.

"She doesn't do a show anymore," she says.

"Okay. But what if it's somebody else. Can we please not do CNN or Fox News?"

"Sure," she says. "Let's pretend it's . . . Reese Witherspoon!"

"Oh, yes," I whisper, "I love Reese!"

"Good! She's going to love you too once she meets you."

I put my hands together and face the camera. I have no idea what I'm going to say, but I need to start pretending.

"So," she says. "Let's begin with the most obvious question."

I nod. My hands are sweating so much, I think I'm going to drown. My sister is going to drown, too. She doesn't even have a lifejacket. My heart is starting to pound. It's so loud, I swear the neighborhood can hear it. I'm starting to get worried about my little sister drowning. I'm . . . terrified. That's what it is. I'm absolutely terrified of cameras. And my sister drowning in a pool of sweaty palm sweat.

"I can't!" I yell out. "I can't do this!"

My sister freezes. She glares at me. "Yes. You. Can." She says this through her teeth.

Now, I'm more scared of her than I am of her drowning. So, I stop sweating.

"Okay," I mutter. My mouth is drier than a ninety-year-old you-know-what. "Okay, I can do this."

"You will do this," she commands.

"Okay," I whisper. "I will do this."

"You have no choice. Famous people do interviews. And you're going to be famous."

"Okay. I'm ready," I say.

I'm not.

But if I say it enough times—out loud—I might be.

Star clears her throat and starts acting like Ellen DeGeneres. "Max McMillan! You've had a very successful week! Your book has outsold the Bible. How does that make you feel?" Star says this like she believes every word.

"I . . . I feel pretty damn good," I say, shyly.

Star glares at me. "You don't use the d-word on camera. Try it again."

"Okay," I say. "Okay."

So, we try it again. And again. And again.

Damn, I hate famous people.

Chapter Four

Star makes me do the interviews several times a week for a few weeks. She asks me the same questions every time and tells me the same thing. It's very repetitive. Out of frustration, I start to say things that make sense. I guess when you do something enough times, it becomes second nature.

Practice makes perfect. It's why a cheater who's been cheating for so long gets so good at it. You know, once you start believing your own lies, it gets much easier to lie. It's people like me, who never lie—*no, we do not*—who get into the most trouble. You ask me if I'm a virgin, and I'll tell you. I don't give a damn what anyone thinks.

One time, a girl asked me how many women I'd slept with—and I told her.

"Zero," I said, all cocky.

She was shocked.

"How in the actual hell?" she muttered in disbelief.

"I'm a romantic," I told her.

She didn't believe me. (Girls never believe you when you're telling them the truth.)

"You look like a cheat," she said. "A real good time."

She said this all sexy and shit, like she wanted to screw me right then and there.

But I was a virgin so there was no way in hell I was going to have sex with her.

Why would I? I just got done telling you I'm as romantic as they come. If I don't love you—and that takes time—I'll never do anything with you. Simple as that.

She began to twirl her hair and brush her hand against mine every other word, trying to warm me up to her.

I saw right past that seductive Cleopatra crap like I was Jesus equipped with MRIs from the future.

"I'm serious," I told her. "I'm . . ."

Anyway, to make a long story short, she let me go after that. Not entirely, but somewhat. You tell a girl you're a good guy enough times and you'll scare the living hell right out of her. Girls are terrified of good people. Trust me. All the bad boys I know have been married ten times over. It's the good who die young—and virgin. (They never tell you that part. But I will. Because I don't care. And I say whatever the hell I want.)

So, the girl gets scared and stops twirling her hair around me . . . *and I guess I start liking her.*

I'm telling you this because it's a true story. But you never really know with me. Sometimes I tell people things they want to hear. And if you want to hear something, you might walk away with an impression that comes straight out of your own head, having little to do with this book or me or whatever. People are like that—full of impressions coming straight out of their own judgmental heads. It's why I don't trust most of you. You won't understand me. And I don't blame you. The last time you said the truth, you were just a good kid trying to make it in this world. But you learned, didn't you? And so, you're here lying to yourself, lying to others. It's easy. Lying is. I get it. I lie to people, too. People like you. I don't lie to my friends. I don't lie to people I love. But you're just a stranger, and there's no way in hell I'm telling you the truth.

The truth is earned. You earn it from me. You earn respect. I don't hand it to you. And I don't think I'm ready to tell you the truth. That's why I'm lying so much—it's because I'm surrounded by people who hate me. And I hate you in return. I'm not lying about that. I already told you I only love five people, right? I wasn't lying about that, either. *I do love five people.*

But you aren't one of the five.

So, that means one thing and one thing only: I don't love you.

And I'm sorry about that. I wish I had more time. I wish I had more love in my heart. But I don't. I can only love five people at a time. That's my limit.

I suppose I should ask you a question as well. I don't know why I'm doing this, but sometimes I ask random people questions.

What's your limit?

Are you at five?

I don't know. Maybe you're kinder than I am. It's possible. Or maybe you're just lying to yourself. It's a lot easier to lie to yourself about how loving you are. Some of you who claim to love anything and everything are crueler than . . . well, Scarlett O'Hara from *Gone with the Wind.* She was a real piece of work.

A girl once told me she loved me—and then proceeded to act in the cruelest ways possible. I didn't stick around long enough to know what she did to people she *didn't like.* I suppose she buried them somewhere in her part of town, Seattle. If you dig up a body in your back yard there in the Pacific Northwest, it's probably someone she once loved—or didn't. You never know with people like that. They just bury people for fun, I guess. But I'm no psychopath, so I wouldn't know.

Like I said, I'm a good person. Well, not entirely, but I'm good to the five people I love. Isn't that enough?

Anyway, I hate talking about myself like that. I feel so vulnerable and exposed. You know, telling people things that are uncomfortable is never fun. On occasion, we all need to be reminded of how shitty most of us are. I suppose Heebuz Jeebuz was right about one thing: people need Jesus. They really do. Some of the folks you see in church would be serial killers without Him. I promise you that much.

But we should probably get back to my sister, Star. She's really the star of this chapter, the darling.

She has me do those videos over and over and over again. And, I swear, I get so good at it, I start to believe the crap I'm spewing.

And—get this—I become terrified. I'm so scared of lying to so many people.

"Max McMillan! Your book is now outselling *the Bible*, *Fifty Shades of Grey*, and *Poor Richard's Almanack* combined! How do you feel?!" Star says in that reporter-journalist voice of hers.

"I feel incredible!" I reply with a voice so artificially flavored that it might as well be Jim Jones' Kool-Aid. "And it's true! My book, the number one chart-topping *New York Times* bestselling, international sensation *Loaded Diapers* is breaking records stacked upon records that have been squared to the second power!"

"There are more books being printed—right now—than there are printers! Your book is truly a miracle! How can there be more books printed than there are printers?"

"I don't know," I say, truly dumbfounded. "I suppose not everyone is gifted in the mathematics department. Four out of three people are bad at fractions."

Star laughs. Giggles. Smiles. She's giddy as hell. She really believes the nonsense coming right out of her mouth.

"Tell us how you wrote the book. Where did the writing take place? Who inspired you? Do you have any quirky writing habits? Spill the beans like it's Taco Bell!"

I let out a laugh. "Wow, so many lights, cameras, questions," I say. "Well, where should we begin?"

"Let's start with the one the audience—which is numbering at twenty-five hundred strong just in the studio alone—an incredible number, obscene even! Wow! How did they fit these people in here? —who inspired you? Tell us. Please. We are dying to know."

I pause for a second because I want to be honest as hell. And, if you're famous, I suppose, you're never honest. So, this may be my last honest moment. Maybe ever.

"Come on, Max McMillan!" she says. "You've got the entire audience on the edge of their seats!"

"Well," I begin, tears welling up in my eyes. "I suppose it's *you*."

"Me?" Star asks, stunned.

"Yes," I say.

The room goes eerily silent.

"You," I whisper again.

Man, I'm so terrified of telling the truth, it hurts. My palms are sweating . . . and my heart is racing . . . and I'm swimming in emotions that are coming at me from angles I did not know existed.

"But . . ." Star begins, her lips trembling. She brushes a tear away. "But I . . ."

"You're better than most sisters I've ever known," I say, quietly.

"I'm . . ." she stutters. "I'm the only sister you have." She laughs nervously. You can tell she doesn't want to get the makeup wet with tears, but they come nonetheless. Just streaming down her face. Her hands are shaking as she tries to brush the tears away.

"You mean it?" she says, her voice quivering.

"Of course," I whisper.

She doesn't know, does she? How loved she is. How I worry about her. How she's one of the five people I love in this world. How I pretend to always have McChickens for her— "leftovers," I tell her—but really, I just buy them for her.

It's hard to be honest with someone you love. Mostly because once you start, there's no telling where it'll all go. You start talking about McChickens and end up with tears pouring down your cheeks, ruining hours and hours of makeup. That's what love is. It's *a makeup ruiner.*

She gets up from the director's chair and comes at me. Hugs me tightly. She didn't know it then, but she knows it now. She's made the top five. She's one of the five. And it's all on video. There's no way I can go back on this.

Damn, I hate loving five people at once.

Chapter Five

My sister takes me to church. On the way to church, my friend Jack calls me.

"Hey," I say.

"Hey," he says.

"I'm going to church," I announce.

"Church?" he asks. "But you're not religious . . ."

"Star is."

"She's not religious either," he replies.

"She is now," I state, matter-of-factly.

Everything these days is matter-of-fact for me.

"You serious?" He's very confused.

"Yeah."

"Okay. I mean, no offense or anything, but you were a raging atheist when we met. And, well—I suppose change is possible."

"Not for me. I'm just going there for support."

"Ah," he mutters. "Gotchya."

"Look," he says. His voice sounds sad. "I'll talk to you later. When you're not going to church."

"Sure," I say.

I hang up and look over at Star.

"How's Jack?"

"Fine."

"He ask about me?"

"Yeah," I mutter. "Just wanted to know why you're Christian all of a sudden."

"You didn't tell him."

"No. I mean, you heard me." I'm annoyed.

"Okay," she says.

I look out the window and try to think my way into a better attitude. I need to really focus on becoming a good person. I hate being nasty. Sometimes I wake up and I'm a real piece of work. Other days, I'm quite the grand pleasure.

"It's going to be fine, Max," Star murmurs. She's always trying to make me feel better. She still has no idea how bad things are for me—well, in my head, at least. I'm depressed. I'm such a pathetic human being, it's crazy. I don't even know how people like me exist. But we sure do.

My mind goes on these tangents. I don't know how to explain it, but I guess I'm a real writer. Words fill my head like a flood. When it's raining—in my mind—it's like pouring sentences. Imagine periods and commas and semicolons dropping out of the sky. Just falling hard like snow or something. And then you have random words being shot out like lightning bolts, right into the fertile soil below. And, of course, this mess then becomes a novel, or a poem, or some such thing. That's how writing is for me. It's a storm of letters, numbers, paragraphs blowing around in my head. Ten thousand mile per hour winds. Hail, rain, snow, thunder, lightning—all of it going off at once. And then a hurricane comes through and flattens the entire thing onto a sheet of paper, lays the letters down one at a time, and a sentence, a paragraph, a chapter is born. You let the storm roar for a few months, and you end up with an entire novel.

There's a hurricane going off in my head and I just want it to shut up already. I want the winds to stop blowing.

God, I think, *if I could just off myself right now.*

I'm thinking such depressing thoughts on my way to see Heebuz Jeebuz with my sister. I suppose if He's real, I'll have some Come-To-Jesus moment and the storm will pass. But I've never had such a thing. Ever. It's why I'm an atheist. I don't believe it till I see it. My middle name is Thomas. I'm basically one of the apostles.

"Everything all right, Maxy?" Star asks. She looks worried. Worried about me.

"Sure," I reply.

"You're not lying?"

"Maybe."

"You don't have to lie to me. If you're not feeling well, I can turn around and take you back home," she offers.

"It's fine," I say. "Really."

There's silence.

"I mean," I begin. "I'm a little depressed."

"Why are you depressed?"

"Oh, I just . . . you know . . . don't feel like being much of an asshole today."

"Well, that's a good thing, isn't it?"

I shrug. "Maybe. But it makes me feel like something's wrong with me."

Star parks the car and shuts off the engine. She turns to me. "If you're feeling up to it, let's listen to the sermon and see how it goes."

"Yes," I hear myself say. "I think I need a sermon."

"Agreed."

"I won't believe any of it," I clarify, "but I'll definitely think about it."

We get out of the car and walk into the church. It's this massive, stadium-like building with a black interior and pipes that run above our heads. In the middle of this massive complex is a stage with lights, fog machines, and a bunch of AC/DC-looking rock stars. Rock music is blaring from the speakers. I can't tell if I'm listening to "Highway to Hell" (with the name of Jesus tossed into the salad like garlic croutons) or "You Shook Me All Night Long." In any case, I like rock music, so that makes me feel better already.

We take our seats. We're late. The rock concert is ending, and someone is making their way to the pulpit. It's a woman. She's wearing an orange hippie dress with enormous loop earrings. Her red, flaming hair is bouncing with curls. She's energetic as hell on stage—dancing, moving, floating, bouncing her way to the pulpit. I'm in love with her already.

"Welcome, Church!" she shouts. She has a nice voice. It's romantic. I detect a subtle Southern accent, and it reminds me of Georgia peaches. And, my God, do I love peaches.

I don't even notice it, but I'm clapping, smiling, shaking hands with strangers. Before you know it, I'm about as Christian as they come. If you had walked into church that Sunday, you would have thought I had been going there my entire life.

Star is smiling. She's laughing. God, she loves this woman.

And I don't blame her. I'm sitting ten thousand feet away and I feel like we're being intimate. One-on-one. It's almost like we're on a date and she's dropping magical secrets on me.

"The love that *gets* you married is not the love that *keeps* you married," I hear her say. "*One* act of cruelty destroys *five* acts of kindness. Don't be cruel." She's dropping truth bombs on me, and I'm just being torn to pieces right here on the spot.

Wow. I'm breathless.

Could a person be so insightful?

I need to start taking notes.

I pull out my iPhone and open Notes. I start writing. And I don't know where to stop. I feel like I'm just transcribing the entire sermon.

"Now, Church," she shouts. "We need Jesus to help us fix our cruelty."

I'm nodding. It's like she read my mind.

"You need a lesson in reorientation," she continues.

Reorientation? What's that?

"Look," she says. "We, human beings, think tens of thousands of thoughts per day. And what do we think? We think about repetitive things. The same things, over and over and over. It's the nagging, the Why-Don't-You-Do-Your-Own-Laundry already! It's the Is-He-Cheating-On-Me? It's the I-Am-Worthless. It's the I-Am-Not-Good-Enough. It's the I-Will-Never-Be-As-Good-As-X. It's the same thought that starts in the morning and lasts well into the evening. And, like the proverbial pig returning to its own shit—yes, I just said shit during a sermon! —you keep returning to your filthy thoughts about your neighbor, about your partner, about yourself; a dog returning to its own vomit. That's what Second Peter 2:22 says. You heard me. That's in the Bible. And that's you, Church. And you've got to stop! You've got to stop thinking the same filth repeatedly. Stop it! And how do you stop thinking nasty thoughts?

You need to reorient yourselves. Reorientation. Here's the first lesson in reorientation. Redirect your thoughts, take your mind elsewhere. 'Well,' you say, 'that's easier said than done.' Oh, yes, I know that. I'm human too! Start praying The Lord's Prayer! Start praying the Serenity Prayer! Start reading the Bible! You've got to reorient yourselves. And it's not just once a week or once a month. You've got to reorient yourselves every day. You have ten thousand thoughts, and a few of those need to be your own. You've got to reclaim your mind. Reclaim your thoughts. Make them belong to you. You are not a slave to your mind; your mind is a slave to you."

She's marching up and down the stage, waving her hands, yelling at us, shocking us into reorientation.

"Repeat after me," she says into the microphone. "I belong to the Lord."

"I belong to the Lord," I whisper. I'm in a trance.

"My mind belongs to the Lord. My body belongs to the Lord. I am the Lord's."

Star and I repeat the mantra. It's empowering—and I say this as an atheist.

"Prayer is a form of reorientation," she continues. "It's why the monks pray all the time. They are out there in the desert, in the wilderness, praying. They are reorienting themselves to the truth. They know they are God's. They know they were made in the image of God. *Imago Dei.* You know this! You know this, right? Come on! But they must remind themselves every day who they are. It's not easy. Look, a wife needs to be told every day that she is loved. Not once a week, not once a year. Every day. You love her. You cherish her. And you tell her, 'I love you.' You reorient her every day to your love for her. That's reorientation. And that's prayer right there. The best kind of prayer. You hear me, Church?"

I hear *Amen!* and *Hallelujah!* and *Praise Jesus!* explode all around me. A couple in front of me embrace and kiss. It's heart-warming.

"Wow," I whisper to Star, "I actually don't mind this pastor at all."

She's beaming. "I told you," she says, squeezing my hand.

"I don't mind coming back," I say. "Not if it's this lady on stage."

"She's my queen," Star whispers in-between claps.

Everyone in the auditorium is clapping. It's loud as hell in here. An electric guitar amp turns on, reminding me that our ears are about to take a pounding.

"You want to go?" I suggest.

"Let's stay for worship. It's only a few more minutes."

I hate worship music, but I agree. "Okay."

Damn, I hate Jesus music.

Chapter Six

Star is pretty, maybe even gorgeous. I say this because they hunted her down and tried to get her on *America's Next Top Model,* but she turned them down. She's like that. Star is.

She's sitting in a coffee shop, drinking a non-caffeinated beverage. I'm a stimulants guy, so I'm hammering down one light-roast coffee after the other. It goes down like water. I feel alert, oriented, and ready to write a five-hundred-thousand-word novel in a single sitting.

She's playing on her phone, rolling her eyes, sighing.

"What's going on?" I ask.

"These assholes," she's saying.

"What?" I ask.

"They're trying to get me to sign all my rights away."

"For what? Who?" I ask.

"Oh, nothing," she says.

"What do you mean by 'oh, nothing'? It must be something if you're huffing and puffing about it."

"Ohhhhhh," she says, her mouth wide open as she's reading something on the phone.

"What's up?"

She finally looks up from her phone.

"I might be famous before you," she says.

"How so?"

I'm interested.

"*America's Next Top Model* wants me. They're gonna interview me today. Again."

"You've already had an interview with them?"

"Yeah."

"Why didn't you tell me?"

She waves a hand. "I thought nothing of it."

"That's great news," I say. "I mean, isn't this what you wanted? You spent years posting all those model-looking photos on Instagram . . ."

"Well," she begins, "I thought it's what I wanted but now . . . now that it's happening, I'm scared. They want me to pose naked."

"Well, isn't that what models do?"

She nods. "Sure, but it sounded cool until they sent me paperwork stating as much *in writing*. Like, 'You're going to be naked—and we own your nude pics. Bye.'"

"You didn't like that?"

"No," she says. "The thought of being seen naked by random people." She shivers. "It grosses me out."

"But all of your followers on Instagram? I mean, you have so many . . ."

Then she says, "I think I'm going to delete my account."

"You sure? That took years to . . . to grow, to build . . ."

I don't care for my sister's modeling pictures but I know how hard she worked to get to where she's at. Being a real model, wasn't that her dream?

"I guess when I did the interview and read the fine print . . ." She pauses. "I guess it's like when you dream of something for so long, the idea of it sounds so, so good. And then it happens to you, you know. And you realize, in a single moment, this gut reaction that comes out of nowhere, surprising even you: I don't want this."

"I hear you," I say. Then I add: "What if that happens to me?"

"It won't. You love attention."

"I do?"

"Yes, Max. You do."

I relax into my chair. "Huh," I mutter. "You really mean it?"

She nods.

"But . . ." I reply. "I'm scared too."

"Of what?"

"Of becoming famous," I whisper.

She waves a hand and laughs. "You're very different from me in that. You'd handle fame well. You love attention, and you've never been laid. This would be your dream. The getting laid part, I mean."

I laugh uncomfortably. "Maybe you're right."

"Look at you," she says. "You're basically a virgin writer on the cusp of success. A few girls, a few hits, and you're going to be a Casanova."

I nod to her Casanova remark. I might be stupid, but I'm not that stupid. I know all about Casanova. It's a salad. I always order one at Olive Garden.

"One of these days, you'll get laid, and you'll realize it's not everything it's hyped up to be. And then you'll become depressed, or become gay, or whatever. That's life. You live and you certainly learn."

We both laugh. It's an uneasy laugh, but we manage anyway.

"I don't think I'll ever become gay, but I suppose everything in life disappoints," I mutter.

"You've never been laid, so you've never been disappointed," she says. "You should be proud of yourself."

"Oh, I suppose I don't really care all that much. I'd rather sell a million copies than screw a million girls."

"That's the attitude," Star says, all serious. "You need that mentality going into fame. Bang girls, make money. That's what everyone in Hollywood says. You get caught up with the girls, and you won't have any money."

I laugh. "If I were to be that, you know, playboy or whatever, it'd really be a . . . a stretch. I'm not cut out for it. I, you know, I'm too romantic for one-night stands."

"Money changes people."

"You really think so?" I ask.

"Sure. Look at James. He hit it big. And we've never heard from him since."

James was Star's friend from high school. He played guitar and ended up with a folk pop hit. It wasn't a bad song, and it blew up like crazy. Next thing you know, everybody and their mom was playing it. It got a billion streams, and now he's in the Hills snorting coke off Latina pussy.

"Screw James," I mutter. "He never had money. And I had a feeling once he got it, he was gonna go off his rocker with the arrogance."

"Yup," she says, all sad and shit. "He sure went off his rocker."

"He really didn't call or write or anything?"

"Nope."

"Not even when . . . when you helped that song take off by giving him some modeling pictures for the album cover?"

"Nope."

"You should sue him. That's you on that cover. Make a million and run."

"I don't care to." She shrugs. "That's on him."

"He's an asshole, Star."

"So, what are you going to do with *America's Next Top Model*?" I ask, returning to the original discussion.

She shrugs. "I don't know if I want any of it anymore."

"Existential crisis?" I ask.

"Maybe."

"What about your identity? Everything okay with that?"

"I'm changing things."

"Like what?"

"Oh, you know, starting to reorient myself like the pastor said."

"So, you're serious about . . . Jesus?"

"Yeah."

"Going to go off into the desert like a monk?" I ask with a smile.

"It's possible. Why not? What's holding people back from leaving society?"

"I don't know. The red and orange notifications we get from Instagram and Facebook."

"The dopamine rush, the attention-seeking."

"The repeated thumbing of the refresh button. That's what it all comes down to," I mutter.

"Yeah, that—and drugs."

"Sex and drugs," I correct.

"No," she says. "All drugs, no sex. People aren't having sex these days. One-night stands don't count."

"Humans are little lab monkeys sitting around a banana-flavored soda machine, refusing to see *actual* bananas hanging from nearby trees above."

"That belongs in a book," she says. "I'd quote it."

I laugh. "Put it on your forehead and walk into a meeting with *America's Next Top Model.* The irony would be lost on them."

"We're such shit talkers," Star observes. "You and I."

"Thank God you didn't say 'you and me.' I would have corrected your incorrect grammar."

"You'd do it even if I were depressed?"

"Thank God you didn't say 'even if I was.' The 'were' there is in the subjunctive mood. The 'if I was' would be acceptable only in the conditional past tense."

"I take that as a yes."

"Of course."

We both laugh.

These days, we're always laughing. Most of the time, for *no reason* at all. It's better than being depressed, which often creeps up on you for *no reason* as well.

"You heard anything from Dean Koontz?"

Star's eyes light up. "Oh my God!" she exclaims. "I totally forgot!"

She digs through her purse. She hands me a sheet of paper.

"A few days ago, he handed me a sheet with his agent's name and number," she says.

I take the paper and look at it.

Sure enough, there's a name and number.

"Should I call her?" I ask, nervously.

"Right now?" Star says.

"Well, when?"

She shrugs. "I guess it doesn't matter. Dean said he enjoyed the manuscript. A lot. Thinks it'll be a bestseller right from the get-go."

"Really?"

"Ding-dong. If Koontz says it, it's happening. One hundred percent."

I nod. I glance at the number again and reach for my phone.

"I can't believe I'm doing this," I mutter.

"Only one way to find out, Max McMillan," she says, taking a drink.

My heart starts beating wildly.

"Damn," I mutter out loud.

I'm getting nervous again for no reason. My palms are so wet, I can barely use the phone. It's drenched in sweat.

I hand the phone to Star.

"You call," I say.

"Why?"

"My hands are all wet."

She takes the phone and dials the number.

The agent picks up.

"Hey," Star says.

The agent is speaking. I can't hear her, but she sounds . . . I don't know. Excited?

"Yes, this is Max McMillan's sister. I'll hand the phone to him right this second."

Star is smiling. Ear to ear. It's good news. It must be.

"Hello," I say nervously. I can feel the sweat running down the sides of my torso. My palms are sweating and now my armpits. It's a shitshow.

I can barely hold the phone. I'm sweating so much, it slips out of my hands like a fresh-caught Alaskan salmon.

It crashes to the floor with a loud smack. Screen-first.

"Shit," I mutter.

Star is glaring at me.

Here I am supposed to be a famous author and I can barely take a call from an agent.

I pick the phone up and say, "Sorry, my phone just fell."

"That's okay," the agent on the other end of the line says. She sounds sweet as hell. Immediately, I feel better.

"I'm so happy to hear your voice, Max McMillan," she says. "I read your book, *Loaded Diapers*. And I have to say: it is one incredible, hilarious, and original work. I absolutely found it entertaining, funny, fresh, and, most importantly, insightful. I mean, it has acute insights into the human condition! And at such a tender age! How old are you, by the way?"

"Twenty-one," I say, my voice shaky with unexpected excitement. I feel like a virgin getting laid. It's happening.

"Well, I must say: You're off to a great start! I can see this book really taking off. And when I say 'really,' I mean there's going to be an all-out bidding war from the Top Five on this one. We're talking a seven-figure advance, Max. And I plan to get it. I mean, I'll take twenty percent. It's more than other agents, but I'm going to take this one and really go to war. I mean, nuclear weapons, Max. We're going to start World War Three and you're going to help me nuke these guys, Max."

She says my name so many times, and so intimately, it's like she's been saying it all her life. I feel . . . at ease.

"Okay," I say.

I don't know what else to say.

"Okay," I repeat.

"Uh-huh," she says.

She really likes to talk. A lot.

"I'm going to nuke these guys—and when I do, there's going to be radiation and nuclear fallout. You're going to be grabbing Benjamins right out of the sky."

There's a brief silence on the other end of the line.

I'm stunned. I cannot speak.

"Max?" the agent asks. "Max, you have any bags? You'll need lots of bags for this one."

I picture myself with bags, catching hundred-dollar bills right out of the sky. It sounds like a dream.

"Sure," I say. "I have bags."

"Good," she says. "You're going to need them."

Damn, I hate bags.

The Deception

Part Two

Chapter Seven

My first encounter with fame didn't go as planned. I guess when you dream about being a famous writer, you tend to dream in particular colors. For example, when I thought about how it would be when I'd be famous, I never thought it would involve being stranded buck-naked in a Boston alley. But there I was, naked and vulnerable.

That night, I was giving a lecture at some library. I don't remember what the name of the damn place was, Metropolitan Something or Other. I was wearing a suit and I had my hair all gelled up, like some teenage kid trying out lube for the first time, right after discovering Latinas did porn. I had those blue eyes all girls go crazy over, but I never did appreciate them as much as they did. Did I say my hair was black, almost onyx? Well, there you have it. You know more about me than I know about myself.

So, suit and tie and gel and fame and all, I had just finished giving the best damned speech in the world. I left the library and walked down the dark streets of Boston. I talked about myself and my book, of course. And what could be better than that?

If you don't believe me—which you probably shouldn't—I was recently lauded by *The Washington Post* as "this generation's greatest writer." And, while I'm boasting (and, please do let me boast, because the rest of this story is an epic fall from grace), *The Paris Review* called me "a literary genius of almost-magical quality." I don't even remember what *The New York Times* called me, but it wasn't better than either of those two, so I promptly forgot it.

Now, and this must be made very clear from the get-go, I was a recent phenomenon. The subways and billboards still had my face plastered all over them. I think in one of the advertisements, you could see me smiling and holding a book. I never cared about smiling much—I, personally, find all people who smile for no reason guilty of subterfuge—so I never felt comfortable in that photo. And, if you looked at it just right, and with the right attitude, you, too, could see how fake and insincere my smile was. God, I hated that smile.

So, I walk out of the library, or whatever, and I turn a corner. Before I know what's happening, several dudes surround me. At first, I thought they wanted my autograph.

"Hey, fellas," I tell them, jokingly. "My hands are tired. I just got done signing a ton of books. But I'll be speaking tomorrow at—"

Boy, was I wrong or what?

"Wallet, keys, chains, anything valuable," the shortest guy in the group said with a sneer.

I was startled.

Holy shit, I thought. *These Bostonians sure do know how to ruin an author's wet dream.*

Being the cocky son-of-a-gun that I was—at least at the time—I tell the short pug, "Hey, fella, I got a few hundred bucks. You all hungry or what? I could buy you dinner. Hell, I'll even write you into a short story one of these days."

I wasn't even through speaking when the little prick threw a right uppercut and I fell to the ground like a dog playing dead for the first time.

I had the audacity to say something like, "Holy shit," on my way down. And, let me tell you, that didn't go over so well.

One of the gangbangers—a hunk of a dude who probably ate babies and steroids for lunch—kicked me in the groin. Then this dude had the balls to take my suit off. He really did. And as if that weren't enough, he ran a hand through my lubed-out hair and called me, "Cutie." I was about to sucker-punch the guy in the damn face, but then I remembered how my health insurance expired and the lady called me a week ago saying, "Your insurance expired, Sir. Would you like to renew?" I put the phone down because I was busy masturbating to some stupid porn I found online, and the poor lady was interrupting that. I told her I'd call her back. Well, I forgot. Sue me. I guess you think of stupid shit like that when you're down on the ground getting the daylights, taillights, and whatever-lights beaten out of you. Hell, I didn't want to end up in the hospital with no insurance. So, no sucker-punches for me. Oh well.

"Okay," I tell the dudes. At this point, I probably have like three blue eyes. I don't even know how many dudes there are at this point because my vision is all blurry and out-of-focus. "Can one of you tell me what is going on here?"

I guess these hobos don't speak any English because the next thing I know, I'm getting my ass dragged along the pavement. These hobos, I swear, are pulling my pants off. So, there I am, famous writer and all, wearing all my bling and all, getting my ass handed to me in some dark and pitiful Boston alley. God, I hate Boston. I don't think I've ever been back since.

Once the harassment is over—and they have my wallet, keys, Breitling watch, and clothes—I assess the situation. My hair—believe me—looks like crap, like I came out of some asshole just before getting robbed. I swear, if it weren't for that damn lube in my hair, I wouldn't have looked half as bad.

I need to get to the nearest open store, I tell myself.

But I look down and see that thing swinging between my legs. And, my God, I didn't know you could get an erection from all the excitement. But there it goes. I'm getting a hard-on in an alley.

Of all damn places, I think.

Now, the story doesn't even end there. It gets more outrageous. I walk and see this little store still open with its lights on.

I walk in—birthday suit and all—and I see this cute girl who's probably my age. And I'm like thirty-two or thirty-three at this point. And the horror that comes over her face. God, you should have seen it. So, I start laughing. I laugh my ass and balls right off.

She covers her eyes and screams. And I'm standing there, with an erection, trying to explain to her that I'm that famous writer, Max McMillan. I ask for some clothing. She runs away and grabs me something. She brings me yoga pants. I put them on. I guide her out of her dump-of-a-place and point to a bookstore that happens to be right across the street.

Thank God for bookstores. That thing saved my life like you wouldn't believe.

She looks and nods. "That," I tell her, pointing my fingers at the billboard like it's the holy grail, "right there is me."

In my excitement, I must confess, I'm probably yelling. The poor thing. I should go back and apologize. But, hell, I'm such an asshole. Or, at least, I used to be. So, I won't apologize. But maybe I'll send her a copy of my new book, autographed, narcissist that I am.

Fame gets to your head. It really does. Everybody says it'll never happen to them. You know, they say things like, "Oh, when I'm famous, I'll be the sweetest thing to walk the streets since Lily Collins."

And then they become famous. And they're the nastiest piece of shit like you wouldn't believe.

Anyway, I end up getting that girl's number. Her name is Lola Something or Other. (I can never remember names.) We still talk. She calls me occasionally. We talk about that night in Boston. We talk about the weather. Sometimes, when she's drunk, she'll mention the size of my—

But nothing ever happens. I don't even live in Boston, and I'd probably suffer from post-traumatic stress disorder if I saw her again. I doubt I'd magically get aroused by her or whatever. I really do doubt it.

But she'd probably like me. I tend to look fairly attractive when my hair is all done right, you know. Sure, I'm no George Clooney or Paul Newman, but I do look good when I clean up. At least one woman, my mother, thinks so. I guess that counts for something.

So, yesterday, she calls me. I pick up the phone.

"This is Max," I say.

"Hey," she says.

"Hey, Lola," I reply.

"You hanging in there? No nude scenes as of late?"

We both chuckle.

"No, no," I tell her. "I stopped getting naked in public."

Now it's her turn to laugh.

"How's Jack doing?" (Jack Gillman is my friend. A good writer. Much better than me. But he's still, as of now, unpublished.)

"He's all right. I saw him a week ago. He's working on another novel. He's calling it *The Final Romance*. It's quite an ambitious work."

"Uh-huh."

"Yeah," I say. "It's actually quite good. Really good if I'm being honest. It's so good, it'll never get published. It'd run the critics out of business. I mean, they'd have nothing to criticize. We need bad writers. It gives the critics something to do; endows their shitty lives with meaning."

"Yeah, well, you're not so bad," she says. "I mean, I enjoyed your last book."

"Which one?" I ask. Not that it matters, because I already know, but I try to be courteous and make conversation.

"*Loaded Diapers.* It was funny," she says.

"Yeah, that book. It was easy to write. The shittier the novel, the easier it is to write. And the more the critics like it."

"*The Great Gatsby*, anyone?" she sighs.

"Yeah," I say. "The critics didn't see that one coming. I mean, they trashed the book."

"I sometimes wonder if critics know how to read."

I laugh. "I've had my suspicions. Nobody knows anything, William Goldman once said. And he's right. The only people that know anything are critics—and what they know is wrong. But they don't know they're wrong. And that's what makes them silly."

"So, how is Jack? Did he submit again?" she asks with worry in her voice.

"Yeah, he did. But, like I said, he'll probably get turned down again."

Sometimes I wonder. If Jack would attend a Pentecostal church. If he could just learn to speak a little bit of that gibberish. I mean, if every third word made no sense. He could write then. And the critics would love it. They'd read that crap so fast and call it "a masterpiece of immense ambiguity" (or something like that).

"Have you looked at the latest Rotten Tomatoes stuff? The critics and the audience just can't seem to agree on *anything.*"

"Oh, yeah. It's like God these days. If the critics like something, it's guaranteed to be junk. You know, they're getting paid off or something. No way in hell people can be wrong all the time—and still have jobs. Imagine a doctor being wrong about ninety percent of her recommendations. I mean, she'd lose her license in a heartbeat."

"Maybe critics should be licensed," she says.

"Maybe."

We end up chatting for another five or ten minutes. Mostly trash-talking the critics. It's one of our favorite subjects.

Anyway, if the critics ever read this book, I hope they don't take things personally. I mean, it's not like they have personality to begin with . . .

When we have the time, I'll tell you all about the book I'm currently working on. It's called *Pick Your Ass, Then Pick Your Nose.* I have a feeling the critics will love this one. I'm thinking of dedicating it to them. It's full of all kinds of wonderful advice.

Damn, I hate critics.

Chapter Eight

Star comes over to my mansion. I have to say this because the last time I mentioned her I was a broke writer trying to eat Fentanyl, recording videos while pretending to be famous. Those were the good old days. They really were. Sometimes my eyes mist over just thinking about them.

Damn, I hate crying. But if you catch me in one of those emotional moods, I'm crying like you won't believe.

"Did you see yesterday's paper?" she says.

"No," I say. "What's in it?"

She hands me a copy of *The Wall Street Journal*. "Take a look."

I can't believe my eyes. "Max McMillan to be nominated for the Pulitzer," I read the headline out loud.

"That's ridiculous," I blurt out.

I can't lie to my sister. That'd be stupid. She'd see right through my bull. I don't reply to the headline with a "No duh."

"Well, ridiculous or not, somebody at the top wants you," she says, settling down into an expensive white couch I had custom designed in France.

"You sure it's not a joke?" I ask. I'm as pathetic as they come. I really do want to win the Pulitzer.

"I don't think so, but maybe some lady wants your dick inside her."

"A *quid pro quo*?" I say, eyebrows raised. I'm already fantasizing about it. You know, I've never been with a Pulitzer-prize committee woman. I have no idea how it'd go, but I'm sure I'd learn fast.

Star takes a cold drink from a refrigerated compartment inside the couch. She opens it and takes a long sip. She crosses her legs. These days, she's dressed in designer clothing and crosses her legs a lot. "I suppose you could call it that," she says, casually. "Everybody is paid off. That's life. None of it is earned."

Star is cynical these days. She works for my company, gets paid a ton, and knows the business inside out. "Back in the day, I had to hound a few journalists, pay for roundtrip flights to Bora Bora before they'd so much as cover you favorably," she recalls.

I take a seat next to her. "Yeah," I say. "We've come a long way."

"It's life, Max. That's how it goes. You suck and fuck, and that's how you end up on top. It was only last year that I found out you had to buy a slot to be an opener for a larger act. It's a bidding war even for that. If your band has the money, you can open for Taylor Swift. It doesn't matter if you're good or if you suck. Just cough up the million and you're the opening act. It's as easy as one visit to the bank."

"Yeah," I mutter. "The corruption runs deep in our part of the world, in our industry."

"So," she says, looking me over. "How have you been? It hasn't all gone to your head, has it?"

I shrug. "Who knows?"

She laughs. "Maybe a little?"

I chuckle. "Yeah, I suppose. I've become more of an entitled prick. But I'm working on it."

"What's that supposed to mean? You opened up a charity or something?"

"Thinking about it."

"What you gonna call it, *The Cancer Can Fuck Itself Foundation by Max McMillan*?"

We both laugh.

"Yeah," I reply, "that might be the name of it. Why not? It should go fuck itself, shouldn't it?"

"You have a point."

"You seeing any girls?" she asks.

"Somewhat," I say.

"Lola?"

We both laugh. She knows my Boston alley story.

"No, not Lola," I say. "We just talk on the phone sometimes. I have trauma from that experience."

"You haven't been back to Boston since, have you?"

I shake my head. "Nope."

"Damn," she whispers, "it really must have destroyed you."

"The entire city just reminds me of that, you know . . . that experience."

"I hear you," she says. "Trauma does that. Ruins entire cities for us. You get raped by some ex-boyfriend in Seattle and it'll never look quite the same to you. The entire city becomes 'City-In-Which-You-Were-Raped.'"

"Seattle's awful," I mutter. "I hate it."

"I hate it, too."

"The worst city I've ever lived in."

"Agreed," she mutters.

"The rain, the people, the traffic, the roads—everything about it sucks."

"Seattle sucks," she says.

"I love Los Angeles," I say.

"I know," she replies. "You've always had a soft spot for Hollywood beauties and balmy weather."

"There really are a lot of beautiful women in West Hollywood. The Spanish girls there are much prettier than they were in Seattle. The ones in Hollywood—they're charming, loyal, even kind. Not cold and cruel like the ones in *that* shithole."

She laughs. "Your ex-girlfriend really did a number on you, didn't she?"

"Yeah," I mutter. "Screw her."

"Well, at least you'll write about her. And when they write about you, they'll know what kind of piece of shit she was. That's what's going to happen. She'll be remembered for being the cruel, inhumane person she was. Nobody will remember her kindly. Nobody, Max. But they'll remember you. Because you're going to start that charity and you're going to write some incredible books."

I want to believe it, but who knows? "I don't know, Star," I mutter. "I believe you. Like, I do. I mean, I've had so much success already. But . . . I feel like there's this big hole in my heart, you know. Like something good and wonderful and fulfilling is missing. I lack something, but I don't know what it is."

She takes a long drink. "That's called living life and realizing you need Jesus."

I nod. She's really stuck with Jesus this entire time. I suppose it's good for her.

"Now," she says, "I know you're going to start with the entire I-Don't-Believe-God-Exists stuff, but hear me out."

"Sure," I say.

"It's obvious you were made for something more, something bigger, Max. Look at your life. You have it all and you're still walking around the mansion in underwear, eating a bag of Doritos, talking about how miserable you are. You really need to reorient yourself. Take a closer look in the mirror."

"Well," I say. "I've been meaning to do it, but it's much harder when you're this big. And how does God fit into all of this?"

"God fits into this because you're lacking something—and you don't even know what that something is—and maybe it's not of this world. You know? Like, I don't know. Maybe it's like you were born with a hole only God could fill."

"Star," I reply, "I've heard this all before. I just don't know if this stuff will work for me. I'm too . . . rational."

"What does that have to do with anything?"

"Reason. Rationality. Logic. Science."

"You need to live less with your head and more with your heart."

"I already do that!" I retort. "I'm always putting my heart first."

"Well," she begins, at a loss for words, "maybe you need a wife."

"Like a wife would solve my problems!"

She rolls her eyes. "Yeah, don't ever marry for happiness. You'll never find it that way."

"You have to be happy first, on your own, prior to any marriage. Everyone knows that. Happiness comes from within."

Star chuckles. "Remember Caroline?"

"Yeah," I mumble. "The girl from Montana, right?"

Star nods.

"Well, what about her?" I say.

"She married for happiness."

"It didn't work out?" I ask.

"Nope."

"Huh."

"She ended up taking this happy-go-lucky guy—Henry, I think—marrying him for money and his good sense of humor. Well, then they both became depressed. He was miserable with her. Not only did he not make her happy, she ended up making him as miserable as she was. He almost offed himself, last I heard. Ended up on Prozac, in therapy, and divorced. He's much happier now. Much happier without her."

"Sometimes a depressed person doesn't become less depressed in a 'happy marriage.' They just make the other person miserable as well. The world had one happy and one depressed person. After marriage, another depressed person joined the ranks."

Star smiles. "I felt bad for Henry, her husband. He was a good man. She just couldn't see it. A depressed person can't see shit."

"I remember you in your depressed days," I say, reminiscing. "Nothing I said really mattered. When you hit those lows, you went low. And everything became shit. It wasn't anything in the world itself. It was just your attitude towards it. You saw things as you wanted to see them. The glasses you put on were of a certain mood, a certain tint, and you wore them out."

"Yeah," she says, lost in thought, "now look at us. Just two legends." She pauses. Then adds: "We made it."

"If I were drinking, I'd say cheers to that."

"You haven't been drinking as much lately?" she asks.

"Off and on," I say. "I was pretty much drunk for an entire year after *Loaded Diapers* came out. Nothing but Hollywood parties, you know. Then I decided to take it easy. I may be dumb, but I'm not dumb enough to do something that'll land me in a hospital. You know I'm terrified of hospitals."

Star gets up. "I gotta run to another meeting. It's about a book you wrote, Mister," she says.

"Tell the idiots at the publishing house they better be wearing their socks for this one," I say, grinning.

Star looks at me. "There," she says with a devilish twinkle in her eyes, "that's the arrogant son-of-a-bitch I know. Maxy is back. And he's better than ever."

"You tell 'em that, little Sis!" I tell her on her way out. "You tell 'em!"

Damn, I hate publishers.

Chapter Nine

You might think I'm bipolar or something. Today, I don't feel all too well. I'm a little depressed and feel like being emotional.

For example, my friend called me. Jack did.

He says to me, "I've been working on *The Final Romance*, Max."

"Oh, yeah," I say to him. "I guess that's something."

I mutter some inconsequential things.

"Everything all right?" he asks, concerned.

"No, of course not," I retort. "Of course not."

"Well, what's the matter with you, you famous writer?"

So, I tell him.

"I'm not feeling good today is all. Just don't feel like my perky and usual asshole of a self. Today, I feel like I'm Jesus Christ or Gandhi or something. I feel like going out in the street and being crucified for something, anything."

"Why?" he asks. He probably already knows why but is just trying to be nice to a depressed person.

"Oh, I don't know, Jack," I confess. "Last night, I was feeling all dipper and dapper and stuff. Now, I woke up on the wrong side of the bed it seems. Everything has lost its glow. I can't even drink coffee without thinking about crying and stuff. I threw away the coffee grounds and cried. I cried because I couldn't believe it was over for them. They were such beautiful coffee grounds."

"Are you sure you're okay, Max?" Jack asks in that cautious voice of his. "I mean, you're taking your medications, right?"

"Oh, I don't know, Jack," I lament. "I've been feeling like shit lately. All the praise is getting to me. I know I'm a hack. I know it like I know the sun is up right now. And I just want someone to call me—anyone—and tell me that. Would you tell me I'm a hack, Jack? Please yell it in my ear or something. I need to hear it, I swear."

Jack coughs into the phone and laughs softly. "Okay, pal, here it goes. And you asked for it: You are a hack, Max. An awful hack."

"My God, does that feel good. Say it again. Only this time, say it louder. I don't know, shout it or something."

"You're a hack. A hack!" he yells.

"Okay, Jack. Now you're making me depressed."

I look around the room and sit down. "Shit, I do feel depressed, and a little dizzy," I tell him.

"Look, buddy," he says. "If you need anything, or anyone to tell you that you suck, feel free to call me."

I hang up the phone and look outside.

I'm still in my underwear, and I don't feel like putting clothes on.

I'm rich and famous, and everybody should be honored to see me in my underwear. But, oh, to hell with it, I still feel depressed and worthless.

"Okay," I whisper to myself. "I'll put some pants on and go outside. I need to go to the lake or something."

I live in a mansion. Did I tell you? I'm not kidding you. It sits on a lake. I'm not going to tell you which state I live in or anything, because I don't want you coming over and stalking me. (I did that once. Got stalked, you know. And it wasn't any fun.)

I live in this big house. Sometimes I have girlfriends come over. I don't ever keep girls around for very long. They all bore me in a few weeks. I trade them out like socks. I don't know. Maybe socks wasn't a good analogy, but it's true. I'm very insecure when it comes to women. So, I just let them all get away. It's easier that way. If a girl starts dreaming about marriage to me, I do something stupid. One time, I told a girl I was gay. And I had to pay a dude to come over and kiss me just to prove it to her.

She left after that.

I was depressed for a day.

Then I found another girl. Or, rather, she found me. I walked into a coffee shop, and they were, by chance, selling a book of mine. She recognized me. It was a collection of my romantic poems. It was called something like *Poetry for the Chicken Soul.* I almost got sued for plagiarism. I guess there's a book out there with a similar title. I didn't know. I don't read much.

I never liked books. They don't make any sense to me. I have a hard time keeping up with all the new words people keep adding to the dictionary or lexicon or thesaurus or whatever the hell they're calling it this year. It's like a full-time job being a writer these days. I swear. They send out a list of all the things you can and cannot say.

For example, if I were to say, "My day was queer today. And I didn't like it," I'd get sued by someone. Queer means weird. You know, as in, "That is a queer way of talking about chicken soup." But words keep getting added and changed and people keep arguing over what the word means this year. And now they have this new system in place called "Word of the Week." So, they're telling us, writers, which word means what during which week. It's getting out of hand. God, I miss the days when the thesaurus was updated by some fossil like once or twice a century. Now it's being updated every damn second.

So, the girl I was telling you about. The one impressed by my romantic collection of poems.

She asks me, "Hey, aren't you that famous writer?"

I say, "Yeah, I guess that's me. But I didn't check the papers this week. Am I still famous?" I ask this nonchalantly.

She says, "Oh, my God. You're so funny. Here's my number. Come over and screw me."

No, I'm kidding. She doesn't say it that way. Rather, she says, "Oh, my God. You're so funny."

At which point, I just slide a napkin her way and write a few numbers on it. I wink at her and tell her, "If you can figure out which number mine is, I'll take you on a date and write my next book in your honor."

She figures out my number and we talk. She comes over that evening. And I hate one-night stands. But, oh, to hell with it, after a few drinks, we screw like rabbits. And she's rather surprised that I'm damn good at sex, or lovemaking, or whatever-the-hell the Word of the Week is. I think it's the first time she ever cried during sex. Yeah, I'm not even kidding you. I have to give her Kleenex and hug her. She won't stop crying. Then she gets on top of me and just keeps on crying. But I don't mind, because she is doing things to me I have never experienced. I mean, I guess she's teaching me what a good cowgirl round of sex feels like. (I'm going to start calling her Cowgirl Up.) She cries the whole time, during sex, and I guess I get all sentimental and start crying, too. I get like that sometimes, all emotional and shit.

God, I don't ever want to have kids. I'd probably never stop crying. They'd come home and say, "Daddy, I got a C today." And I'd just start crying for no reason. I'd probably walk over to my wife or whatever and say, "Did you hear? Johnny got an A today." I'd fudge the grades a bit. And we'd both start crying together. I don't know. I don't think I'd be a good dad. I'd spend too much of my time wiping my eyes and nose. I'd be a wreck.

Anyway, I hope I didn't just get this girl pregnant. But if I did . . . God bless her.

I really don't know if I'd ever be a good dad. I feel like all the good dads are taken—and only applications for bad dads remain. I would apply for the job, but I don't know if I'd pass the background check.

I get so depressed thinking about all the bad dads that exist—who do dumb shit, who never say I-Love-You to their children, all those evil pricks—that I decide to go outside. I just need to take a walk and get some air.

I walk no more than twelve feet, and already I can see my little old lady of a neighbor pushing her oxygen tank and all, rushing towards me. She probably had a cane but threw it in the bushes right after she spotted me. I swear. She's probably trying to impress me.

"Go—od morning," she sings. Or croaks (depending on how you look at it).

"Good morning," I say. But I keep on walking. I'm making a beeline for the docks to see the ducks.

"Do you have a minute?" she asks.

Oh, my God. I swear I hear her pulling out books or something out of the—what the hell is that? —a trash bag? A purse? A parachute? Oh, my God.

Her hands are shaking and she's such a sweet thing. And I . . . I feel like such an asshole, I almost tear up. I walk up and help her with the books. Her little, fragile wrists are all veiny and stuff. And she's so awfully thoughtful, she even brought a permanent marker. And she's so, so happy to see me. Hell, at this point I don't even want to see ducks on the dock. I just want to see happy old ladies running me down in the streets.

I'm telling you: I really get excited over stupid stuff.

"How's your day going, madam?" I ask with the most charming voice I can pull out of my ass.

I sign a copy of *Loaded Diapers*. Then I proceed to sign a few other books. I can't remember the titles because then I'd be a real narcissist, and I'd have to shoot myself. God, I hate narcissists.

"Oh, it's so pleasant," she says. I can hear her dentures moving in her mouth. And the asshole part of me wants to reach in and adjust them. But, of course, no sane person would ever do that. And I'm quite sane.

I just look up at her and smile. And she smiles back. And, I swear, we fall in love right here and now. For the briefest of moments, of course. Then she coughs or sneezes, and her little dentures fall out, as I imagined they would, so I help pick them up off the ground, wipe them down using my clean, Versace shirt, and hand them back. I even help find her lost cane in the bushes.

No, I'm not that good of a guy. I'm only jesting.

We say our goodbyes, and I'm sure I even catch her tearing up a bit afterwards, but it may be allergies. Who knows?

Sometimes when you think someone is crying because they missed you so much, it's just allergies. I swear it really is.

Hell, I'm even guilty of it myself. I love taking girls on dates next to blossoming cherry trees. I do a little romantic picnic or something. See, I'm allergic to cherry tree pollen. So, I read the girl some poetry, straight out of my lame-ass hack of a book, and then I tear up. And the girl thinks I'm crying. But, really, I'm just a hack.

She holds me tenderly and says all kinds of sweet little things that ultimately mean nothing. And I tell her all kinds of sappy bullshit. And then we go back to her house or my mansion (or my "crib"—whatever the Word of the Week is), and we watch a movie . . .

And then we you-know-what. But I could be fudging my numbers even here.

With all the thinking that's going on in my little obnoxious head, you'd think I would be crazy by now. But, I swear, I'm perfectly okay. I walk over to the dock, as I promised I would, and sit at the end of it. My feet almost hit the lake waters, but I keep them swinging at just the right angle. No water on my shoes anytime soon.

The little ducks I was going to tell you about come out. They are adorable creatures. Ducks are. They can do all kinds of amazing things, like make you feel loved. One quacks a few times, probably saying something like, "Oh, that's that famous writer. Let's go chat with him" in Duck-Speak. I scoot over and the duck just plops down next to me.

"Quack," it says. "Quack."

"It's all right," I say. "I won't hurt you, little one. You can sit next to me. We could watch the lake and the sky and the sun together. Just you and I."

"Quack," he (or she, or whatever) says.

"I've never talked to a duck before," I confess. "But here I am, crazy old me, just talking to animals in public."

The duck remains silent. I can see it close its little eyes and enjoy the sun. Or maybe it's just enjoying my company. Imagine that.

I stop speaking. Maybe the duck wants silence. If it does, well then, so do I.

After a few minutes of sitting in silence, I figure it's unbearable. So, I get up and leave.

Damn, I hate silence.

Chapter Ten

Somebody set off a fire alarm at three in the morning. It must have been the neighbors. I was sleeping. Was is the keyword. Then I woke up and, my God, I'm not lying: I felt like committing suicide.

Screw it, I told myself. *Instead of committing suicide, I'm just going to save children out of a burning building and die that way. Heck, at least they'd say a few nice things about me.*

I'm a morning person. I wake up early. I hate waking up at night. So, when I say I am being Gandhi, I mean, *I am being Gandhi.* I, begrudgingly, begin to put my pants on. Then I spend twenty minutes figuring out which shirt to wear (you know, just in case the TV people show up and I'm dead and shit and I need to look good for the camera). I spend like thirty or forty minutes deciding between Yale and Harvard. I attended both schools and can't settle on one or the other.

All I could think about are headlines. "Yale alumnus dies in fire, saves twelve children." Or, better yet, "Harvard alumnus dies in fire, saves twelve children."

I start to worry about what I would look like Out There. Sometimes I get like that. I worry about what others may think.

I start trying on various outfits. I mean, gosh, children are dying in a fire, and I must look good for the event. I mean, imagine if this goes on Instagram or, God forbid, it ends up on YouTube.

Of course, if I'm being honest, nobody really cares about children dying in a fire. Everybody just wants to give the impression of caring. It's like when we say, "How are you?" And someone says, "Good." They don't ever mean it. If you think about it, a lot of people probably answered that question with "Good"—and then went and hanged themselves.

People are weird.

But, honestly, I'm one of the few good people. I really am. I am up at three in the morning thinking about laying my life down for little brats that annoy the living crap out of me.

Like this one time. I swear. These kids came to my house, knocking on my door at two in the morning. Who does that? I guess it's a game called "Knock—."

Oh, whatever, I can't remember what the hell it was called. I have memory issues.

It's not my fault they made me this way. I mean, who wants to wake up at three in the morning and rescue children? Nobody. Except Jesus, or maybe a firefighter.

I'm neither a firefighter nor a hero. I'm just a good person tainted by little bits and pieces of original sin.

Finally, by five fifteen, I'm ready. I have settled on Yale. I don't know. Something about my undergrad Yale years makes me nostalgic.

I step outside, and when I do, I realize it's all over.

I ask the Little-Old-Lady-Who-Throws-Canes-in-Bushes, "Hey, madam, what happened here?"

She says, "Oh, the firefighter said it was just some burnt popcorn."

Burnt popcorn? You gotta be kidding me.

I'm so disappointed, I want to kill myself. But now I'm so angry, I won't do it. I had decided on how I would die: *a damn hero saving children from a raging, massive, hot fire.*

And now, little Miss I'm-Going-To-Ruin-Your-Party is telling me that I'm not going to die, much less die a hero? How dare she?

I want to slap the little old lady so hard, she is going to become young again.

God, now that I think about it, I'm just getting cranky. So, I pat her on the shoulder, sign another copy for her, and help her back to her house. I'm not going to be an asshole (at least not tonight). I'm going to save that stuff for later.

God, I hate waking up at three in the morning to save children from burning buildings. It's not easy being me.

(You're all probably wondering when I have time to write all the genius stuff I write. Well, welcome to my life. It's not easy being the most famous writer in the world. Not at all. I have responsibilities, too.)

Well, I have news for you: Jack emailed me today. I swear, it's true. I have no idea why he wrote me. I guess jealousy hasn't ended our friendship . . . yet.

I start reading the opening paragraph to his epic novel, *The Final Romance.*

> *The warm autumn night laid its blanket over the earth and brought with it memories of hearth and home. Beneath the stars, ones he could almost reach out and touch, Luke Anglewood sat, reading from an old book. A shiver near his heart reminded him of the one time he fell in love. He closed the book and lifted his eyes. He could see The Big Dipper and*

The Milky Way and a thousand other lights splashing across the dark waters of that night sky. Had he really forgotten her, and so soon?

It's stuff like this that I absolutely hate. Stars and shivers and stupid sappy lines that everybody has already used, like "the dark waters of that night sky."

Honestly, who am I kidding? If I were writing this introduction, here's how I would do it. And, of course, I hope you can see why I sell more books than he does:

Luke Anglewood sat on a chair in the middle of the field. It was a warm autumn night, and he was reading from an old book. He closed the book and began to think about the love of his life, Laura Smith.

I throw out half the shit Jack wrote—and make it worse.

Hell, who am I kidding?

They pay me the big bucks so I could take poetry and turn it into toilet paper prose. Stuff you can use three times a day, consistently, without leaving a rash.

And, as my agent tells me, make sure the prose is soft. They love that word these days. I'm not even kidding you. Last week, I spoke to my agent. And you want to know what she told me?

She said, "You need to write another novel. Make it about love. And make sure it's one of those soft romances."

That's exactly what she said. *Soft.*

What the hell does that even mean? The entire time, I was under the impression that women love things hard (if you know what I mean). (I wanted to write "wink wink" but that would make the entire thing in-your-face.)

Back to my introduction.

You might ask: "Why is Luke sitting in the middle of the field?"

Oh, but why not? First, it's to be understood that he is *seeing* the stars. If you live in the damn city, where all the light pollution pollutes the living shit out of the "dark waters of that night sky," you can't see stars. Period. That's a fact. The only way you can see stars is by running so fast, you run your damn head into a wall. There. Now you are seeing stars in the damn city. And it's not even evening yet.

God, I hate the pretentious pricks who live in New York. All these so-called editors. They have no idea what they're saying.

So, the only way Luke Anglewood could possibly see stars is if he's sitting in a chair in a damn field that is in the middle of nowhere.

Second, and this is important, Luke is sitting in a chair that is in an open field—at night, mind you—because it's *not what you would expect.* Who sits in a chair in the middle of a field in the middle of the night? Nobody. And, that, my friends, is called "the element of surprise."

I'm done trashing my poor friend's work. I could never write like him. I always tell him that. I mean it. I'm a hack. I know it. I'm not even ashamed of saying it anymore. I write stuff that is banal, boring, and bitchy. I have no idea how I do it—"nobody knows anything," William Goldman quipped—but I do it.

I finish reading the first paragraph from his epic novel and call him up.

"Hey, friend," he says.

"Hey," I say. "So, I just finished your book." (I'm lying. I only read the first paragraph. But why the hell does it matter? Nobody reads past the headlines and titles these days. Books sell with good introductory paragraphs. If Jack gets the first fifty words right, he'll have a bestseller on his hands.)

"Oh, wow," he replies.

He's happy. He knows I'm lying but acts like I'm not.

"So, what'd you think? I mean, I just sent it to you an hour ago. You sure you finished it?"

There's some doubt in his voice, but I'm a good liar.

"Look," I tell him, "it was unputdownable. Once I started, I couldn't stop. I read it from the moment I got the little bing-sound when your email came through."

I'm lying a lot at this point, because I check my email once or twice a week, and all my settings are set to "Do Not Notify." I have everything turned off. I just happened to check my email an hour or so after he sent it. And, to be honest, I was still reading the last sentence of the paragraph when I called him, and he already picked up—

Shit, I think. Realization dawns on me.

It's like he waits by the phone for me to call him.

Pathetic.

(That's what happens when you're famous and your friends are not. I'm such an asshole. I should be better than this. But—oh, to hell with it!)

"So? How did you enjoy the ending?"

"Ending?" I ask.

I didn't read the damn book, and here he is asking me about the ending. I open the email again and say some stupid crap that buys me some time.

"The ending was, and I know you're not expecting this, I mean, you who are such an amazing writer. I really wasn't expecting such an . . . ending."

I'm still scrolling through my emails.

Crap!

I can't find his email.

Oh, I deleted it.

I gotta look in my trash.

"It was something else. I mean, Luke. He really is a character. A real hero. I mean, a hero like you wouldn't believe. He really was something else. And the love story. My God, all that talk about stars and nights and fields and . . ."

"Fields?" he asks.

"Oh, you know what I mean," I say, brushing off his remark.

I find the email. It was in the trash. I open it up. I scroll to the end of the book. I read the last line. Damn! It's such a beautiful line, I almost tear up.

"My God, Jack," I say. "I feel like I finally understood it just now."

I'm not even ashamed at this point. I mean, at least I'm being honest with him.

I just understood the ending.

That is true.

And, if I'm being honest, I was getting all teary-eyed just reading that last line, so props to him.

"Yeah, it took me a year to write and rewrite that last line," he says, nostalgia creeping up in his voice.

"Well, I can tell. I read that last line and it made me cry. It felt like a year's worth of tears," I say.

I read him the last paragraph. It really is beautiful. Rich, gorgeous use of language. Something no one will ever appreciate (but I don't tell him that). I'm like Jesus. Bruised reeds I do not break. No siree.

"Thanks," he says.

In his voice, I detect pride. I'm glad he is proud. He should be. Another novel that is good. Fantastic, even. But, alas, one that none of these critics will read. Most of them can't even read English without Google Translate, anyhow. I don't blame them. Life must suck when you don't know the A-B-Cs and your job is to review long, thick books. I don't blame them.

"You're welcome," I say.

And, this time, I really do mean it. I guess getting all teary and shit makes me get all authentic and sentimental.

"Man," he says. "I'm so glad you enjoyed that book."

He sighs.

I wait and he doesn't add anything. "How's Jane?" I ask. (Jane is his wife. She's his high school sweetheart. She's also dying from breast cancer.)

"She's doing okay. We just finished another round of treatment. Chemo and radiation. She lost all her hair now." He starts to sob.

I don't know what to say. I don't like cancer. Who does? I don't even know what to say when people say things like, "I have cancer." Shit. I really don't know what to say. I'm such an asshole when it comes to words and people. But I never say anything when it comes to cancer. I can't. It's just not a good thing to say anything about. It's like nothing you say makes any sense anyhow. So, I just don't speak. I prefer silence when it comes to the subject of cancer.

"You still there?" he asks.

"Yeah," I whisper. "I'm sorry."

That's all I can say.

Sorry.

Sorry for what?

I didn't give her breast cancer. I'm not responsible for it. Hell, language and humans are so weird. Cancer just had to come and screw things up.

God, I hate cancer.

I get on my iPhone and look at my ApplePay account. I have a hundred thousand just sitting there. God, I hate cancer. So, I send him a hundred thousand dollars. I was going to buy another Corvette, one of those Z06s. With the rims and shit and the roof thing that drops. I forget what they call them. Convertibles, I think.

"Max," he says. "Did you send me some money just now?"

"Yeah, I did," I say.

"You know I can't have you keep sending me money like that. She's got health insurance. It pays for the treatments."

"I know," I say. "But she doesn't work, you don't work, and your two kids still need to have some fun." Cancer sucks.

"Well, sheesh," he says, a little more relaxed. "I guess thanks?"

"Yeah," I say. (Nobody really likes to talk about money, especially when they're receiving it from a rich asshole like me.)

"You still getting that Vette we talked about?" he says, changing the subject.

I want to be an asshole and say, "I just sent you the Vette money" but that would be mean, to make fun of a dude whose wife is dying from cancer, who can't even get a book published to pay for something, anything.

God, I hate cancer.

"Yeah," I lie. I'm such a good liar. I swear I am. "I'm buying it tomorrow." (I'm not. I don't have any money. My next royalty check for *Loaded Diapers* doesn't come in until the summer. It's spring now. So, I must wait, like, two or three months.)

"I'm so happy for you," he says.

I'm sure he is, but I don't really believe it. He must be jealous of me. I'm the rich and famous one.

"Yeah," I say, "I'm going down to Los Angeles to pick it up tomorrow. That one we looked at. The yellow one with the red interior and the black rims. It's also got that custom-colored red and yellow and black top."

I describe the vehicle inside out. I mention stupid things like how much horsepower it has, and how the tires have all kinds of special shit in them. Of course, I'm lying through my teeth, but it makes me feel like I really am driving it tomorrow. To be honest, I'm sure Jack wants to hear about cars and tires and Vettes and shit, because if I'm not talking about that, then we're talking about his wife dying, and it's like the shittiest thing to be talking about. I swear I hate cancer.

"Will you let me drive it?" he asks.

He's joking. Mostly.

Of course, I'll let the unpublished loser drive it. He deserves to drive it. I'll probably donate it to him, anyway. I'll write it into my will.

I plan on killing myself soon. I don't know how yet. But we'll get there, I guess. Before I do kill myself, I'd like to make the world a little bit better. I don't know how yet. I'm still thinking about it. Like, if I eat a lot of Fentanyl, I could probably die. But then I wouldn't want Jack's kids not knowing Uncle Max. I'm probably the best thing that ever happened to those two kids. They're coming over today. Lucy and Nathan. Lucy is four—and she's head over heels in love with me. And Nathan is eight. He's shy but he's a good kid. I like him.

I usually pay for anything and everything, as they are incredibly broke. I wrote them into my will. They'll get all kinds of money when I die. Hell, my death would be a kind of event, I guess. If you think about it just right, I could even become a kind of saint when I die. I mean, here I am thinking about killing myself and about and how I could impact the world, and I haven't even thought about how the two events could be related. I swear I'm so stupid.

The reason I haven't killed myself yet is simple: I'm still *thinking*. Still thinking about how I could make the world a better place. At this rate, I won't find out till a hundred. And, I figure, if I live to one hundred, I might as well just die naturally. I mean, I could probably get constipated. Or maybe I could sit on the toilet for a week straight and, once it comes, tear myself another asshole from the straining and just die that way. I think something like half of the people in old age die from constipation-related injuries. I read it in an article somewhere.

I hear a knock on my door. It's Lucy and Nathan. Jack is dropping them off.

I put on some clothes. (I was naked when talking to Jack on the phone.)

I open the door, and the two kids run in and each one attacks one of my legs and hugs me tightly. Lucy jumps up into my arms and hugs me so tightly, I swear she's trying to kill me and collect on the life insurance policy.

I don't trust kids these days.

You know, kids are incredibly smart now. I read about a two-month-old who assassinated her mother. I'm not even kidding you. Baby was a prodigy of sorts. It happened in Alaska. I guess the place is known for child prodigies. So, the two-month-old starts talking at like a week or something. By three weeks, she's already reading books. And when she finally does walk, she goes to the library on her own and checks out a book. (The father found out later, after his wife's death, what the title was. Now, I won't keep you all waiting. It was: *How to Kill Anybody and Get Away With It.* I swear babies are dangerous.)

Anyway, I say hello to Jack, but he's in a hurry. He leaves and I'm stuck with my two favorite rascals.

"Hey, sweetie," I say to Lucy.

"Uncle Max! Uncle Max!" she shouts. "Could we watch *Frozen*? Please! Please! Please!"

"No!" shouts Nathan. "You watched it last time on the big screen. I want to play *Call of Duty* with Uncle Max."

"All right," I tell the kids. "Let's just go to the store and buy another TV."

"The store!" Lucy shouts, excited.

"The store!" Nathan agrees.

I guess it's the store.

I let the kids hop into my Corvette, before realizing it's two of them in the passenger seat.

"Uncle Max?" Lucy says. She's got these huge puppy eyes that are the color of almonds. I swear if she asks me for an arm or a leg, I would probably give it to her.

"Yes?" I ask.

"Could I drive with you?" she says.

"Like, with me?"

"Yeah," she says.

"No, sweetie," I tell her. "You have to wear a seatbelt."

She starts crying. God, kids are so crazy. But I love them anyway.

"Okay, kids," I say. "Let's hop into my G-Wagon. It'll fit all of us."

They've never been in my Mercedes. It's really a piece of shit. I'll probably trade it in for something like a Honda Civic, or just gift it to Lucy or Nathan once they're old enough to drive. What is it? Twelve years old? I don't know. Fourteen? I can't remember. But the car would be worth shit in a few years. They'd probably be embarrassed to drive it. It'd be like the stupidest car to own in the future. The more I think about it, the dumber my thinking sounds. I'd rather gift them something better, something that won't make them feel all insecure like I did back when I was in high school driving a crappy Toyota Tercel that had half an engine.

We pull up to the store and I get the kids out of the car.

"Uncle Max," Nathan says. His eyes are glowing.

"What is it now?" I say, rolling my eyes.

I already know it's something stupid, like "Can we eat ice cream?" or something outrageous like "Can we go to Disneyland?"

"Could we go to Disneyland?" he asks.

How did I guess.

Lucy starts crying. Again. For no reason.

"I guess we could go," I say, shrugging.

I call Jack. "Hey, Jack," I say. "Kids want to go to Disneyland. Can I take them?"

"When will they be back?"

I look at the kids and they are looking at me as if I am Jesus or Gandhi or Santa or God (or all three, four, five—whatever the number is). (I don't like counting anyhow.)

"Tomorrow?" I say. I'm not even sure. I've never been to Disneyland. I didn't even know the place existed until Lucy or Nathan mentioned it.

Jack sighs. "Let me ask my wife."

Jack always sighs right before he says yes.

There's some noise on the other end of the line. I think I can hear Jane throwing up in the background.

God, I hate cancer.

I look at the two kids and wink. They know Uncle Max has got them covered. In their little minds, they're already in Disneyland. I guess that's what happens when you have an adoptive uncle who's a rich and famous writer. God, I wish I had an uncle like me when I was growing up.

I hang up the phone, once I get the okay, and look at the kids. They're staring up at me with those romantic and childish eyes that are ever hopeful and full of wonder.

I frown. And Lucy starts to cry.

So, I just stop pretending and shout with excitement, "We're going to Disneyland!"

Lucy keeps right on crying. At this point, I'm not sure if they are tears of joy or whatever, so I just pick her up, kiss her on her puffy and salty cheeks.

"Shhh," I tell her. "It'll be all right."

I give my babysitter a call. I have like twelve of them. I never trust babysitters. They're all crazy. I usually have like two or three. I don't know. I swear they don't ever pay attention to the kids. It's like they're all eighteen years old and can't lift their damn eyes from their stupid-ass phones.

"It's Max. You want to go to Disneyland for a few days?" I ask.

"Yeah," she says. "I can do it. Finals are over. I'll be there in ten."

Liz is twenty-one. She's a college student. She's unattractive, but I never tell her that. I think she's studying to be a doctor. She's poor and has average grades. I created a secret scholarship just for her. I called it *The Miranda Acres Scholarship for Struggling Girls*. I then told her about it. She applied. And she got it. Well, I don't know if she *got it* got it, but she certainly ended up getting it. It's what happens when you work for a famous writer. Scholarships just pop out of thin air like snowflakes or raindrops or whatever. I don't know where I was going with that.

I pick up the phone again and call Evelyn. "Hey," I tell her. "I need you to help me with the kids."

"Can't do it," she says. "Busy working on a research paper."

What a liar. I can tell she's lying. I swear I can hear her boyfriend screwing her. I'm not even kidding you. One time she brought her idiot boyfriend over and she was stupid enough to leave six dirty condoms on my bed. I promise you kids these days don't know how to clean up after themselves. I made her come back and clean. I swear if these kids reproduce, our society is doomed. But I love them all anyway.

I'm so stupid when it comes to love. I swear I am. I just love everyone for no reason. It's probably because I've never been loved in my life. Well, except for Star and Jack and Jane and Lucy and Nathan. I just love everyone because I know how much people need that shit. Besides, I'm a famous writer and all, so I might as well set a good example for the next generation of famous, Pulitzer-Prize winning hacks.

Research paper, my ass! I'm still hung up on Evelyn's comment.

Evelyn's probably researching which condoms tear in which hole and how fast. But I'm not judging her. I swear I'm not. I used to do that myself.

We get back into the car and head home. At home, I have Liz and Sarah waiting. (Sarah, my other babysitter, said she'd do it.)

"Get the kids ready," I say to them. (I'm a famous writer and I'm used to giving commands to all kinds of people. And if they don't listen to my commands, I don't know. I guess I do things myself then.)

Liz is on her phone. Sarah is on her phone. I don't even know if they hear me. I hate being ignored, but oh, well. Sometimes, even if you're hella famous, people still ignore you.

I get the kids ready—pack their clothes and dolls and snacks—and we all jump into my private jet and fly to Disneyland.

No, I'm kidding.

I'm not that famous. Plus, I just sent Jack the last money I had. Now I have to buy shit using my credit card, which, mind you, *does* have a credit limit. It's the little stuff that upsets me. I buy us first-class tickets only because I don't want the kids being miserable. (Of course, that's just an excuse. I'm a rich-ass prick who doesn't want to mingle with the poor people crammed in the back of the plane like twenty sardines in a can made for two.)

God, I hate poor people. It's like, are they serious? Why can't they all drive Lambos and C8s? The world would be a much better place if everyone would just be rich and pretty and in a C8. God, I swear I hate everyone. Almost as much as I hate cancer.

We end up going to Disneyland. I'll tell you about it someday. It was quite the event.

I mean, I don't do this often, but I ended up going to jail right after Disneyland.

And it's not what you think.

I swear it's not.

I just lost it. I swear I'm not having a mental breakdown or anything. I just got really, really upset when this fake-ass hack wanted to ruin my day with the kids. God, we were having such fun until this prick came in and wouldn't leave us alone. This prick kept chasing us around all over the park. He was taking pictures of us. And always apologizing. God, I hate people who take pictures of me almost as much as I hate cancer.

He kept saying, "I love you, Mr. McMillan."

He wanted to take pictures *with* me, *on* me, *by* me, whatever. I asked him to leave us alone. And this prick wouldn't leave us alone. So, after I've had enough, I punched him so hard, he fell out of a roller coaster and died. I swear. Little prick.

Heebuz Jeebuz.

I might end up going to prison. All because I punched an annoying prick in the face.

Damn, I hate Disneyland now.

Chapter Eleven

I said I'd tell you about my Disneyland experience.

Well, here she goes.

So, we're all having a wonderful time. Sarah and Liz, my two wonderful and unattractive babysitters, are doing their job today. Like, not just doing it partially and with that eye-rolling annoyance but are "actually" being pleasant and affectionate human beings.

It's hot here in California or Florida. I'm not sure where exactly. I mean, it could be *either-or* or *both-and.* Maybe we're in both states at the same time. I think it's California. I'm pretty sure Disneyland is in California. But I could be wrong.

And all I know is Lucy is having the best time of her life. She loves all the Disney characters, and she's in love with all the Cinderellas that pop up in the most random places. Every time I try to do something on my own, like stare at some attractive waitress and sign my autograph on her left or right breast (or both; sometimes, they ask for two autographs—and I comply); anyway, anytime I try to do anything suspicious, Lucy starts crying. She wants all my attention. I swear it's like she's madly in love with me or whatever. It's hard to breathe around her without making her upset.

When I walk with her, I give her my index finger and she holds onto it with this ferocity that I've only seen once or twice. I watched a National Geographic episode once. And it was about this monkey that could climb all kinds of places. I mean, it could climb up skyscrapers, right up the shiny windows. Anyway, that's the way Lucy is clinging to my finger. I swear she's in love with me. I don't know if she's a cyborg or a human being. Sometimes, I imagine she's half robot or something, and her hands and fingers are made from some crazy metal, like titanium.

I have a theory about Jack and Jane's kids. I'm pretty sure people who have cancer can't make babies. I don't know. But I've always found it odd that people who have any kind of disease have kids. If their bodies are diseased, why are they having kids? I just don't get it. I wouldn't be surprised if their kids were adopted from some agency. I don't know what they'd call the damn place, but I'm sure they wouldn't dare put "Kids for Cancer Patients" in the name. But, oh well, I do swear such a place exists. At least I'm fairly certain of it.

I also have another theory. It's entirely possible Jack and Jane's kids aren't even human. This one time, I swear, when Nathan was five or whatever, he played a round of *Call of Duty* and beat my ass. He beat my ass so badly, there was no way in hell you could convince me it was fair and square. I swear these damn kids are robots or something. You should have seen how he used the remote. It's like it was attached to him or something.

I don't trust kids these days. I swear I don't. Half the time, you don't even know if they're yours. I mean, how many of the kids living in American homes belong to their parents? Think about the last family you saw. Did those kids look anything like their parents? Probably not.

You know, at the hospital, kids are switched out all the time. I swear it's true. I remember talking to this nurse this one time, and she told me they had no staffing ratios. Like, one day, a nurse could have one patient for twelve hours, and the next day, she could have half the hospital. I swear it's true. Look it up. They don't have laws regarding safe patient staffing. The only law they have literally says, "hospitals should provide adequate staffing." What the hell does "adequate" mean?

So, these nurses are always running tired and late and have like zero time to take a piss. One time, I swear, I caught a nurse pissing in my urinal. It's like they don't even let these guys take a break or something. And, my real point is this: nurses are confusing your babies. They're mixing them up. It's not even their fault. They're so damn tired, have you seen the bags under their eyes? They mix babies up all the time. I asked a nurse once what the baby-mix-up rates were. You know what he told me—and it was a he (I didn't even know males could be nurses)—he said: fifty percent of the babies in this hospital have been mixed up.

Fifty percent?! Can you believe it?

Hell, I got so frightened by his statistic, I immediately called my dad's funeral home and asked to speak with dad.

The Funeral-Home-Dude says, "Your father died thirteen years ago, Sir."

I say to him, "I know, but this is important. Can you do like a séance or something? I need to speak with him."

He puts me on hold and asks around. I swear this guy is an asshole. I can hear it in his voice.

He gets back on the line and I can hear he's out of breath. I bet he went and masturbated to some nasty porn or something. No way in hell he's out of breath from asking around if they have anyone who could perform a séance.

"Hey," he says. "Yeah, strangely, there's this woman who could come by and do it. She charges one-fifty."

I laugh my ass off. "Tell her I'll pay three hundred."

I swear I hear him choking on the sound of money. "I'll give her a ring right now."

"I'll wait," I say.

"No need to," he says.

"I want to," I say.

"Okay," he says.

An hour later, after I shave and do chores around the house, I finally hear something on the other end of the line. It's some woman with a weird voice. The woman is saying all kinds of abracadabra weird shit. Anyway, I ask "dad" if I'm his child. And then "dad" says, "Yes, you are my son."

I tear up a bit, and I want to hang up the phone, relieved. But I don't. I'm a famous writer now, and I'm pretty smart. I speak with the lady again and I detect something very fishy. The séance lady isn't even a lady. It's the same guy who works at the funeral home pretending to speak in lady-voice.

"You piece of worthless shit!" I yell.

"Screw you, you dumbass!" he yells.

God, I'm so mad. I hang up the phone.

Anyway, I swear babies are swapped out in hospitals. No way in hell my dad was my dad. I look nothing like him. And he was hella dumb. My dad was. He couldn't even spell. How could someone who couldn't spell give the world a soon-to-be Pulitzer-Prize winning author? I swear my real dad was Ernest Hemingway.

I've done the calculations. I swear I have. If Ernest Hemingway stored some of his semen in a semen bank or whatever, I'm sure my mother, who worked at a fertility clinic, had access to his stuff, you know. I know it sounds crazy, but I think thoughts like Hemingway, and I even write like him. I mean, don't you feel it? You feel that Hemingway vibe, eh? I know I have it. If you don't think so, then you're not a real Hemingway fan, and you should go and shoot yourself like he did.

Anyway, Lucy is excited. She's holding onto my finger and we're busy having too much fun to pay any attention to the crazy prick who is cutting in line, trying to get to me.

Nathan is shy, as usual. I bought him a t-shirt that reads Disneyland on it. He's eating a popsicle and playing on his phone. Liz is on her phone, too, probably sending nudes to her boyfriend.

And Sarah is busy eating potato chips. I watch her from the corner of my eye. I want to tell her that the chips will clog her arteries, that she should care about her diet, but what I say instead is, "You should get a larger bag next time and share it with everybody."

She rolls her eyes at me and keeps on munching away.

God, I'm such an asshole. I shouldn't care about how others look or what their diets are. But I do. I'm such a *caring* person. I really am.

The prick finally makes it to us and starts snapping photos of me. "Mr. McMillan!" he yells excitedly.

I pull the hat down and make sure my shades are still on my nose. I tell him to shut up.

He keeps yelling anyway.

So much so, others start to take notice. I hear some dude behind me whisper to his girlfriend, "That's the guy who wrote that big-hit

Loaded Diapers." His girlfriend takes a selfie without my consent. I want to slap the phone out of her hand but think better of it.

The woman who was checking our wristbands and such hears Max McMillan is in line. Her jaw drops. I notice a change come over her. She drops everything she's doing and comes running my way. At this point, half the line has their phones pulled out and wants pictures of me, next to me, by me, with me.

I try to be nice and say, "Piss off," like three or four times but these pricks don't know I'm having a bad day, and that I don't want to sign any books or boobs or whatever.

I lift Lucy, kiss her on the cheek, and use her as a shield. I hope people can't see me now. I don't know if it's ethical to use little kids for things like that, but I never said I was an ethical person. So, use away I do.

Lucy wants me to put her down. But I tell her that Uncle Max really needs her to stay quiet.

The prick is basically in my face now. He keeps yelling things like, "You're my hero!" and "I love you, Mr. McMillan!" He's screaming so loudly, I swear people once-deaf can magically hear again. The deaf man behind me, I swear, I saw him stick a finger in his ear and swirl it around in there. I'm sure he *heard* something.

Sometimes, I think I'm like Jesus of Nazareth. Wherever I go, crowds gather. And then people magically get their hearing back from all the noise. I guess if I die, they could say I was a miracle-worker of sorts.

I tell the dumb prick to shut up. He doesn't listen to me. He keeps recording everything on his phone. I smack it out of his hand. He picks it up off the ground and keeps recording.

At this point, we're at the front of the line and we get on the roller coaster. He sits in front of me and turns around. He keeps recording us like he doesn't care.

Once the ride starts, I get so mad, I smack the phone out of his hand again.

It falls.

And the little prick is stupid enough to remove his safety belt and dive after it.

He dies.

I watch him fall to the ground like a stupid sack of potatoes. I cover Lucy's eyes and tell her to think about *Frozen*.

She does.

Anyway, they eventually take me to jail because of all the smacking I did today. Apparently, they are saying I was assaulting the guy.

Can you believe it? The prick wouldn't stop bothering me and I was the one blamed for it all.

Once they book me, I get to make some lame-ass phone call. I left Lucy in the less-than-competent hands of Sarah. I tell Sarah that if something happens to Lucy while I'm gone, I swear I'll smack her so hard, I'll end up in prison for a solid twenty.

Sarah says, "Okay." And then she also rolls her eyes and I almost smack her, but I'm not really a violent guy. I swear I'm not.

"Jack," I say.

"Yeah?" he says.

"I'm in prison." I'm lying out of my ass but prison sounds like so much fun. I mean, jail is like kindergarten for criminals. Prison is for people who are dangerous with pen or sword. I'm obviously the former.

"Wait. What?" he yells.

"Stop yelling," I tell him. "You'll wake up my roommate. He's probably a rapist or serial killer or something."

Jack says, "I'm not stupid, Max. You can't make phone calls from a prison cell. Not directly."

"Well, in this one you can," I lie. "I'm in a high-security prison." I'm lying so much, and I'm so good at it, he believes me.

"How are the kids?" he asks.

He doesn't even care about me. Here I am telling him I'm in a high-security prison and the first thing he asks me about is whether the kids are safe. I swear this guy wouldn't care if I died. He'd be the friend watching *Oprah* and eating bonbons. And when the TV lady would say, "Famous writer and legend Max McMillan is dead at 33," he'd yawn, switch channels, or whatever, and not even care. I swear I hate him.

"Jack, are you hearing me?" I yell. "I'm in prison. Come bail me out."

"Dude, calm down," he says. "What'd you do? Run a little old lady over?"

"No, I killed a man," I say.

"Sheesh." His voice is now getting serious. I'm really enjoying this now because it sounds so cool. Like, Jesus, how many famous writers have been booked for murder? Like, zero. And here I am, the first guy who actually killed someone on live TV or whatever. I feel like a dangerous criminal.

I look at the jail guard and wink at him. He glares at me. "Are you sure these cuffs are on properly?" I ask him.

He comes over and tightens them.

I say, "That's much better. Now, when I do escape, you can say you tightened the cuffs last. And, my dude, you did a good job."

He glares at me again and rolls his ugly eyes.

"Max, who are you talking to?" Jack yells.

"Stop yelling!" I say. "I swear the rapist is waking up in the cell next door. You want to be responsible for the next asshole getting torn? Let the poor son-of-a-gun sleep. Sheesh."

"Why are you in prison? Seriously. Stop telling me stories."

"Look," I tell him. And now I'm lying out of every orifice. "I swear they have special prisons for famous writers. They're worse than prisons for regulars, like assassins and rapists and mass murderers. Those are just regular prisons. I don't qualify for regular, Jack. You see, they lock us up like rats in cages. You see *Silence of the Lambs*? Well, I'm literally Hannibal Lecter. Except I'm significantly more attractive and I get more women."

Jack sighs. He's always sighing when he knows I'm telling the truth like Abraham Lincoln or Cato.

"Look, us, writers, we can escape anything. They know we have high IQs or whatever. It's like in the high eighties or something. Most people are in the fifties. I don't know, something like that. I'm a solid eighty."

I'm peacocking now. I'm hardly an eighty, but I do hit that when I'm next to cute girls. It's an evolutionary reflex. Girls love smart dudes. They really do.

"Look," I begin again. "We can escape anything. You give us a pen and we'll write our way out of prison. Any prison. Alcatraz. I don't know. I'll write a bridge into existence and walk right across the bay."

Jack laughs.

"Why are you laughing?" I ask. I'm literally offended that he's not buying my bullshit.

"What's your bail, Max?" he asks.

"It's ten thousand," I say.

"Okay," he says. "I gotta go. I'll stop editing *The Final Romance* just to do this. I hope you appreciate that."

"I do," I say.

I hear his wife saying something. She's probably worried about the kids. I haven't even told her about my theories—how the kids aren't hers. I just don't want to be an asshole to her. I'll let her know once she's dead. I'll whisper it to her at her funeral. I'll walk right up to her casket and say, "The kids aren't yours, madam." I doubt she'll believe me. But, hey, it's worth a try.

"Say hello to Jane for me, will ya?" I say.

"Okay," he says.

I hang up the phone.

"What are you doing now, Mr. McMillan?"

It's a different guard now. This guy looks friendly. I eye him. "Nothing—and you?"

He laughs. "I saw the video."

"Which one?" I ask.

"The one that went viral. The one where the guy jumps out of the roller coaster after seeing you."

"What?" I ask, confused as hell.

"They're letting you go," he says.

"Why?" I ask. I'm genuinely offended at this point. I thought I was a criminal who would be chained for life. And here they're telling me I'm being let go? How?

My throat goes dry. "Why?" I ask again.

"Because they reviewed the footage. The kid who was harassing you wasn't wearing a safety belt and he literally dived out of that thing of his own accord. The video just shows you smiling with that little girl next to you, and you raise your hands and then the kid's phone falls out and he plunges to his death."

"So, I'm a hero?" I stutter.

"I guess you can say that." He's smiling now.

"Why are you smiling?" I ask.

"Oh, no reason," he says. "There's just an entire crowd outside waiting for you. Lots of people came to see you. I mean, something like thirty thousand out there waiting for you to come out and sign their books."

I'm so astounded, I don't even know what to say. "Shit," I whisper. "Should I call my friend back and tell him not to come?"

"Yeah, you might want to do that."

I guess they check me out of prison. On my way out, they give me my clothes, my keys, and my wallet, and they let me leave with a tight asshole. I guess that's all that matters. No horror stories for me to write about. And here I thought I was going to be a famous criminal, like Bonnie and Clyde.

God, I hate city jails. They are so awful. They wouldn't even give me the pleasure of escaping.

The first person to hug me is my favorite rascal, Lucy. When she sees me, she starts crying. Some *New York Times* photographer captures the moment, and it makes front-page news the next day. The headline is "World-renowned writer McMillan released from jail, nation rejoices—all charges dropped."

I spend several hours outside the jailhouse signing books, boobs, and stuff. All kinds of people are crying. Everybody is happy to see me.

One old lady confesses that she burned all my books when she heard that I murdered a teenager. (I guess the rumor mill turned the prick into a teenager. Prick looked like he was at least thirty.) I hug the old lady. She hands me ten of my books, all brand-new.

She says to me, "After they cleared you of the murder, I knew I had made a mistake, so I went and bought all new copies of your work."

I smile at her and sign the ten books. Behind her is a twenty-something girl. She looks a lot like the old lady, but younger.

"Meet my niece," she says. "She loves your work, especially *Loaded Diapers.*" She winks at me. "You should meet her after," she whispers in my ear.

I sign a copy and leave my number in it. I guess if she wants to screw me, she could reach out or whatever. God, I'm thirsty for a blowjob.

I proceed to sign away. A few famous people show up. I see Leonardo DiCaprio in line, too. (He's scheduled to star in my novel-turned-film *Bathroom Stalls.*)

He gives me a hug and says, "Man, I'm glad you made it out of this mess."

I laugh and say, "Thanks for coming out."

He winks and says, "God, the movie is going to be so good. It's my favorite role. Ever."

I'm so happy Leo likes my film. I almost tear up.

"Thanks," I whisper. "You're the greatest actor of all time."

"Thanks, Max," he says, tears in his eyes. He really appreciates me saying that.

Then I ask him to step aside because there's like at least ten hot girls right behind him wearing shirts that read, "Screw Me, McMillan."

He winks again and mouths, "I brought them here."

I laugh my ass off. (He's always doing nice things like that for me.)

Once it turns dark, we all get into a plane and head home. Since it's already late, we all sleep at my mansion or whatever.

The next day, I wake up in the morning and realize I didn't buy the Vette I promised Jack I would.

So, I get on the phone and get to work.

I call a rental place.

"Hey, you guys got any Vettes?" I ask.

"Yeah, like a boatload of them," a dude on the other end says.

"It's Max," I say.

"Wait? *Theeeee* Max McMillan?" he asks, surprised.

"Yeah," I say.

There's a silence on the other end of the line. "Oh. Ma. God," I hear.

"Please come in, Max," he literally shouts. "Just sign a book and I'll give you whatever car you want. I'm the owner of the store."

I agree to it.

"Look," I tell him, "I need this car to be yellow and it *has* to have a red interior."

"We don't have that right now, but I know a guy who could make it red."

"How long?" I ask.

"Give us a few hours. Till noon."

"Okay," I say.

I make breakfast for all the kids. Sarah and Liz wake up late (as usual) and eat cold cereal.

"Sorry," I say. "I made breakfast at eight."

They don't care. I swear those two girls aren't going to get very far in life. They're always bumping into things, yawning, waking up late, and staring at their phones.

At noon, I get dropped off at the rental car place. I pick up the Vette and drive it home. I leave the kids with the two babysitters.

When I get home, Nathan asks me if he could drive the Vette.

"It's a manual," I say. He looks up at me as if he understands what the hell I'm saying.

Lucy comes up and takes my index finger into her little hand and squeezes it. "Uncle Max," she starts. "Could I watch *Frozen*?" I usually side with Lucy for two simple reasons: one, she's a girl; and, two, I never say No to Lucy. I don't think I can.

Nathan objects, but I tell him it's all right. He had all night to play *Call of Duty*.

Nathan sulks but I know he knows I'm right. I mean, I'm the one who is the famous uncle, not him.

An hour later, Jack and Jane show up. I show Jack my new Vette. He's happy.

"Wow," he exclaims. "Isn't she a beauty?"

I tell him I paid a hundred thousand for it. Of course, I'm lying, but he believes me.

"Wow," he keeps saying.

Deep inside, I'm laughing my butt off. I can't believe he believes me. I'm such a good liar. It's not even my car. God, people are so stupid these days.

I once knew a guy. He pretended to be some bigwig entrepreneur. He would only date supermodels and shit. He'd post all kinds of silly photos of himself and shit with these rich, cute girls all over Instagram.

You want to know how he got them all? The guy had zero talent. He just rented expensive cars and expensive beach houses. During the week, he was like some truck driver or something. During the week, he'd always tell the girls he was out in Tokyo or something ("on a business trip"). And they'd believe him. Of course, he was just in Kentucky delivering a load. (And not a sexual one, mind you. No pun intended there.)

I swear people believe anything you say these days. It's like the older they are, the dumber they get.

You have these old folks looking at Instagram profiles and shit. They're like, "Oh, my! He's got twelve million followers!" And you have some intelligent two-year-old take one look at that profile and say, "Fake followers. Next!"

I don't trust old people. They're so gullible. Everybody knows the Internet is as fake as firm double-Ds on a two-hundred-year-old chick. I swear the boobs can't be that hard at that age. But you can make old people believe anything. It's why you have these two-year-olds killing their parents all the time. It's like they're little psychotic geniuses. I swear. Did I already tell you the story about that one baby? My God, I think I did. Anyway, I don't trust people. They're all full of shit.

I once bought a million followers on Instagram or Twitter for like a thousand dollars. I ended up getting a million more followers for free after that. Just because all the dumbasses thought I was somebody special. Anyway, I guess I'm just a hack and nobody seems to know any better.

I've been a hack for so long, I'm an expert. I can fake my shit into any butthole. I swear people will take anything up their ass these days.

Jane starts crying. She's holding Lucy and is getting all emotional. Jack is right: cancer sucks. Jane looks like shit, but I don't say anything. It's not her fault. Cancer is such a bitch. It'll take supermodels and turn them into freaking Frankenstein's monsters.

Jane asks if I could take a picture of her with her daughter. (I still haven't told her about my theory. I don't think I will. I don't want to make her cry more. She already cries all the time.)

I take a picture of her, and I want to cry, too. God, she looks so . . .

(I swear I'm sending Jack a million next month so he can take her to see a plastic surgeon. I don't care how much it costs, but he better make his wife look like what she looked like before. Cancer is a piece of shit. Damn, I hate cancer.)

Jane holds Lucy close while Lucy points at me and tells her how much she loves me. I start crying. Before you know it, we're all crying together. Even Sarah and Liz join us and get all teary-eyed. (But, hell, who knows? It's still spring and maybe Sarah and Liz just have allergies.)

We all sniffle and whatnot. Before long, we decide to grab lunch at some posh café. I tell Jane I'm paying. She doesn't object these days. She knows it's going to be over anytime soon, and she doesn't want to waste time arguing with a stubborn rich prick like me.

I let Jack drive the new Vette that I recently "purchased." (He doesn't suspect a thing; he thinks it's mine.) He drives the Vette with his son. I let the two of them have father-son time (even though I'm no longer sure if Nathan is really their kid or some adopted cyborg).

I drive the G-wagon. God, I hate anything Mercedes manufactures. I swear it's the worst car company in the world.

We get the piece of crap from my house to the posh café without event. (It usually breaks down like once a week. That's basically what it's known for. The G-wagon. G for garage. It's always getting repaired in some garage.)

We all order pancakes and Jack starts getting emotional with us.

He says, "I want to just say thanks to you, Max, for being such a great friend."

I hate it when people talk about me in public. It's like, "Goddamn! I'm not even dead yet. Save that shit for my obituary or whatever."

I nod and mumble, "Thank you."

Lucy looks at me and says, "Uncle Max, you need to drink your orange juice."

Jane looks at Lucy and says, "Uncle Max is an adult. He can do what he wants, sweetie."

Jack returns to his monologue, obituary. "Max, it looks like the kids had fun with you. I'm glad you were able to spend some time with them, while Jane and I spent some time at the hospital."

He gets all melancholic when he talks about Jane. It's really cute, actually. I hope he doesn't realize how jealous I am of their marriage. I have nothing but hoes, side-hoes, and side-salads. I've never been loved in my life, so I have no idea what the hell he's talking about half the time.

He looks over at Jane and she looks at him. They act like we don't exist. Then they make out for like two minutes and I just look at Lucy and Nathan and tell them to finish their food.

I'm glad Sarah and Liz left. They don't have to see this soppy crap. They don't need their little delusions burst like bubbles. I'd rather have them believe in eternal love and stuff. Not this sobby, cancer-filled romance that I'm being made witness to.

God, I hate cancer.

Jane is kissing Jack on the mouth, and I'm just getting all sick of watching them because I know Jane will be dead soon.

Anyway, I'm glad Liz and Sarah are still stuck in their delusion that life is pink cotton candy and full of roller coasters and theme parks with sex that lasts from dusk till dawn and pussy that's always wet when it needs to be.

God, I hate posh cafes.

Chapter Twelve

I see Jack the following day. He comes over to drink some scotch with me. The kids are at home with their mom. I'm wearing a pair of underwear and just walking around with a stain right where my you-know-what is. I don't even care anymore.

"Another girl?" he asks, eyeing the evident stain.

"No," I say. "Just some good porn."

He laughs.

"What are you laughing at?" I ask.

"I don't know. I'm just not even amazed anymore. You never told me about jail."

"You heard about it, didn't you?" I say.

"Yeah, I did. I mean, it was all over the papers."

I pour us some scotch and take like ten shots on an empty stomach. Jack follows suit. We're both drunk off our eyeballs a few seconds later (we're drinking that Highland Park 25; it hits you like a train even if you just smell it, I swear).

Jack is smiling now. His face is red and he's loose as a goose. "Tell me about that cocksucker you killed?" he says, barely pronouncing his words.

"Well," I say. "He was trying to kill me. I swear. He was jumping in my face. Trying to take pictures of Lucy and me. And I just got really protective of the kids."

He starts crying and wraps his arms around me and then kisses me on the mouth.

"You're a good friend," he says. "There's not a single person in the world that is more honorable than you."

I don't believe a word he says, but I pretend to. So, I cry.

I hug him and say, "You know I'd do anything for you guys and the kids."

He puts my face in his hands and just looks at me. "You're amazing," he mutters.

I tell him about my jail experience and confess it was anything but an experience.

He laughs.

We take another shot.

I slide out of my chair and I'm on the ground.

Jack slides out, too, and we're both on the ground together.

"Max," he says, all serious.

"Yeah?" I drunk-stutter.

"Can I tell you something personal?"

"Sure," I say.

"I love Jane," he says.

I know he's serious.

"Of course," I say.

He looks at me and gives me this strange look. "No," he drunk-stutters, "You don't get it. I lo—ove Jane." He says it all quietly, like he's saying something sacred.

"I know," I say.

"No, you don't," he says. Then he adds with a quiver in his voice,

"You know, she's the only woman I've ever loved. Ever. I've never been with another woman. I'm not like you. I don't even know how I ended up sleeping with Jane. I thought she'd end up with some lawyer or doctor. Not some damned hack like me. Unpublished. Unwanted. No money. No nothing. Just a loser of a man."

I lay a hand on his shoulder. "You're not a loser, Jack," I say. "Look, you have two wonderful kids. You love them and they love you."

He nods and begins to sob. He puts his head in his hands. "I know, I know," he sobs. "I don't deserve their love."

"God, Jack," I say. "Get a grip on yourself. You're all right."

"No, you don't get it," he mutters. "I'll never amount to anything. I'll never be published." He looks at his hands. "All my life, I've tried to turn Jane into a muse. I've written my best work in her honor. And none of it ever gets published. None of it. It's like they don't want her to exist. It's like the universe hates her. Hates my girl. I don't understand why it's this way. Why? Why can't I get *The Final Romance* published? Why?"

He looks up at me as if I have the answers.

"I told you I could start a publishing house and get it published," I say.

"No, that would be too much. You've already done so much for us. That would be taking complete advantage of you. You'd be responsible for everything good in my life. And I would hate you then. You let me do this on my own. I have to get it published on my own. I have to. For Jane. My Janie."

I listen to him in silence. I don't know what to say.

"She's going to die soon," he says. "Maybe a few more months. It's not all working, you know."

I glance at him and then look away. I don't want to see him like this.

"I have a few months to publish this work. Before she—"

He starts to sob. His entire body is shaking, and I just hold him like a crumpled-up paper cup.

"It's all right," I tell him. "It's all right."

"I only have a few more months, Max. Just a few months. Just a few months to make Jane proud."

"Maybe I could do something," I say, softly. "Maybe I could call up agents and publishers and—"

He lays a hand on my shoulder and looks me dead in the eyes. "No, Max," he says. "I have to do something myself for once in my life. I have to."

"It's a good book," I tell him. "I could write the blurb for it."

He looks over at me and smiles. "Maybe I'll let you do that. Just a blurb. A short one."

We take another shot to that and pass out drunk on my kitchen floor.

Damn, I hate cancer.

The next morning, I wake up on the kitchen floor. My head is throbbing and my neck hurts. Jack is nowhere to be found. He probably walked home. I decide to go out to the lake and talk to the ducks or whatever.

I get dressed and head outside. My little old lady neighbor is out walking her little pooch.

She runs me down.

She's got a cane but I swear it's pimped-out. I think it's got diamonds and shit on it. I assume she's trying to impress me.

"My gosh," she says, out of breath. "I haven't seen you in ages."

I nod. "Yes," I say. "I've been on vacation."

"So, I heard," she exclaims.

She pulls a newspaper out of her parachute-bag.

"Look," she says, holding it up so I can see. "It's you."

I glance at the paper. It's the *Chicago Tribune*.

"What about it?" I ask, knowing this is the beginning of a long-ass conversation.

I try to take my mind off things by paying attention to her dentures. They're all lubed-up or something. They're not even making noise today.

She says, "Is it true?"

"What's true?" I ask.

"That you're a murderer?"

I think it over for a second. Then I exclaim, "Well, of course, it is!"

She takes a step back. "Really?" she asks, horrified. Then she takes another step back and stutters: "But how are you here, walking around?"

I can tell she believes everything I say. And, if I'm being honest, I'm sick of this old grandma chasing me around in the morning, asking me about shit I don't care to share.

"I escaped," I say as nonchalantly as possible. "Plain and simple. Escaped like a motherfucker." I say the last sentence with a serious voice.

She looks me over, examining me as if for the first time. Then she leans in and whispers, "I don't care what the papers say. I still think you're the greatest writer on the planet. You can come over to my place and hide if the cops show up."

She runs a finger over her lips and becomes quiet. "My lips are sealed," she whispers. "Sealed."

I'm sure she just wants me to come over and bang her because she hasn't been laid in something like sixty years. Anyway, I just tell her I appreciate her gesture.

"Good day," I say to her. "I have to go and put that brain to use."

She shouts after me, "I love you, McMillan!"

There it goes again. That silly phrase. God, I hate old people. If I hear another person say it, I swear I'm going to shoot them.

Just when I get to the lake, like a few seconds later, my stupid phone rings. I pick up.

"Max," I almost shout.

"Did I catch you at a bad time?"

It's Cowgirl Up.

An image of her ass flashes through my mind and I immediately get an erection. I'm in public. I don't even care.

"No," I say. "Now is as perfect a time as ever."

"You want to watch a movie tonight?" she asks. We never watch movies. We always end up screwing like rabbits twelve seconds into any damn show.

"What time?" I ask.

"Seven sound good?"

"Yeah, yeah," I tell her. "That sounds good."

"Should I bring anything?" she asks.

"No, why?"

"Oh, I don't know," she says. "Just thought I could grab pizza on the way."

"Pizza?" I say. "Hmm." Then I think about pizza after a good round of pussy. "Yes," I mumble. "Pizza sounds fantastic."

I scratch my nuts and glance around. There's old Grandpa Gene watering his dead flowers.

He waves at me.

I wave at him.

I put the phone down and proceed to scratch my balls. I don't care if Grandpa Gene is watching. He's so old he can't see crap from where he is. He's so blind, he still thinks his roses are alive—and there. (They're not.)

I feed the ducks while scratching away. It's been ages since I've been laid.

I go back to my mansion and watch TV. Then I take a nap. I wake up a few hours later and there's Cowgirl Up standing over me.

"You look cute," she says.

I rub my eyes. "Damn!" I say, "Is it seven already?"

"Yeah," she says. "There's a few slices of pizza left for you."

"You ate it without me?" I ask.

"Yeah. Why?"

"Oh, I don't know. I just thought we'd eat together."

She laughs. "You'll be eating pussy soon enough."

She's got all kinds of jokes. Cowgirl Up does.

I eat the pizza and ask about her day.

"It was awful," she says. "Had all kinds of mean clients."

"Uh-huh," I mutter while eating a slice. "Tell me about them." I say that to pretend I care. I really don't. I don't give two shits about her clients. I don't even know where she works. I figure she's a prostitute, judging by how good she is at sex. No way in hell a normal girl could . . .

"Oh," she says, playing with her hair. "Nothing really to tell. One of them wanted dental implants but his insurance wouldn't cover them, so he took it out on me."

"Dental implants?" I ask, eyebrows arched.

God, I had no idea she was a dentist.

Are all female dentists this good at sex and fixing teeth?

"Max, stop being silly. You know I have my own dental office."

"Oh, yeah," I mutter.

My God, what was I thinking hooking up with a dentist?

"It's been a long day. I just want to relax right now and have fun."

She's getting all sexy and I'm still nibbling on my pizza.

"Uh-huh," I mutter.

When did girls become so damn demanding? Always telling us men what they want and when.

So bossy. I love it.

She starts taking off her clothes.

Oh, shit.

She's really serious.

Her shirt is off, and her tits are all in my face.

God, I'm still swallowing pizza.

Next thing I know, her panties are on the kitchen table and she's already bending over.

Hell. This girl. I swear. Why doesn't somebody marry her already?

She's naked and bending over the kitchen table. She turns her head and looks at me.

"Meow," she says.

I take a sip of Pepsi and quickly start throwing my clothes off.

"Goddamn!" I mutter. "I'm harder than a physics exam."

She finds the joke funny and starts to giggle.

God, I'm going to go ham on her.

We do the deed. I don't even wear a condom. (She says she's a feminist and believes in the whole pro-choice thing. I don't really care what she believes. To each her own.)

After ten minutes of hard lovemaking, we move from the kitchen table to my room, where she proceeds to do some incredible things to me.

Once we're both spent, she lies on my chest and reads from my unfinished novel, *Snow in California*. It's the only one that I ever cared about. Hence why I never had the balls to publish it. It's a mature work, one the critics would trash. I'm terrified of them trashing my baby, so I just let the girls I make love to read it. They love it so much, it's insane.

It's like they go home and tell all their girlfriends about McMillan's "new and never-before-seen romance novel." And then their girlfriends knock on my door and . . . shit gets crazy then. I'll leave this one to your imagination.

I swear, I'm never publishing it. It's like a pipeline the size of Big Oil Texas that brings girls my way. I get so much you-know-what from this unpublished thing, it's crazy. I'm really making up for all the lost time.

You should read the comments about it on Reddit. It's like there's an entire community of women who hooked up with me and read selections. I swear they reconstructed like half of it already. I just might have to release it.

Snow in freaking *California*. Who would have thought? I counted the girls who made contributions to that thread. You want to know the number? You're gonna have to sit down for this and make sure your dick doesn't hear what I'm about to say.

Oh, to hell with it. I'm not going to embarrass you with my numbers.

I'm always fudging them anyway.

Nonetheless, I feel like a damned whorehouse.

Cowgirl Up looks up at me and smiles. "I love that last paragraph of chapter three," she says.

"Read it to me," I say.

I grab some cigarettes from a nearby drawer and light one up. I don't even smoke, but I do on occasion, usually to get laid. Women love guys with something in their mouths. It's like if a guy is caught in public using his mouth, it translates into something else. I don't know.

I cough like a dumb bastard, and blow smoke at the ceiling.

> *I remember the last time I saw you. You were holding a little umbrella in your fragile hands. Those hands once held a pen and wrote me letters. Love letters. Those hands—your hands—once held onto me. I'd do anything to become that umbrella for you. Oh, may it rain again—so that you may hold me.*

"You really like it?" I ask.

"Yes," she whispers.

Then she slides her tongue into my mouth, and we go at it again. Round six. I swear *Snow in California* is the greatest unpublished novel of all time. No question. At least in my humble opinion.

We have another round of sex, and at this point I am thoroughly exhausted.

I get up from the damn bed and use the restroom. I look down at my dick and, lo and behold, thing is as red as a sports car. I swear women drive me crazy.

Cowgirl Up meets me in the bathroom. I'm brushing my teeth.

She looks at me and says, "You have back dimples."

"Yes," I say. "I do."

"How sexy," she murmurs.

A second later, she runs a finger down my back and stops at my butt cheek. "I love your body," she whispers. "It's so much better in person."

I turn around, and at this point, I have another hard-on, and it's pressed up against her.

She meows like a cat.

God, she's a freak—and I love it.

We go back to my room and we're about to make love or whatever, and she says, "I can't believe you just bang so many girls. I mean, aren't you a romantic?"

The question takes me by surprise. I swear nobody has ever had the courage to ask me that before.

God, this will require a cigarette.

(I swear, I really don't smoke. I just want to act cool and say things that will sound believable. Everything is more believable if someone is smoking a cigarette.)

I light the damn thing and inhale some cancer-causing smoke.

God, I hate killing myself this way.

"Okay," I tell her. And I can tell she's looking at me all serious. Her breasts are soft lumps of clay, just sitting there. I look away because her sexuality is so alluring. "I once was in love."

She leans in and kisses my chest. Then she looks up at me with her large eyes and says, "Keep going."

I hate being so sentimental. I'm an awful human being and she wants me to talk before having more sex. I hate interrupting my sex. Hell, women these days! They're so awful.

I blow some smoke and look at the ceiling. "I once was in love with a girl. I spent a few years of my life chasing her. Devoted some of my poetry to her. Thought about her every day. Her name was Ruth. I loved her like no man ever loved a woman. I worshipped her. Everything I did was for her, in some way. We ended up dating for a little bit. Nothing too serious. Well, I was always the one who was more in love. She taught me that men should never love women. I learned that best from her."

Cowgirl Up nods. "And?" she whispers.

I exhale some more smoke. "And she cheats on me. I end up coming home to her one day, and there's another guy leaving. She didn't even care that I saw him or anything. I remember I couldn't walk home or drive home that day. A friend had to come pick me up. That was the only time in my life I ever felt dizzy, like my entire world was going black into swirling darkness. I drank for a few months. I think I even cried. Haven't cried since. After that, I realized it was mostly bullshit. Love, family, loyalty, values. Most of it. Just a crock of crap. I mean, don't get me wrong, some of it is real. Some people have love, like my friend Jack. But that's rare. Almost everybody I know isn't in love. It's all just, I don't know, some form of bullshit, I guess."

"Just one girl? All it took was one girl?"

"Yeah," I say. "One girl. Didn't take much to turn me into an asshole."

"And you've never loved since?"

"Nope. Never. I just bang until I can't bang no more. Then I send her home. If she likes me enough, we'll bang again. If not, I got another girl coming. It's an adventure every damn day."

"What about family? Don't you want to have kids someday?"

"No, I'm not going to be a good father. I'm an awful example."

"What makes you say that?" she asks.

I turn to her and shrug. "Look," I say, "I'm not an example. I'm not Jesus or Gandhi or whatever. I'm just a dude that got screwed over. And it's not my fault the girl I loved never loved me. It's all about her. Always has been; always will be. *Snow in California* is for her. I just can't get it right. That's why I'm not publishing it."

"Why can't you make it be about somebody else? It sounds as though you still haven't moved on."

I light another cigarette. I'm starting to get nervous as hell. I normally don't do pillow talk with girls I make love to. God, but I need this. Nobody really knows my story. They all think they do. I've buried the truth in a hurricane of words. That's really what I did. A novel every six months or so.

Damn, I hide a lot.

"I don't know. I've tried replacing her with somebody. Believe me, I tried. But I can't. I spent ten years of my life chasing her ghost. I try to find her in other women. It's unfair to them. That's why I just send them home. I screw them, love them, then I kick them out. I don't want them knowing."

"Knowing that you are capable of loving somebody else?"

"No! Knowing that I am always looking for Ruth. That's what I'm doing. I don't see you for you. I only see you as a vehicle for Ruth. It's not fair to you—and you should never pretend it is."

She looks at me longingly. "I could be your Ruth," she whispers.

"Don't say that," I say.

"I mean it," she says.

"Don't make me kick you out."

"Just try," she whispers.

This girl. I swear. I blow out the cigarette and stare at her hair. Her head is on my chest and she's starting to doze off.

I inhale her scent and realize she smells like peaches. That was Ruth's favorite shampoo. Effing peaches.

Crap. I swear this is why I hate everybody. I hate everybody because they always remind me of Ruth. Why did she have to go and put peaches in her hair? Crap.

God, I hate peaches.

I look at her blonde hair. I run my hand through it. She smiles softly and says, "Goodnight, you."

I say, "Goodnight."

I still can't remember her name.

I look at a bracelet on her hand and bring it to my lips.

I kiss her wrist.

She says something sweet like, "Thank you."

But I'm just reading the name engraved on the bracelet.

Jessica. That's what it says.

Jessica.

This entire time I've been hooking up with a Jessica?

My God, and I didn't even know it. I swear I'm the worst piece of shit you could ever meet. I'm famous and I get laid all the time. But, damn, women should really choose their men carefully.

I turn the lamp off and stare at the black ceiling. I can hear Jessica breathing. She's sound asleep. At least she seems that way to me. I don't know. I hate the idea of having someone tell me I'm wrong. I know I can't possibly love again. I only love Star, Jack, Jane, Lucy and Nathan. That's it. I don't love anybody else. I hate everybody, in fact. I have a soft spot for the ducks, of course. And I do enjoy my fans, from time to time. And, if I'm being entirely honest, I might like Jessica, too.

Not love, just like.

God, I hate peaches.

There was this one story I must tell you. It happened to one of my professors back when I was an undergraduate studying psychology. He told the class this story I cannot get out of my head. I've been thinking it over ever since.

He was in college studying biology or whatever. And he knew this one girl—her name was Linda or something. Anyway, he didn't really pay attention to her or anything. He never had any romantic feelings for her. And then, one day, he's out in one of the college buildings talking to a bunch of friends. And everybody used to call him by his last name, Moeller. They'd never call him Jim Moeller or James Moeller. Everybody always called him Moeller. So, he's talking to his friends—a bunch of loud-ass dudes—and somebody yells, "Moeller!" He turns around and looks at whoever is shouting his name. And as his eyes move over the crowd, he sees Linda standing there, looking at him. And in a single moment, in that very sudden instant, he falls in love with her. And what's funny is he knows she's going to be his wife. Just like that. One second, he's not even remotely interested in the girl; the next second, his eyes meet hers, and he just knows. It's like God comes down and says, "Yep. She's the one, Moeller." And there's nothing he could do about it. He marries her. They have, like, five kids together. Anyway, their story doesn't end so well. He loves her like crazy. He loses her—and all their children—in a car wreck. It's unfortunate because it seems like that's what happens to every good couple. If things are too good to be true, you better bet your ass they are not true—and it'll all be taken from you in a heartbeat.

Anyway, I've always been fond of his story. I've always wondered if such a thing, like love, was possible. I mean, to glance in someone else's direction and just know—truly know—that they are meant for you.

I'm thinking over this story, just lying in my bed, smoking a stupid cigarette—still pretending to, at least—when it happens. I swear it does.

Jessica moves in my bed, and I glance at her and notice for the first time how pretty her eyelashes are, and how her jet-black eyebrows seem to sleep on her face.

And I swear to God I hear what the hell Moeller talked about. I swear.

It happens just like he said it did. One second, I'm smoking cigarettes, thinking about something stupid—and the next, I know I'm going to stop all the stupidity and marry this girl.

Damn, I hate Moeller.

Chapter Thirteen

I wake up and Jessica is making me breakfast. I don't know why she's making breakfast. I didn't even give her the morning wood.

Well, not yet, at least.

Maybe I'll deliver the bone in the kitchen. God, I'm such an animal.

She says, "Hey, Sleepy Head! I made you breakfast."

She's wearing this sexy purple robe with little pink flamingoes on it. God, she looks as good as Marilyn Monroe and Betty Crocker. You know, that's like the best combination ever. Sexy-Kitchen-Girl is what I'm going to start calling her. No longer will she go by Cowgirl Up. I don't know if I'm falling in love but maybe I am. At any rate, I don't even care because it's my ass that's having breakfast with this beautiful thing.

"God, that looks wonderful," I tell her. And I'm being all sexy and classy, just winking at her and staring at her like I know something she doesn't.

"Why are you looking at me like that?" she asks.

I sit at the table and look at my bowl. God, it looks wonderful. Then I lift my eyes and look at Sexy-Kitchen-Girl again.

"What's the matter with you?" I joke. "You're the most beautiful thing in this room."

I have no idea why I'm getting all sentimental and romantic with her. I hate myself for it.

God, I should probably lay off the sexy-nice-guy shit and just resume Normal Activity Mode, where I swap the hoes out every two hours or so.

I keep telling her silly things like, "My God, you have the most beautiful hips in the world" and "Your cooking is better than my mother's." And this girl is blushing in colors that are as red as any Rudolph the Red-Nosed Reindeer. And she's really, really cute when she blushes. I think a part of me melts or whatever whenever she smiles at me like that.

You know what's crazy? What's crazy is how good it feels to make somebody smile like that. It's like our roles have reversed. I'm the little old lady chasing me down in the street, asking for an autograph, making a famous person happy.

Jessica doesn't even know it, but she's literally famous. I know you probably didn't see this coming, but Jessica has been a muse of mine for a very, very long time. And what's surprising is I didn't even know she was a muse of mine until about a minute or so ago. It's like I just glanced at her, and she changed. It's like Apostle Paul said, "in the twinkling of an eye."

I swear that shit is real. I have no idea how or why. But it's all true.

God, it must be my erection. Or it must be the food. Damn, women are always deceiving men, making us fall in love with them for no apparent reason. I mean, what kind of reason is it to fall in love with a girl who is (a) a dentist; (b) beautiful; (c) good at sex (like really, really good); (d) makes amazing breakfast; (e) and can wear a purple robe like she's Julius goddamn Caesar?

Damn, I hate purple robes with little flamingoes on them.

I swear I'm falling in love with this woman already.

"Is everything all right?" she asks, softly.

I put another spoonful of cereal in my mouth—and is it amazing!

"How did you pour the milk on this bowl of Frosted Flakes just right?" I ask.

She laughs. "Don't be silly, Max. It's just a bowl of cereal."

"My God, it's the best bowl of cereal in the world!" I tell her.

She blushes.

(I'm always making women blush.)

"Thank you," she mouths.

My! Her mouth looks so delicious from here. I swear, I want to kiss this Sleeping Beauty.

Shit.

I'm falling in love or something.

God, I hate Frosted Flakes cereal. I swear this shit makes you do stupid things, like believe a girl who made you the bowl is fated to be your wife.

"Why are you staring at me like that, Max?" she murmurs. Then she wipes her chin and looks at me.

I finish eating my cereal and look at her.

"I think I'm going to marry you," I tell her. I'm probably lying about it but I'm so damn good at lying, she probably believes me.

"Oh, wow," she whispers. "I mean, I don't know if that's such a good idea." She repositions her legs and keeps staring at me.

I realize she's got these big, pretty, green eyes. I didn't even know they were green. I mean, her tits and ass were always so nice. I swear, I looked only at them. But, dang, her eyes are so nice, too.

"Max?" she says.

"You might be right, Jess," I say.

She blushes. "Why are you calling me Jess?" she says.

"Why? I can't?"

"No, it's fine," she says. "I just—" She pauses. "I haven't been called that in a long time."

"Ex-boyfriend?"

She gets all serious. "Yes," she says.

"I'm sorry," I tell her.

She waves a hand. "It's all right. I mean, it's been three years, so—"

"What happened?" I ask. And I probably shouldn't ask stupid questions like that because most of the time the asshole part of me never means it. But here I am truly caring about this Jessica girl and am feeling like a regular human being who might be falling in love (a little).

"Well, I guess we just weren't right for each other. He was a nice guy. He really was. I think we just didn't get along emotionally. Like, he wasn't wordy or anything. He never talked about his feelings. It was always hard to figure out what he wanted. It's like he wanted me to read his mind all the time. And when I did something wrong, he was always the guy blowing up in my face and stuff. Then he'd say sorry and punch a hole in the wall. He wasn't really a bad guy, he just couldn't express his emotions. Always kept everything bottled up and expected people to figure things out on their own. And when I didn't—"

"God, that sounds like a piece of work," I say, throwing my napkin down on the table. "He sounds like he's got some kind of emotional issues."

"Yeah."

"You want someone emotional. Someone who cries and is able to talk about his feelings well."

"Yeah," she says.

"God, and who might that be?"

"Well—" she says.

"Oh, I think I might know of a guy for you. Jack Gillman!" I exclaim.

"He's married," she says.

"Yeah, I know," I say. "But his wife will be dead soon and—"

"How can you *fucking* say that??" she shouts, her face burning with anger.

There.

I must have said something stupid.

At least she can leave and go home now. I don't want to marry her. God, that was the stupidest idea I ever, ever had.

What the hell was I thinking? Marriage to a goddamn awful dentist? What a dumbass Max McMillan idea. I swear I'm as stupid as a pile of rocks.

"How can you be so emotionally insensitive, Max? How?"

She must be really upset, because she just stood up and threw a plate in the sink. I swear it broke.

I get up from the table.

"I think you should go," I say.

She's silent for a minute. Then she turns and says, "He used to say that to me, too." She wipes a tear from her eye.

"Dammit," I mutter.

"Thanks," she mutters and begins to leave.

"Hey," I tell her.

She's not listening. She leaves.

I hear her crying and she's packing her clothes.

I run upstairs to my room.

"Hey," I say.

She's really upset and she's not even looking at me.

God, I'm such a piece of work.

God, I'm such a piece of shit.

"I'll marry you," I whisper.

God, I swear I mean it.

She stops what she's doing and looks at me. She shakes her head.

"Max, I don't know when to believe you," she says. She wipes her cheeks and sniffles.

God, I love her sniffles.

"I don't want you crying. Ever," I say.

"You've made me cry more times than once," she mutters. "I just hid it."

"When?" I ask.

"The one time you left me in the rain when a crowd of fans ran up to us. We were on a date. And you conveniently forgot about me."

Ouch.

Shit.

"I did that, Jess?" I ask. Now I'm really feeling like trash.

"Yeah," she mutters.

She's sobbing again.

Tears are dropping onto the floor.

I come up to her and wrap my arms around her and kiss her soft neck.

"I love you, Jess," I whisper.

"But you always make me cry, and you make me feel like I'm not a good person," she sobs. She's shaking, and all I want to do is make her feel warm and loved and cared for. And, my God, all I want to do is make this girl stop crying because up until a minute ago, she didn't mean a thing to me. But now—I don't know.

I want to marry her—and now I think I want to have kids with her.

"I won't make you cry anymore," I whisper.

(But what I really mean to say is that I won't ever hurt her intentionally or whatever. I'll probably make her cry. Like, if she's having my baby or whatever. She'll probably be in pain during labor and she'll cry. And I'll cry, too. And we'll all cry together. We'll be a family that cries.)

She finally puts her arms around me and goes silent. And I just hold her like that and keep telling her that I love her; that she makes the best cereal in the world; that if she ever cries again, it'll be when our son or daughter or whatever is graduating from Harvard; that I'll finish writing *Snow in California,* and I'll dedicate it all to her.

She doesn't want any of it, she tells me. She says she wants to fall asleep in my arms and wake up in them too.

And it touches me for some strange, dumb-love reason, so I start crying too. And we both cry.

And she says, "I'll marry you, Max McMillan." And it's the most serious thing she's ever said in her life.

I get on my knees and ask her to marry me.

"Of course," she says.

But I'm so stupid, I propose without a ring in my hand.

What a dumbass.

I go to my closet and pull out this ring that my great-grandmother once stole from Queen Elizabeth One, Two, or Three. It's a huge diamond. I give it to her, and she starts laughing. (She knows the story about the ring. I wrote about it in *Loaded Diapers.*)

She puts her hands on her face and keeps saying, "Oh my God, Max!"

And I start grinning like a toothless two-year-old.

"I love you, Jessica," I whisper. And the asshole part of me is finally dead because I get Jessica's name right.

"I love you, Max McMillan," she says seriously. Then she kisses me hard, looks me in the eyes and says, "You'll never sleep with another woman again. And you'll always spend evenings with me."

And I think it's such a wonderful idea that I start crying again. And she's happy. And I'm just happy she's happy. So, I get even happier.

And the asshole part of me dies a little more.

I push her away. "My God, Jess!" I exclaim.

"What?" she asks, surprised. "We have to plan a wedding! Let's ask Star and Jack and Jane for help!"

"Let's put some clothes on first, silly," she says.

We put clothes on and head out in my old Vette. (I had to return the new one. But I might have to rent it again occasionally, to make it look like I own it. For Jack's sake, you know.)

We pull up to Jack and Jane's place and I make a mental note that I'm gonna somehow donate more money to them so they can buy themselves something that is more suitable to the likes of rich and famous people like me.

We knock on the door and Lucy greets us.

She's kissing me, and I guess I'm falling even more in love with people. I hug her and tell her to meet her new auntie, Jess.

"Auntie Jess?" Lucy asks, confused.

"Yeah," I whisper. Then I point at Jess and say, "She's going to be my wife."

Lucy starts clapping with excitement. She turns and runs back into the house, screaming, "Uncle Max is getting married! Uncle Max is getting married!"

Nathan runs up—and, at this point, we're in the house, but still by the door. He hugs me tightly and then jumps into Jess's arms.

Jess is holding Nathan, and Lucy comes running back, bringing Jack and Jane with her. She's pointing fingers and saying, "Mommy! Daddy! That's Auntie Jess!"

Jack and Jane are a little surprised, but they've met Jess a few times, so they know her.

"I heard the news," Jane says with a smile.

We all shake hands, hug, kiss.

They congratulate us and we start planning the wedding.

"Well," Jack says, once we're all sitting in their tiny living room, "I'm glad Jane and I can participate in this marvelous event." He looks at Jess. "I'm so happy for you two."

Jess sits close to me, and we hold hands and giggle like teenagers.

"So, where do you want this event to take place?" Jane asks, once everyone has settled down.

I look at Jess. "Whatever you want, honey," I say.

She looks at me and says, "Whatever *you* want, *honey.*"

So, we look at one another for a few more seconds. Then we get tired of looking, so I start kissing her. And it's like we're kissing for the first time. I swear, we are so in love, it's crazy.

"When do you want to have the wedding?" Jack asks, concerned.

Jess says, "This summer would work for me."

She looks at me and giggles.

And it feels like a thousand years of assholeness just made its way out of me. I feel so damn good, I think I'm going to marry this girl once a year. Hell, I would marry her once a month if I could.

"Hey, I have an idea," I say. Everybody looks at me and they know I have a great, soon-to-be-famous idea because I have a glow and spark in my eyes that only comes but once or twice in most people's lifetimes (more in mine, since I'm famous, and most of my ideas are impressive).

"Yeah?" everybody says in unison.

"Let's just get married once a month."

Everybody is listening now.

"What do you mean, Max?" Jess asks. She's obviously stunned.

"Well," I say, "I don't mind marrying you in multiple locations. We could say our vows once a month—for at least a year straight."

Jess looks at Jane. And Jane just smiles.

She's used to Max McMillan crazy.

"Sure, I guess," Jane says.

Jack looks over at Jane and he's laughing. "Honestly, if there ever was anyone in the world who could pull it off, it'd be you," he says to me.

I nod. "Why not?" I ask. "I love Jess and she loves me. We will celebrate this love once a month. Hell, I'll even write a book about it. I already have a title. *Twelve Weddings in Twelve Months: The Crazy and Unending Love Story of the World's Greatest Romantic, Max McMillan.*"

Jess laughs. She covers her mouth and giggles uncontrollably. "You're going to be the craziest husband in the world," she says.

I nod. "Duh."

Everybody laughs.

Lucy comes into the living room and jumps into my arms. "I want to be in Uncle Max's wedding," she announces. "I want to be his wife," she adds.

"Honey," Jane begins, "you can't be Uncle Max's wife, but you could be his flower girl."

I kiss her on her little forehead and brush her hair away. "Yeah, sweetie," I say, "you can be my flower girl."

She's so excited about this, she runs out of the room and heads upstairs to tell the news to her brother.

"You're going to be such a great father, Max," Jess murmurs. She leans in and kisses me.

I laugh. "I don't know about that."

I glance at Jess and see nothing but sheer admiration in her eyes.

God, I think, *how in the hell did I get to be so lucky?*

Everybody loves my idea of marrying Jess once a month.

Just as we get settled into it, my phone rings.

It's Star.

"Hey," I say.

"Hey," she says.

"What's up?"

"What's up with you?" she asks. "I heard you and Jess might be getting married."

"Yeah," I say, "I'm thinking we get married several times."

"Sounds about right," she replies.

"You don't think it's crazy?" I ask.

The kids in the background are making a bunch of noise. They're excited as ever.

"Are you at Jack's?" Star asks.

"Yeah," I say. "We're all here."

"Okay," she says, "I'll be there in a bit. Love you!"

"Love you!" I say and hang up.

"Star's coming over," I announce.

"That's great!" Jess says. "She's so sweet."

Everyone is excited to see Star as well, especially Lucy.

"Auntie Star is on her way! Auntie Star is on her way!" Lucy shouts while running in circles.

"Shhh, darling," Jane tells her. "You don't want to wake the neighbors up."

"But they're not sleeping, Mommy! It's too late to be in bed! Even I know that!"

Jess coaxes Lucy and seats her on her lap. She kisses her cheeks. "Lucy, sweetheart!" Jess says. "Star will be here soon, and you need to be on your best behavior. It's okay to be excited, just not too loud. Okay, sweetheart?"

Lucy nods. "Okay."

The doorbell rings and Star walks in. The kids run over to greet her, each one grabbing a leg and hugging it tightly.

"Aww," she says, "you two lovebugs!"

"Uncle Max is getting married!" Lucy whispers, trying her best to hush her childish excitement.

"He is," Nathan chimes in, as if the news needs confirmation.

Lucy has Star stoop low and whispers something into her ear.

Star blushes and smiles.

"What's she saying?" Jane asks, curious as all mothers are about their children's private lives.

Star waves a hand and takes a seat beside me. "Oh, she's the cutest thing in the world," she says. "She tells me, 'Uncle Max is getting married—for the first time ever!'"

"Everyone knows Uncle Max is getting married except for Uncle Max," Jack says, trying his hand at humor.

He's funny, but not like me. I laugh at his jokes only to be polite.

Everybody knows he doesn't stand a chance of making the ladies tear up from laughter like I do. It's why I'm getting married and he's not. It's obvious why. I'm funny as hell.

Jess plants another wet kiss on my lips and I'm trying hard not to get a boner. These days, I get boners just by sitting beside her. She's so damn attractive to me, you'd catch me boning her over Lily Collins any day.

Jess has no idea that I'm sitting in Jack's living room with a boner. It's pathetic as hell, but there I am surrounded by people and trying to hide that shit from the entire circus.

"Jess," I whisper. She looks me over and screws up her face. "What?" she asks. "Is everything all right?"

"My . . ." I mutter under my breath. And then I look down at it.

"Oh," she whispers. "Should I leave?"

"I don't know," I reply. I've never been in this situation before.

She scoots farther away from me.

Every inch she scoots is an inch lost.

A minute later—with a loss of a few inches—I'm back to normal.

"What's going on over there?" Star asks, eyeing the two of us with suspicion.

"Wedding planning!" we blurt out simultaneously—then giggle. We're both like two kids getting caught in the act of passing love notes to one another in the first grade.

Damn! We're both so talented when it comes to lying. I'm so proud of how far we've come. We could deceive the entire world and they'd never notice.

"Sure doesn't look like wedding planning with all of that whispering!" Jane observes, teasingly.

I clear my throat. "Well," I say, "Jess was just telling me how she wants to do something outrageous for the wedding."

"What's outrageous?" Star asks.

Jess and I look at each other. We didn't get that far.

"Well," I begin, lying through my teeth. "Jess and I have been thinking of maybe skydiving out of an airplane and saying our 'I Dos' on the way down."

Jess glares at me. She's got that No-Way-In-Hell-Did-I-Agree-To-Go-Skydiving-On-My-Wedding-Day look.

Jess really can make me change my mind. Besides my sister, Star, she's the only girl in the world who can change a stubborn mind like mine.

"Well," I begin again, "maybe skydiving isn't such a good idea, *sweetie*," I say, glancing at Jess.

I'm heavy on the "sweeties" these days. Everything I say to Jess ends in "sweetie" or "sweetheart." I can make her do anything when I say those words.

One time, she wanted to watch a romantic comedy and I insisted on a horror flick. The moment I said, "Let's watch a horror movie, *sweetie*," it worked like a charm. The word is a magical *abracadabra* if you ask me. You say it enough times, and you can get your woman to do anything. I swear, people just need to start manipulating others by using sweet words. They call it sweet-talking. I picked it up from a book I never finished in high school. I've been calling every girl I've tried to manipulate *sweetie* or *sweetheart* ever since. If you ever see me out and about using those words, know this: Max McMillan is getting his way—and he's manipulating people left and right.

"Baby," Jess whispers. "Baby?"

I snap out of my train of thought about manipulating others.

"What?" I ask.

"Where'd you go?" she says. "We lost you there for a long minute."

"I was just thinking about words," I tell her.

"Words?" Star asks.

The kids are busy with something stupid, like they always are. They're running around; here one second, gone the next. Jane and Jack adjust positions and lean in to hear me better. They're always eager to hear things that come out of my famous mouth.

"I'm all about a lesson on words," Jack says, crossing his legs. "I need juicy details for the next chapter I'm writing."

"I guess I was thinking about human beings and how we manipulate others, you know," I say.

I can't believe I'm being honest again, but they're my friends and I love them. So, honesty it is.

"I was thinking about how, you know, if I say to Jess 'Can you get me a glass of water, sweetie?' that could be a form of manipulation."

"How so?" Jess asks. She wants to know how I'm manipulating her. Women always want to know things like that.

"Well," I say. "The word 'sweetie' functions as a nudge of sorts, right? It's a nice way of threatening someone. Do this . . . out of my love for you. In abusive relationships, the dominating emotion is fear, so you use force, violence. That's a different form of manipulation, but it's manipulation nonetheless, right?"

Jess shakes her head. She's disagreeing with me. Soon-to-be-wives always disagree with their soon-to-be-husbands when they're right. "People choose to do things of their own volition. The difference between doing things out of love and out of fear is the dividing factor. It's the difference that makes all the difference. When you ask me to do something, and you ask nicely, I know you really do love me—and I do things for you out of love. You aren't coercing me. That's not true."

Star nods. "I see Jess's point," she says. "I also see your point, Max. But I think you're wrong."

Now I have two women opposing me. It's getting ugly. I'm starting to get nervous. There's only one more woman left and she looks like she's going to side with the girls.

Jane clears her throat.

I can hear a disagreement being formed.

"Well, Max," Jane begins. "People make choices every day. If I make a choice to wake up today and do the laundry, or make breakfast for the kids, or go to work, that's a choice I'm making. And if I choose to lie in bed all day and not do anything, that's also a choice. We engage with other people every day. And other people influence our behavior. But the people we surround ourselves with—my husband, Jack, or you and Star and Jess—these are choices I've made as well. And—here's the real kicker—if I listen to your advice, your so-called 'sweeties,' your nudges, that, too, is of my own volition. I am free to listen, and I am free to not. So, I disagree. I don't think by using the word 'sweetie' you are manipulating anyone. At least if your intentions are pure and coming from a good spot. And I know you're a good person, Max. We all know that. The world may not see it that way—you're rough around the edges and you make up stories about yourself—but we see past that. We're not stupid. You're not fooling anyone. In fact, you've never fooled us. Not once."

Star is nodding, as is Jess. Jack is crossing and uncrossing his legs, listening attentively, digesting the wisdom his wife delivered *ex cathedra*, seemingly out of nowhere.

Hell, I had no idea she was this smart. But here we are.

My mind is scrambling to say something, anything, but nothing comes. I'm stunned into silence, even submission. The three women, like the great Trinity, have smashed me into nothingness. I'm mute.

"I like how you put it," Jess says, after a long pause. "I like it very much. Thank you for sharing that with us, Jane. Seriously. Max's brain just operates on a different level. And, as Star points out, he needs a lot of reorientation. Right, Maxy?"

She says this so sweetly, I'm starting to get a hard-on again. "Sure," I mutter. "Reorientation."

Damn, I hate women.

Chapter Fourteen

The next day, I take Jess to the courthouse, and we fill out the marriage paperwork.

I swear this has been the best time of my life.

Last night, after Jess gave me all that sass of hers, I almost lost my virginity again. I swear I'm writing a book about it. I had no idea wives-to-be could go wild like that. It was out of this world. More people should get married.

I swear I'm getting married twelve damn times this year. At least!

Just look at me. I got myself this wife-to-be, and suddenly, I feel like a million bucks. Look, I'm not saying everybody should get married. All I'm saying is God was right when He said, "It is not good for man to be alone." It doesn't get any clearer than that. God wants us to procreate. He's all about procreation. I mean, parts of the Bible are nothing but a whorehouse if you think about it. It's got all kinds of sex scenes. I swear God was the first porn director. I'm obviously kidding here, and I don't mean to offend anybody, but God is really into all kinds of strange shit. There are angels banging people in Genesis chapter six, and then there's Lot banging his daughters in Genesis chapter nineteen. I swear there's nothing but crazy-ass sex in the Bible. I'm not into that biblical stuff. I'm not.

Some of you think I'm crazy and wild, but the reality is: I would never read Genesis chapter six, personally. And I'm certainly never letting *my kids* read about angels banging humans and people having sex with their daughters. That's just plain gross.

Anyway, Jess and I walk into the courthouse and there's a thousand or so fans waiting for us. I wanted this to be a private event, but word gets out fast around these parts. I shake a few hands and sign a few books. I literally have to say, "No titty signatures anymore" to all the girls still trying to hook up with me.

I'm constantly pointing at my soon-to-be-wife, Jess. Like, "This here is my wife. Please respect her. Don't show me your tits. I don't want to sign them anymore."

Jess is laughing because she knows that I used to be "one of those guys." She doesn't care. And I don't either. I just sign books and leave little notes in them. Like, "Love everything and everyone."

Hell, I swear I'm so romantic these days, it's crazy.

Jess is wearing a red dress that reaches the ground. She's got these black high-heels on and I can't even believe she's going to be my wife. How crazy is that?

I hold her little hands in mine and keep kissing them. I don't even care. All the paparazzi are watching us and I'm so proud of this girl who knows how to make a great damn bowl of cereal, I'm just on cloud freaking nine. I swear I am.

I kiss her wrists and then kiss her on the mouth. And she's so awfully pretty, it's giving me a headache. I just want to go home already and cuddle with her.

We sign the paperwork and we're officially married.

Jack and Jane—along with the kids—make their way through the crowds just to get to us. Star trails them, tears glistening in her eyes.

I have to be an asshole (but only for a little bit) to a few of my fans. I yell at them and ask them, kinda-politely, to move out of the way. They do. Jane finds me and congratulates me. Jack is holding Lucy in his arms. He puts her on the ground and she's kissing Auntie Jess like she's known her all her life. I'm actually a little jealous. I thought I was Lucy's favorite uncle. But, to hell with it, I love Lucy and Jess and Jane and Jack and Nathan and Star—and everyone.

I start waving at the fans and cameras and some desperate man comes rushing at me yelling, "I love you, Mr. McMillan."

So, I sucker-punch him in the face and he falls flat on the ground. The cameras get active right then and there, and they leave us alone. That's how I escape the thousand or so crazy fans.

I swear people these days are nuts. I'm not even kidding you. A man wants to get himself a wife, and they come at him as if he invited them. I swear I didn't invite a single soul. I just wanted to marry the love of my life. I'm never getting married again. I don't ever want to go through that again. No, I don't mean not have a wedding. (I'm having twelve of those, at least.) I mean, I hate going to the courthouse to get any kind of paperwork signed. I seriously hate courthouses. They're the most boring places on Earth. I swear I could bomb one of them if I ever go crazy.

My wife looks at me and she's smiling. I tell her I have a surprise for her. She's used to all kinds of surprises.

"There's a helicopter waiting for us," I say. "I'm taking you on a tour of the skies."

It's sunny out, and it's basically sunset in an hour. The sky is already turning red and orange and whatever. All that sappy romantic fluff is in the air.

Jess is happy. She keeps looking at Queen Victoria One, Two, or

Three's ring repeatedly like it's precious from *The Lord of the Rings*. I swear women are all crazy. Why stare at a piece of glass all day long? (Diamond is nothing but an expensive piece of glass. I mean, I should have given her a windshield instead.)

But I don't even care. She's my wife now and I'm going to make sure she gets treated like the wife of Max McMillan.

God, I hate Max McMillan. I swear he's ruining my life.

I get us into the helicopter and start it right up. I hate helicopters more than I hate anything else. And, I swear, in a moment, you'll understand why I hate them as much as I do.

We take off and I'm using all the control thingies like I know what I'm doing. (The night before, after we made love in the doggystyle position, and Jess went to sleep, I got a helicopter license online. I swear I did. *But I also cheated.)*

The helicopter starts spinning out of control. And the crowd is below us. I swear it is. And I think to myself, "Damnit, McMillan. You're going to get us killed."

My wife, Jess, is holding onto me tightly. I can tell because her little hands are turning white from all the gripping they're doing.

Anyway, the helicopter starts to drop like a rock.

Right before it hits the ground, I look over at Jess and we both start laughing. We start laughing so hard, I let go of the control thingies and somehow the entire thing just starts ascending like a cock on Viagra. Man, we go up into the sky like a—

Jess is crying tears the size of my balls. And we're laughing because we both thought we were going to die.

She's got this crazy idea. Jess does. She takes my pants off and I'm like, "Goddamn, this woman is a God."

I look down and she's got my cock in her mouth and we're like twenty-thousand feet up in the air and the alarms are all sounding off and I'm literally about to cum. I swear this woman is going to be my wife forever.

Anyway, I finally cum and I have no idea how to land the damn thing. I look at Jess and Jess says the craziest thing in the world. She says, "Your turn."

She literally bends over, and I realize she's not wearing panties. Goddamn, I swear, she wants me to deliver a load on a helicopter that's dropping out of the sky?

Wow. She's crazier than I am. I'd be the dumbest man since Einstein to ever think of divorcing this woman. She's God Himself.

You bet your ass I delivered (as the helicopter dropped out of the sky).

Well, the good news is that we did land the damn thing. The bad news is we landed in a pond. (I swear ponds look like helipads from up high.)

So, I swim with Jess to shore and it's muddy. We're like two teenagers exhausted from all the first-time-ever sex. We get to shore and we're huffing and puffing, and Jess is all black and brown. And I got mud all over me. And she's laughing at me, and I'm laughing at her. Goddamn, I swear I want to marry her all over again.

She lies down in the mud and starts to make a mud-angel. I lie down next to her and do the same. We're laughing our asses off when an old man and his wife run out of the house and come our way.

This old grouch wants to ruin my day but I'm not having any of it.

He says, "Hey, what are you two morons doing?"

His old hag is standing by him, wearing some overalls like a cowgirl from a spaghetti western. She's chewing on leftover something or other and he's got a shotgun in his hands. I stand up and I'm like, "We survived a helicopter crash."

The old man is astounded. But not at the helicopter crash (he couldn't care less about helicopters dropping out of the sky into his pond below).

His jaw drops. He realizes it's me. Yes, me.

"Max McMillan!" he yells. "Well, I'll be darned, son!"

My wife gets up at this point and she's wiping her cheeks and she looks like some soldier in some war pit who's crawling out of Afghanistan or something.

The old hag is . . . not so old and haggy. She starts smiling at us and says, "Jess McMillan, is it really you?"

"Yes, ma'am," Jess says in that awfully sweet voice of hers.

"I just saw them on TV," the old lady says, looking at the husband, who's still shocked at the real and actual sight of me.

The old man puts the shotgun down and says, "Hell, come in for dinner, you crazy sonofabitch."

We walk into the house and shower. Then they give us some used clothes and we put them on. We are fed pot roast with carrots and peas and mashed potatoes. And, my God, it's the best pot roast in the world.

After dinner, the old man, who's named Bernie, takes us into the living room and shows us the books he has. I swear it's nothing but rows and rows of Max McMillan books. He's got every edition.

He looks at the books and says, "*Loaded Diapers*. Now that was one helluva novel. Yes, sir. That one was a beauty."

He asks me to kindly sign all his books. I sign them, and when I'm done, he says, "Hell, it's late. Why don't you spend the night with us?"

I look at Jess and she looks at me. We both shrug and say, "Sure, why the hell not."

We go to sleep on the first floor, in a room that looks like it was built twelve hundred years ago. The hardwood floors are all creaky.

And then I wake up to some crazy sounds.

I look at Jess. "Hey," I whisper.

It's like three in the morning.

"Are you awake?" I add.

"Yeah."

"You hear that?" I ask.

"They've been keeping me up for a while now," she whispers back.

"What are they doing?" I ask.

"Screwing, of course."

"At that age?" I ask.

"Why not?"

I put my hand between her legs. "You want to?" I ask.

She's a little wet.

"Were they turning you on?" I ask, amused.

"Maybe," she mutters.

"Goddamn," I whisper. "I had no idea you were into grannie porn."

She laughs softly. "You can be disgusting with me, husband." She turns and faces me.

She purrs like a cat.

Goddamn, I swear I hate cats.

But, to hell with it, I've never been one to turn down a session of rolling in the hay in a stranger's house.

I start making love to her, and we start going all crazy. You must excuse me since I've never been with a married woman before.

Anyway, the sex is wild. I'm having a great time and the bed is literally slamming into the wall like a bull in a china shop.

A few minutes into our crazy rendezvous, the floorboards break—and we fall through the floor.

Dang, I hate cobwebs.

So, there we are in the middle of the night stuck under a house that looks like it could be in one of those haunted house movies or whatever.

Jess is all freaking out, which just adds to the excitement. And, what's weird, I'm still hard as a steel pole.

She starts feeling around in the dark.

"Jess," I whisper.

"What?" she whispers back.

"Follow me."

She grabs hold of my hand, and I guide her out.

We run through the back yard and find an old trampoline.

"I'm tired," I say. "Let's just sleep here."

It's dark but the moon is out. It's one of those tiny crescent moons.

Jess agrees to sleep on the trampoline.

We lie down on it. After a minute, she starts to shiver.

"I'll go back to the house and steal some blankets," I whisper.

"From the bed?" she asks.

"Yeah," I say.

"Okay."

I go back to the old, haunted house and grab the blankets. I return to Jess and we get all cozy.

Once we're all warmed up, I whisper, "God, what a night."

She doesn't say anything. She's already sleeping.

Damn, I love Jessica McMillan.

Chapter Fifteen

We wake up bright and early to the sound of a rooster crowing away. I promise you it would have been great if it was just the rooster waking us.

But no.

That's not all that happens.

The sprinklers turn on and do their goddamn sprinkling. A minute later, we're soaking wet.

We run into the old, haunted house, just in time to see Grandma Bess and Grandpa Bernie making breakfast.

Bess smiles at us and says, "I see you two are continuing your crazy honeymoon."

She winks at my wife.

"Bess, I'm sorry for the bed and the floor," my wife says. "We'll send some carpenters in for repairs."

Jess looks over at me and I nod.

"Of course! Not a problem!"

Grandpa Bernie starts laughing. He's laughing so hard, his mustache is twitching and jerking like Miley Cyrus on-stage.

"You guys are a hoot!" he hollers. "My God, I'm opening a museum!"

Jess and I look at each other.

"A what?" we ask, simultaneously.

"A goddamn museum!" he says, laughing.

"Why?" I ask.

"Simple," he says. "I'm gonna call this place, 'Max's Hideout.'" He runs over to Bess and gives the nastiest sloppy wet kiss I have ever seen in my life.

"Look," he says, still excited. "Imagine this place being a museum. We could sell your books. We could have people go down into the pond to see the helicopter you crashed. Then, we could give them a tour of the bedroom and bed and floor you two broke on your honeymoon. Hell, we could make it a bed and breakfast!"

He is so goddamn happy, you should see him.

I just smile, nod, and wave—and act like I'm not the crazy one.

Jess is okay with it. She says, "I can even help out with the layout and design of the place."

Bess is happy, too. "Yes," she exclaims, "you can come on over—once the honeymoon ends, of course—and help me decorate."

I swear old people are crazy.

We have breakfast and get the hell out.

I get us a taxi.

We're standing here, wearing these dirty clothes that make us look worse than we really are. I swear we smell like swine. Jess looks over at me and she's all happy.

"Why are you so goddamn happy?" I ask, irritated.

She wraps her arms around me and kisses me. "I love being married to you," she says. "Why are you so grumpy?"

She starts tickling me, and I just kiss her. After the laughing dies down, I tell her I'm gonna give her the bestest wedding in the world.

"I already have you," she says, her eyes beaming. "I don't even need a wedding."

I kiss her again—and this time I really do mean it.

The taxi pulls up and it's some crazy-looking Indian dude wearing one of those crazy hats or whatever. He's Sikh, you know.

"Hey," he says.

"Hey," I reply.

"Max McMillan?" he asks. He's got an accent.

"Yeah," I say.

"Oh, ma god! Mama Ji!" he says.

I don't even open the door and he's already handing me two or three Hindi copies of *Loaded Diapers*. I swear these people have no manners, whatsoever.

I help my wife get all situated in the back seat and then return to the front passenger seat. I grab the books from his hands once I'm seated.

"What's up?" I say, once we are all settled in, and I have given him my address.

I look at the copies in my hands. Goddamn, I swear people are crazy if they're buying books with titles such as *Loaded* freaking *Diapers*. Heebuz Jeebuz! People are stupid. Hell, I thought Indian people were smart and only Americans were idiots.

"Mama Ji," he says, more excited than an American at the Taj Mahal. "Please tell me you can take a picture with my daughter. She loves your work. It's her birthday today. She's thirteen. It would mean the *vooorld* to her."

He says "world" like it's some goddamn magical spell or something.

Jess is being gracious. She's all smiles and giggles. "Oh, don't be a party-pooper," she says. "Be nice for once."

I roll my eyes. Women—always trying to turn men into something they aren't, like nice.

"Okay," I say. "I'll sign the books and I'll even go to your daughter's birthday party."

The Indian-Dude-With-The-Crazy-Hat is smiles, spices, and butter chicken. He's so excited, he starts dancing in his seat to the tune of some crazy-ass Indian music. I promise you everyone but me is crazy.

Before long, I start to wiggle with dance in my seat and I can feel Jess's fingers touching my neck and rubbing my shoulders.

I Indian-dance my way into a better mood. I swear marriage is already making me a better person. I'm even willing to go places I've never been and do things I've never done—like crash a thirteen-year-old girl's birthday party.

We pull up to this mansion-looking house. And Indian-Dude opens the doors for us like we're goddamn royalty. I, of course, look like shit.

"Don't you *vv-oorry*, Mr. McMillan," he says, accent thicker than my loaded wallet. "I have just the suit for you."

An old fella with white hair and skin as dark as the darkest sunburn I've ever seen comes out. He's very pleasant. He speaks no English, except two of the most beautiful words in the entire world: *Max McMillan.*

Jess and I are standing next to the taxi and this crazy old guy is running around me in circles, measuring me with a tape measure.

He's saying something in Hindi, and I can't understand any of it. Then he says, "Max McMillan." He nods and smiles and then goes on measuring me.

"My grandfather is an excellent tailor," Indian-Dude says,

observing my fascination with the old man. "He's going to make a suit for you and a dress for your wife."

I swear these people are crazy.

So that's what all the measuring is about, I think.

I look over at Jess, and she's laughing like a twelve-year-old who just realized boys never had cooties. This world is full of people who need to be in a looney bin.

An hour later, after shaking hands with nineteen hundred Indian people, we are presented with clothes.

Indian-Dude's-Wife hands them to us and sends us to a private room. I put on my suit and it's the best suit in the whole wide world. It's tan and they even made me a blue tie. I love it.

I look over at my wife and she's wearing this green dress that, I swear, came out of one of those Gatsby parties.

"Daisy?" I whisper.

She gets the reference and says, "Jay Gatz?"

We make out for a few minutes and then she bends over—and I promise you I deliver.

Heebuz Jeebuz! My wife's ass is the nicest thing in the world. And a dress like that? She's going to be pregnant so fast, she'll be delivering babies before she knows it. We're so horny, it's incredible. I won't even lie to you: I love dresses made by Indians.

Best. Sex. Ever.

My wife and I leave the room and join the rest of the crew. They're all outside, doing all kinds of silly things. Everybody wants to talk with us. We get tired of smiling from all the selfies.

Eventually, I meet the birthday girl. An hour in her house and she didn't even see me (she was busy dressing to meet me).

Anyway, this sweet thing walks out with this bright blue dress. I swear everybody in this building is wearing dresses and togas and whatever.

She runs up to me with a group of her teenage girlfriends and we start taking pictures all over again. She's hugging me and she's asking me for autographs. Her friends start bringing me their copies. They make me wait so that everybody can go home and grab their copies, too. After the wait, they come back, and I sign some more. I sign a thousand books.

I'm not exaggerating when I say: Being a famous writer is not as great as it sounds. But I have Jess, and she doesn't seem to care about any of it. She leaves me and she's out doing her own thing, talking to the women about women-things.

Eventually, I get tired of everybody and everything, and I make my way towards Jess.

"Hey, sweetheart," I say.

"Yes, my love," she replies.

"Can we go home and sleep?"

"Why, of course we can, darling," she says.

We say our goodbyes and head home.

At home, we get into my large-ass bathtub and take a bath. She scrubs my back and I scrub hers. We're so happily married, it's crazy.

"Do you want kids?" she asks, while scrubbing my back.

"Yeah," I tell her.

"How many?"

"Ten," I say.

It's a random number I came up with on the fly, but it sounds about right. I wouldn't mind having ten kids. I don't know. It sounds like fun. I have a shit ton of money. I could bribe Harvard ten times over, send them all to school there, and still have enough money to bribe another college for graduate school or whatever. I don't know. It seems like everybody is doing that, anyway.

"I'm being serious, honey," my wife says. "Like, how many?"

I want to be an asshole and say, "Twelve" but I decide to go with a smaller number.

"Okay," I say. "Six kids would do."

"Six?" she asks in a serious voice.

I can tell she's actually considering giving me six children. Who the hell would want to be pregnant six times by the same dude? I swear women are batshit crazy. What? The first time around didn't teach you anything? Insanity!

"Well," she begins. "I guess if I go part-time, we can do six kids."

It's my turn to do the dirty work now. I start scrubbing her back. She's getting all relaxed and stuff and I'm just scrubbing. I kiss the back of her neck because it's so goddamn cute. I swear I love me some back-of-the-neck action.

"Yeah," I say. "About that. I'm really old-fashioned here."

"Uh-huh," she says. I must be hitting all the right spots because she looks like she's about to cum or something.

"Well, I don't want you pregnant and working," I say.

"Uh-huh," she says.

"I mean, I just don't want you, you know, burning out on me anytime soon."

I'm starting to get a little nervous because I know how much she loves doing all the dentistry stuff. But on a serious note, I worry about her all the time now. She's my wife, and I'm all protective over her.

"Well, I could hire a replacement and work like once or twice a week," she says.

I get a little more relaxed, happy she met me halfway.

"Okay, lovebug," I say, "let's go to the bedroom and start making babies."

She says, "I'd love to, but I'm tired."

"Okay," I say. "I'm just going to go watch some porn then."

She gives me a long and hard look. "No, you're not, mister."

"Okay," I say. "I was only kidding."

"Good," she says.

I swear women are all crazy.

We go to sleep, and I wrap my arms around her—and she lets me hold her. I don't know, but the more I sleep with this woman, the more I like holding her. She's the kindest thing in the world. I swear she's been the best wife ever this week. I go to sleep fast and dream about a thousand orchards just bursting with red peaches.

Then, I swear, out of the blue, I start to dream an awful, awful nightmare.

My wife is dying from cancer. And her hair is all falling out. And her breasts get chopped off with surgical knives. She's hooked up to IVs and shit, and she's dying from cancer.

I wake Jess up. It's three in the morning.

Goddamn, I swear these nightmares are nothing but crazy-talk.

"Hey," she says. "What's the matter, baby?"

"We need to go to the emergency room," I tell her.

I promise you I'm worried about her. I can *hear* the goddamn tumors growing in her breasts.

"Something wrong?" she asks. She sits up, turns the light on, and looks at me. She lays a hand on my forehead. "You feel all right, babe."

"It's you I'm worried about."

She's surprised. "Me? Why?"

I get out of bed and begin putting my clothes on. "We need to go see an oncologist right now," I say.

"Is something wrong?" she asks again.

"Yes," I tell her.

Goddamn it! Why do women always have to ask so many goddamn questions? I'm the husband and I get to have a say in your goddamn health.

"Because I'm worried about you," I add.

She's confused now. "Why me? I feel fine, honey," she says.

"I had a nightmare."

"Oh, baby. It's just a dream." She turns the lights back off. "Go back to sleep."

I turn the lights back on.

"Babe, we have to go," I insist. "Right now."

She's getting a little annoyed with me. She takes a pillow and puts it over her head. "I'm not going anywhere," she says in a muffled voice.

She peeks out from behind the pillow and smiles. "Pillow fight me first."

I throw a pillow at her. She throws a pillow at me. We start pillow fighting. After a minute or so of such stupidity, we sit down on the edge of the bed laughing and out of breath.

"So," she says, "why are we going to the emergency room again?"

"Listen," I tell her. "I know this sounds crazy, but I had a nightmare that you had cancer. And I won't be able to sleep until I know—for sure—you do not have cancer. I will not sleep until I know. I *have* to know."

She nods her tired head. "Could we do it tomorrow, honey?" she asks.

"Oh, I don't know about tomorrow," I mutter. "I have no idea if you'll make it till tomorrow."

"I'm not going anywhere, Max. I feel fine. Look at me. Look at *us*. We just got through a pillow fight."

I lie down in bed and cover my eyes.

"I don't know," I mutter. "Maybe you're right. But what if you have cancer, and this is our moment—our one and only moment—to catch it in time?"

She lies down next to me.

"First of all, I don't have cancer, Max," she says, softly. "And, second of all, if I did, I'm sure a day or two wouldn't change anything."

"But what if you have cancer and I don't stop it and if something happens to you, and I end up feeling like I killed you or something? And everyone will laugh at me and say, 'There's that famous writer who was so stupid he practically let his wife die from cancer.'"

"Oh, Max. Stop being silly," she says. "I'm not going anywhere."

"Goddamn!" I shout at the ceiling. "I fucking hate cancer!"

"You're so crazy, honey," she says, laughing. "I mean, bat-shit crazy."

"I know," I say. "You want to know how Kurt Gödel died?"

"Who's Kurt Gödel?" she asks.

"He was Einstein's best friend." I sit up in bed and look at her. "I can't believe you don't know who Kurt Gödel is."

"I don't know a lot of things, Max," she says all seriously.

"Well, you want to know how he died?"

"Sure. But first tell me a little bit about him so I could cry when you tell me about his death. I need to know a little bit about somebody's life first before you tell me about how they died," she says.

"Okay," I say. "He was a mathematician and a logician. He came up with the incompleteness theorems. There were like two of them that he came up with. You know, the Greek thing they call 'the liar's paradox'?"

"Sure," she says. "It rings a bell. I've probably heard about it in a philosophy class of some sort. But that was a long, long time ago."

I can tell my wife is starting to get sleepy again. Women always get sleepy when their husbands start talking all smart and stuff. It's like they don't even want to believe their husbands are capable of thinking vast, big, mathematically precise thoughts as Einsteinian as the theory of relativity.

"So, the liar's paradox is a paradox. It essentially is the following: 'This sentence is false.' If you prove the truth of the statement, then it is false; but if you prove that the statement is false, then it must be true."

"Uh-huh," she mutters.

She's probably sleep-talking at this point.

"So, Gödel set out to do something crazy. He wanted to prove the consistency of a closed system, where all the axioms could be proven. Instead, what he found is that he could only prove the *unprovability* of a self-consistent system. What that meant is that mathematics was not consistent. At any given point, math would have at least one axiom that would always remain unprovable. It's called the Gödel sentence, I think. It essentially says, 'G is not provable in the system F.' If you try to prove G, you can't. All you can do is prove that it is unprovable. It's like the liar paradox. The statement is true in the sense that it makes sense to us. But we have to step outside the statement itself for it to make any sense. Same thing with math. Some things will never be proven. All you can do is assume the truth of a given axiom."

She's already sleeping, but I keep on talking because at this point, I'm the smartest guy in the room, and I don't ever recall being this smart. I mean, here I am in the middle of the night telling my wife about the limitations of every formal axiomatic system. You can't prove zero. You can't. Zero is zero whether you like it or not. You just accept zero for what it is and always assume zero isn't lying.

I hear her move. "So, how did he die?" she mumbles.

I swear she's still sleep-talking. No way in hell she's smart enough to understand the philosophy of mathematics.

"Well," I say, "he was Einstein's best friend. And Einstein only stayed at Princeton just so he could walk home with Gödel; that's how much he loved Gödel. Anyway, one day, when Gödel was fairly old, he started thinking his food was getting poisoned. He became paranoid. And he wouldn't eat unless his wife, Adela, made him food. Well, when Adela got hospitalized, he refused to eat. He would only eat food prepared by his beloved wife. Anyway, he starved to death. I don't know. But I've always found his story romantic. Einstein tried to convince the poor guy to eat. My God, he really did try. But Gödel refused. He was that romantic."

"Aww," she mumbles. "That's sweet and sad."

"Yeah," I say.

She turns over and kisses me with her eyes still closed. "Now go to sleep, you," she murmurs. "Or else I'll stop making you food and you'll starve to death."

I smile. I have no idea why, but I find it awfully romantic. I'd hate to die from starvation, though. I love food too much.

I kiss Jessica on the cheek and close my eyes.

Damn, I love Gödel.

Chapter Sixteen

I wake up, and I swear, something smells like it's burning.

"Jess!" I yell.

I'm not used to waking up with the scent of a burning-down-house in my nasal passages.

"Jess!" I yell a second time.

I hear some noise downstairs. Goddamn, I swear it must be the fire department or the goddamn kids playing another round of Burn-Max-McMillan's-House-Down.

"Yes?" Jess says, stepping into the room. "Why are you yelling at eight in the morning, honey?"

I look at her. She's wearing that purple robe with the pink flamingoes on it. Goddamn, she looks like a Playboy Bunny. I promise you I'm horny as a dog that grew a second pair of balls overnight.

I'm staring at her, still in my ugly Fruit-of-the-Loom underwear.

"What's burning?" I ask, shriveling up my nose like that chipmunk or whatever from *Ice Age*.

"Nothing's burning, babe," she says, walking up to me. She wraps her arms around me. "I'm making you pancakes."

"Pancakes?" I ask. I'm starting to get irritated because I know exactly what this woman is doing. She's crafty as ever. She thinks she can deceive me. Well, no siree, I have news for you: I can talk about Gödel and mathematics and the theory of relativity like a goddamn world-renowned physicist. You could basically call me Michio Kaku. I swear. So, I'm not buying any of it.

"Are you trying to deceive me?" I say. And I'm starting to get angry for no reason (probably because I really am hungry and probably should eat those pancakes).

But, oh to hell with it, I feel like arguing with her. So, damnit, I will!

She keeps rubbing my neck like some masseuse.

"I don't want you starving like that guy you told me about last night," she says, all sexy and crafty and shit. "Come downstairs and eat. And stop talking about Deceive Me This or Deceive Me That."

She's entirely nonchalant about it all, which makes me even more frustrated.

"Okay," I say. "You think you could just distract me with pancakes today?"

"Why would I distract you with anything?" she asks.

"I know what you're trying to do," I say. "You're trying to make me forget."

"Forget what?" she asks. Now she's hella confused and I'm starting to enjoy myself.

"We have to go see the oncologist today," I say, matter-of-factly.

"Sure do," she says, all nice and sweet and stuff.

"Why are you being so nice to me?" I ask.

"Why not?" she asks.

"Punch me," I tell her.

She gives me the Are-You-Crazy look.

I step towards her in that ugly underwear. "I mean it," I say. "Punch me."

She kicks me right in the balls and I swear I fall right over.

"Damnit!" I yell. "Are you crazy?"

I swear I can barely move and she's in the corner laughing her ass off.

"I didn't say kick me!" I yell.

"Stop being such a baby," she retorts, as she steps out of the room. "Come eat your breakfast, Mister Bruised Balls."

I swear that woman is going to get her ass handed to her one of these days.

"We'll be taking *you* to see the doctor today," I hear her add.

I put some clothes on and make it downstairs. I have no idea what the hell is going on, but I think marriage is made for people who aren't as crazy as we are. What kind of husband wakes up and gets his balls kicked in like a door by the FBI? I swear women in America are crazy. They're always kicking something.

I eat my pancakes in relative peace. No kicking or whatever. I'm still partly horny because we didn't do anything last night, but I figure we'll do all kinds of weird stuff once we get done seeing doctors or whatever.

After breakfast, I help Jess wash dishes and we drive to the hospital.

We go to the Emergency Room because it's a goddamn emergency.

"I'm Max McMillan," I tell the lady at the front desk. "And this is my wife, Jess."

The woman looks at us and smiles.

"He wants a mammogram," Jess states matter-of-factly.

The Lady-At-The-Desk nods.

Jess starts giggling.

"Why are you laughing?" I ask, irritated.

"Because you have no man-boobs, honey," my wife explains.

"So what?" I say. "I want *your* boobs examined."

"We'll get them examined," she says. "But first we'll need your balls examined too."

"Why?" I ask.

"For my sake," she replies. Then she gives me those puppy eyes and I know she's trolling the hell out of me.

A few minutes later, an oncologist walks out, and she's roughly forty years old and clearly in love with me.

"Max McMillan!" she exclaims, throwing a hand over her mouth. "Oh, my God! What are you doing here?"

My wife and I gesture to step into a private room.

"Of course!" she says. "Follow me."

We get into one of the hospital rooms and I sit on one of those examination tables.

"I have a small request to make," I say.

"What is it?" she asks.

"I'm getting really paranoid," I begin, almost cautiously.

I feel like giving up because sometimes when you say things out loud, they sound crazy. I mean, who thinks their new bride has cancer three days or whatever after they sign papers and get married? Seriously.

"Okay. So, I have to confess something," I say.

My wife sits down beside me and takes my hand. It's cute.

The doctor stands at the doorway, looking at me as if I'm about to announce that we're pregnant with triplets and they all have cancer or something.

"So, I just want my wife examined. I think she might have

cancer," I finally blurt out so fast, I'm sure the doctor has no idea what the hell came out.

"What?" the oncologist asks.

Yep. I knew it. I'm so stupid, even doctors who specialize in diagnosing stupid cannot understand me.

"I think my wife has cancer," I say slowly.

The doctor looks over at my wife, who is holding in a smile and a laugh and all sorts of other things wives of crazy-author-husbands need to hold in.

"Do you have any lumps in your breasts?" she asks, uncertainly.

"No," my wife states. She glances over at me as if to ask for my opinion on the matter.

Dang it! Dealing with one woman is insanity. Anybody who is stupid enough to get married to a single girl is bat-shit crazy. But being stuck in a room with two goddamn girls, and they're both smarter than you? Heebuz Jeebuz! I swear I'm the unluckiest person in the whole wide world.

What happens when Max McMillan walks into a room with an oncologist and a dentist? I have no idea where I was going with that, but I'm sure the joke would end with me getting a root canal on my ass or some shit like that.

I stand up. I feel much better when I stand. I'm six-foot-one. Not tall, but tall enough. And when I feel like being authoritative and in-charge, I stand up. Right now, I feel powerless. Like, these two females are trying to conspire against me. Me, the great writer, Max McMillan. Me, "a literary genius of almost-magical quality." Me—damnit! I swear I hate being in the presence of smart and intelligent and beautiful women. I feel entirely and totally insignificant. What does it even matter that I am a "literary genius?" These two girls are geniuses. I'm not a genius. I'm a "literary genius." Anything "literary" is a joke. Everybody knows that. If you're specializing in Literary Anything, you're a hack. That's what you are. A goddamn, good-for-nothing hack.

"Okay," I say. "Let's just go home." I look over at my wife, who is basically laughing. I promise you. She's sitting there laughing.

"No, I'm getting the mammogram, honey," she says. Now she's putting her foot down.

"No," I say. "Let's just go home." I'm getting all worn out from trying to act smart in front of these intimidating creatures, and I just want to go home and lie down or something, and maybe just have sex or something.

"No," my wife says.

She has no idea, but she needs to stop being so goddamn bossy with me. She has no idea how attractive it is. I like making love to a girl who could use some good old-fashioned disciplining. I could whip out all my wild stallion tricks on her and subjugate her like one of those royal Saudi Arabian crown princes or whatever. Goddamn, woman! You say "No" to me again and I swear you're going to end up getting pregnant.

I ask the doctor to give us a few minutes "to talk."

The doctor says, "Sure, I'll step out of the room and see another patient. Be back in ten minutes."

Once the door is closed, I look at my wife.

"Why'd you send her out?" she asks.

"Because you're turning me on," I say.

"Oh, really?" she says, all sexy.

"Take your clothes off," I say.

She begins to unbutton her blouse. "Meow," she says, when her tits are all out and shit.

Anyway, to make a short story short, I give that woman some good old-fashioned disciplining in the doctor's office. I'm so hard, I swear. Later she tells me it was "like having sex with a robot." I have no idea what robot-sex looks like, but you can rest assured, I out-sexed those pricks.

The doctor came back in and we're both lying on the examination table, huffing and puffing away like two teenagers who just got caught red-handed jacking off to porn.

"Everything all right?" she asks.

I roll over. "I had an asthma attack," I say.

"I'm sorry to hear that," she says.

"But why are her panties on the floor?" the doctor says, looking at the panties . . . that are . . . on . . . the . . . damn . . . floor.

Oh shit.

"Oh," I say, "she had to perform CPR on me, and the panties were bothering her. They, um, were rubbing her *there.* So, she felt like she needed to take them off."

Goddamn, I'm such a good liar, everybody believes me.

My wife is blushing, but not really. She's not a good liar like me.

The doctor is stunned. "Why were you performing CPR?" she asks.

"Well—" I clear my throat. "Sometimes, when I get an asthma attack, I get congestion, and you have to do chest compressions, and then stuff starts to come up. Like, I don't know. It's something I can't really explain."

"Max McMillan," the doctor says all seriously, "were you having sex in my office?"

I give her one of those excellent What-The-Hell-Are-You-Talking-About looks. She buys it.

"I'm kidding!" she says, laughing. "Anyway, let's get this mammogram over and done with and send you two crazy love-birds home."

My wife grabs the panties from the ground and slips out of the room.

"I'm going to put these back on and use the restroom," she says, hastily.

When she leaves, the doctor shakes her head. "I can't believe it," she says. "Max McMillan." She keeps shaking her head.

I chuckle. "Asthma is getting really out of hand." I cough into my fist.

A minute later, Jess is back. I leave the room and wait outside. I guess Jess doesn't want me to look at her tits. She doesn't want me getting desensitized to them.

It doesn't take too long. She walks out with the doctor and they're talking like they're best friends.

Jess walks up to me, kisses me on the cheek, and says, "Nothing detected."

I feel relieved. "That's wonderful news," I say. It really is.

We leave the hospital and Jess's phone rings.

She picks up.

"Hi, mom," she says. She looks at me and says, "It's mom."

They talk for a few minutes and then she hangs up.

"Mom wants to know when the first wedding is," she says.

"Tell her we need to plan it all out. It's going to be spectacular," I reply.

She takes my hand in hers and we skip out of the damn place.

God, I hate hospitals.

We drive to Jane and Jack's house. I hate driving places because sitting in cars is like a chore for me. Sometimes, I drive and write. I swear I do. This one time, I was busy writing at a stop light and some asshole tried to honk his horn at me. Thank God, I was driving my Ferrari, or some other piece of shit, so the dumb-ass recognized me. I'm sitting there in traffic working on my novel, and this loser wants me to stop writing mid-sentence? What? Does this kid not know I'm writing the next big hit? Shit. He should be honored to sit his lame ass behind my ass.

Anyway, this kid walks over. He's all pissed as hell. I roll down my window and tell this prick that I'm goddamn writing.

This prick, I swear. He recognizes me. So, he runs back to his car and pops his trunk. For a second, I think he's either pulling out dead bodies or guns. I put my car back in gear and I'm about to tear a few holes in the pavement, when I see this loser running at me with twelve books in his hands.

Heebuz Jeebuz!

So, there I am signing copies at this busy intersection. I swear, I have no time to goddamn write. Next thing I know, people are getting out of their cars, bringing Max McMillan novels my way. I swear, famous writers can't even park their cars on highways like normal people. It's like the world is out to get us.

What's crazy is I end up making the news. They get the stations over there and shit, and they're all interviewing people at this intersection. The only good thing that comes of it is the fact that I shut down the highway, and this drunk driver that was literally going to kill people never makes it onto the on-ramp. Next thing you know, I'm a damn hero. They run headlines like "Max McMillan blocks traffic, saves lives."

The next day, I swear these losers won't leave me alone. They have *The New York Times* knocking on my door trying to find out if I'm some prophet of sorts.

"How did you know this mad drunk was on the road raging?" and "Do you listen to police scanners in your free time?" I swear, people are nuts. I simply wanted to write a sex scene in one of my excellent books, and these people take a goddamn Casanova and turn him into Jesus-Christ-Super-Star-Batman-Returns. I swear people just want a superhero and not a damn writer.

So, I'm thinking all these stupid thoughts when we walk in and Jane greets us.

She looks like shit, once again, but I don't tell her. I'm becoming a nice guy. I swear marriage is turning me into God or Jesus or Gandhi or something.

The kids run up to us, wanting something or other. Sometimes, I feel like I'm Walmart. It's like every time I show up, there's some new product that's on sale and it's nine-for-the-price-of-five or something. I swear hospitals bring out the worst in me.

I give the kids big hugs and whatever. And Jess is still perky from all the orgasms she's suffered ever since she got married to her asshole husband, so she's sweet as pecan pie.

"Kids," she says, "will you help Auntie Jess plan her wedding?"

Nathan doesn't really care about weddings, but he nods his shy, little head. It's really Lucy who is out to lunch with wedding planning. She's all hyper and jumpy and all kinds of girly.

"Auntie Jess! Auntie Jess!" she yells, excitement reaching a feverish pitch. "Can we make the wedding in a submarine? We could look at fishies!"

Jess laughs and says, "Of course! We'll see what Uncle Max and I come up with."

Lucy is beyond herself. She's running around the house yelling out things like, "I'm going to find Nemo!" and "Uncle Max is getting married!" I swear kids are almost as crazy as I am.

Jack comes down the stairs and I can tell he's struggling. His eyes are all red and he's rubbing them like he's masturbating the hell out of them or something.

Jane looks at Jack and then back at us. "He's been working on *The Final Romance*. Editing away all night." She sighs.

"You look like shit," I tell him. And I really do mean it.

He laughs. He gives everybody a hug and then stands by me.

"Well, I certainly feel like I'm getting old, Max," he says. "I can no longer write like I used to."

I pat him on the shoulder. "Stop being so hard on yourself. You're not even forty yet," I say.

"I feel like I'm ninety—with nothing to my name." He laughs, but I can tell it's one of those laughs where he's really hiding something.

I tell my wife she can plan the wedding or whatever with Jane and Lucy, while Jack and I go look over his book.

She smiles and agrees.

The girls do their thing, and we do ours. Nathan gets back to video games.

We head into his study, and he closes the door. I settle into a chair, and he sits down in a corner on the floor.

"Where's the damn beauty?" I ask.

He nods at the desk.

I glance and see the papers.

"That it over there?" I ask.

"Yup," he says. "Fifteenth edition or so."

"You've edited this thing fifteen times?" I ask, surprised.

"Yeah," he says. "It's been exhausting."

"Still no word from publishers?"

"Nope."

"Damn," I mutter.

Then his eyes spark up a bit and he says, "But I do have some good news."

"What?" I ask, curious.

"I got a poem dedicated to Jane published."

"Which journal?" I ask.

"Oh, it's not even a journal. It's a blog or something."

"Just a blog?" I ask, disappointed. I don't mean to be an asshole but getting published on some blog run out of a ghetto kitchen isn't exactly the epitome of publishing.

"Well, it's something," he says, shrugging. "Only recognition I've ever gotten, anyhow."

I start feeling tired and depressed just listening to him.

"How's Jane?" I ask.

"She's hanging in there," he says.

"Any news on the cancer?"

"Stage four," he mutters. "Basically, a death sentence."

"Death sentence," I repeat, softly.

"How are the kids?" I ask.

"They don't know," he says. "Nathan may suspect something, but Lucy is—" He pauses. "I don't know," he finally says. "I don't even know how to tell her."

"Goddamn," I mutter. "Anything I can do?"

He shakes his head. "Nothing at this point. Only thing we're working through is all the nasty stuff. End-of-life care. Comfort care. Hospice. All the things you should be doing when you're ninety, not thirty."

I shake my head. I have no idea what to say.

"The wedding planning is good, though," he says. "It helps get her mind off things. She needs some of that in her life right now."

"Well, she'll have eleven more weddings to plan." I laugh.

"Yeah, that's probably a good thing. When's the first one?"

"We're thinking next week. I mean, I want Jane to be there."

He nods.

"It means a lot," I say. "To Jess."

"I know," he says. "I know."

"Such is life," I mutter. "Such is life."

"Yeah, we never thought we'd be here, did we?" he asks.

"Never," I say.

He becomes quiet for a minute and then says, "I've been thinking a lot lately."

"About?" I ask.

"God, you know. How none of it makes any sense."

"Uh-huh," I say. I'm not a theologian, and I've never been religious, so I have no idea what the hell the word *God* even means.

"I've been thinking maybe I should take her to church, you know. Get her prayed for."

I shrug. "Didn't know they still prayed for people," I say.

"Yeah, Elaine, her friend, was saying something about a healing service at her old church."

"You think that stuff works?" I ask, skeptically.

"Who knows?" he mutters. "I feel like we have nothing to lose at this point."

"I don't know," I say. "I feel like if healing services worked, we wouldn't need hospitals."

"True," he mutters. "But even hospitals aren't saving us at this point."

"Well, you do you," I say. "I'm not opposed to anything. I mean, if it floats your boat and helps Jane, I'm certainly all right with that. Look at Star. Jesus saved her."

"Yeah," he says. "That's where I'm at, too. We've tried everything. At this point, I don't care if some character from *Veggie Tales* saves Jane—as long as she gets saved."

I laugh. "Yeah, desperate times sure do call for desperate measures."

We end up chatting for a few more minutes, and then go downstairs and watch some stupid movie together. I swear all the movies released today are as pathetic as they are horrible.

Jess sits next to me and she's eating popcorn. Jack is drinking scotch and he's cheering up a bit. Jane is cuddling with Jack, sipping from a glass of wine. Lucy and Nathan are doing whatever.

We spend the evening together like that and then Jess and I head home.

On our way home, Jess gets the wonderful idea to go grocery shopping. I swear grocery shopping is the sexiest thing a married couple will ever do. Let me explain.

We get to the grocery store, and we start looking at tomatoes and cucumbers and lettuce and shit. And Jess is trying to figure out how to tell which cucumber is good. She's out there touching cucumbers like she's some teenager, blindfolded, feeling out a hard dick in a dark place.

I start laughing because, I swear, it's inappropriate to be doing things to cucumbers like that out in public. After a few minutes of watching her try to find a fresh, hard, good cucumber, I get this brilliant idea.

I grab one of the cucumbers and tap it with my knuckles a bit. Then I put it to my ear and pretend to listen. Jess stops what she's doing and looks over at me. I tap the cucumber again and then put it to my ear.

She says, "What are you doing, honey?"

And I act like I'm the smartest prick in the world. I'm all nonchalant and arrogant like Napoleon Bonaparte.

"What?" I ask her, all serious. "Your mother never taught you how to properly select a good cucumber?"

She furrows her brows and gives me that I-Have-No-Idea-What-the-Hell-You're-Talking-About look. "No, she did not," she says.

I keep on tapping away and placing cucumbers to my ear.

She picks one up and taps it. Then she places it to her ear.

She's intent as hell, like she's operating on a patient at her dental office or something.

I watch her out of the corner of my eye.

She picks up another cucumber, taps it, and puts it to her ear. She's all focused and such, so she doesn't even see me leaning over.

She's listening to the cucumber when I whisper in her ear, "Put me in your pussy."

I swear she jumps. She gives me this bewildered look.

I swear, she thought the cucumber was talking to her.

I burst out laughing like some lunatic.

Goddamn! Women these days are so gullible, they'll believe you when you tell them vegetables talk.

I wasn't lying when I said that grocery shopping with Jess can be a very sexy thing.

We buy some "good" cucumbers and head home. I shower while Jess makes us one of those stupid Greek salads. After I do my thing, I come down, all naked and shit. (I enjoy walking around the house naked.)

She's humming some boring tune, but it sounds like grandma-moans because she can't sing for shit. I wrap my arms around her and kiss her neck. I don't really care about her singing voice. It never featured on my Why-I'm-Going-to-Marry-This-Girl list.

"Are you excited?" I ask.

"Yeah," she says. She stops humming.

She looks up at me and places one of those sexy kisses on my chin—and I smile ridiculously because I know something she doesn't.

"Why are you smiling like that?" she asks. Her voice is all sexy and stuff.

I look at her and chuckle. "What? I can't even smile around my wife?"

"No, you can smile," she says. "I just don't like when I don't know *the reason* for your smile."

"You're the reason," I whisper.

"If only cucumbers could talk," she whispers back.

I kiss her on her mouth.

"Uh-huh. And what would they say?"

"That they want to be inside me."

"Oh yeah, baby?" I laugh.

I can feel myself getting hard.

I press my body against hers and I let her know which cucumber is ready to take on that challenge.

She's all sexy, wiggling away to the sound of her grandma-moan humming. And I know I'm going to have a good night. I swear.

Damn, I love cucumbers.

Chapter Seventeen

It's the day of our First Wedding.

I swear, weddings are overrated.

First, let's talk about something no one ever mentions: the creeps. Yes, you heard that right: creeps. I swear creeps run in groups; there's never just one.

These little sneaky shits run into my house like they own the place. I wake up all naked and shit—and Jess is naked in the shower, playing with herself or whatever.

This sneaky little prick runs in with a camera and starts videotaping all sorts of crap.

I rub my eyes and then place my hands on my dick because, I swear, I'm harder than a stick of concrete.

"What the hell are you doing here?" I shout. I'm so pissed and angry.

"Surprise!" another sneaky piece of shit yells, jumping out of the dang closet.

He's also got a camera.

"What's going on?" I ask, confused as hell.

Jess steps out of the shower, wraps a towel over her boobs, and smiles.

"Oh, hey, Joey and Rene!" she says.

She looks at me. "They're our wedding videographers."

I swear these guys are anything but.

"Videographers?" I stutter. "More like pornographers."

They look offended.

Jess waves a hand at me and acts like I'm a little child who has no idea what he's talking about.

"It's all right, honey," she says. "They're here to take videos of us."

She looks at the two dudes. "Get on with your filming," she says.

They nod their nervous little heads and get back to business.

I swear people these days are all voyeurs. This one time, I heard a story about a guy who ran around filming people. Well, one day, this little prick got his ass handed to him when he stumbled onto a crime scene. He was busy recording something when—out of the blue—this big-ass dude came up behind him and just hit him with a brick so hard, he fell over dead. That was it. The story, like most stories, didn't have a happy ending. The newspapers called it "a true tragedy." What they forgot to mention is that the dude was a goddamn creep. What the hell was he thinking walking around filming shit all the time? Didn't he know he had to look around and shit? I mean, if you're always staring into a camera, you'll never see bricks coming. Never. I always keep my eyes open for flying bricks. That shit hurts.

One time, I kid you not, I almost got hit by one of those bricks. It happened just like in that old movie, *Ben-Hur*. I was giving a great and excellent speech. It was when I was receiving some award. And I did the coolest thing in the world, I swear.

The day before, a *New York Times* journalist wrote a scathing review of my oeuvre. He said: "Mr. McMillan isn't worthy of a Pulitzer. His literature is boring garbage and utterly deprived of anything decent."

For my speech, I mentioned the critic by name. *Mr. Zellister.* I did the unthinkable: I out-criticized him. I went through all my books, one by one, and trashed the living daylights out of them. I left no stone unturned. The speech lasted two-and-a-half hours. It was like sixty pages of single-spaced bullshit. I trashed my work.

After the long trash-talking—my God!—I got a standing ovation. I was my own worst critic. In fact, they saw me for who I really was: a better critic than Mr. Zellister.

The crowd—and critics!—loved it. They loved it so much, they did something unthinkable: they gave me *two* Pulitzers. Just like that, the Pulitzer in Journalism was taken from Mr. Zellister and given to me.

Mr. Zellister didn't like it one bit—so, he threw a brick at me.

I, of course, moved out of the way.

(And the brick hit a lady behind me. Naturally, I was alarmed. But they took her to the emergency room and did a chest x-ray on her. They ended up finding nodules in her lungs and started her on chemotherapy and radiation for lung cancer. And—just like that—I became a hero. She later thanked me for stepping out of the way and letting the brick hit her. She would have died from lung cancer otherwise.)

And so, that's how I was able to make the greatest literary comeback in all literary history. I out-critiqued a critic, dodged a brick, and saved a lady from lung cancer.

What critics don't understand—and this must be made clear—is that they are, inherently, wrong about virtually everything. I swear nobody in the general public even knows what a goddamn Pulitzer Prize is; much less, knows the recipient of such an award. We all know Fitzgerald and his *Gatsby*—and what awards did he win for writing the greatest American novel? None. Why? Because critics don't know anything about anything. Same thing in film. What awards did Alfred Hitchcock win? Did he ever get a Best Director Oscar? No. He was nominated five times. So, I'll give the critics that. They had a partially active and even (possibly?) functioning frontal lobe. They had just enough neurons to make him a nominee—but not enough to get the goddamn job done. And that, perhaps, is why the general public does the opposite of what the critics recommend. Anytime I see "Award-Winning Film," I make sure to never see it. (Of course, special thanks go to the critics for helping me see which films I need to avoid by crowning those films with their nonsense.)

I swear after I won two Pulitzers that night, my sales tanked by half. It's like the moment I was accepted by the critic community, I lost all respectability. The regular people stopped liking me. I had become "one of them."

So, I swear, I did a totally Max McMillan thing. I called in the goddamn voyeurists. I called in like twenty of them. I got them all lined up at my big-ass house, and I pulled out my Pulitzers, along with my huge penis, and I just pissed all over them. Then I raised a middle finger to the hundred or so cameras, and—damnit!—I sold twelve million copies once the newspapers ran *that* story.

I was interviewed the next day. And you want to know what I said? I said, "I'm never accepting any more awards. I do not belong to the critics. I belong to the people."

Goddamnit! I swear I sold another twelve million copies after the newspapers ran *that* quotation.

Random House called me.

They said, "Mr. McMillan. We need you to come in and sign some paperwork."

I said, "What's up?"

They said, "We can only print one million copies a week."

I said, "And?"

They said, "After that brouhaha, we're selling twelve million copies of your work *per week.* We need another publisher to start working with us. In fact, we need several."

So, for a few weeks, The Big Five publishers got together with their Big-Five egos just to print nothing but Max McMillan books.

Random House called me again. "Mr. McMillan, the last time this happened, it was *Fifty Shades of Grey*—and we were spitting out one million copies a week then. But with you, it's *twelve.*"

I swear the number twelve is my lucky number.

The newspapers can't get their shit together. They hate me but they love me because nobody is talking about anything but the stunt I pulled with my Pulitzers. For several weeks, it's nothing but McMillan-This and McMillan-That. I swear I get so many phone calls, the damn lines are lava.

Anyway, I don't trust the voyeurs anymore. They're all just a bunch of pricks. I swear, I hate cameras. I had to dye my hair grey and wear sunglasses for twelve weeks just to take a piss in my own damn house. Things were bad. Really bad. I had cameras out by my house for a quarter of a year. I had to move to Mexico City because shit got out of hand.

I have another story for you. This one happened in Mexico City. I swear that place has the most beautiful women in the world.

I'm living like a cockroach; sleeping by day and writing by night.

Get this: one night, I get the strangest call in the world. Some girl calls me. She's got this angelic voice, and she sings like Aretha Franklin.

She says, "Mr. McMillan, the Mexican Authorities need you."

I say, "Who the hell is this?"

"Agent Garcia."

I swear half the people in Mexico are Garcias. What is this place? I swear everybody is banging someone by the name of Garcia.

I roll my eyes and say, rather sarcastically, "Okay, Agent *Garcia*, who the hell gave you my number?"

She says, "The Mexican Authorities."

I say, "Prove it." I'm rolling my eyes but, hell, I've got nothing better to do. Besides, I'm starting to get a little horny and maybe Agent *Garcia* might help me with some of that.

She says, "In fifteen minutes, your hotel is going to go up in flames."

I say, "What the hell is this, some kind of prank?"

"No, *señor*," she says. "It's true."

What the hell? Since when did I become a *si, señor* kind of fella? I'm Max McMillan and nobody calls me in the middle of the night about—

Oh, to hell with it! I might as well dress up and get the hell out of this place. If I get kidnapped, it might be a story worth writing about.

So, I put my clothes on and step out of the hotel.

I swear it's like in those movies. I see this hot Mexican girl who's all curvy and shit, and she's wearing a *sombrero de charro*. She's got that Mexican hat all on her head and it's not even sunny out.

I can tell by the way she's observing me she's either naked or getting there. She tells me to follow her, and I'm stupid enough to do it.

We go to the pool, and in the moonlight, I can tell she's naked. So, I assume this is one of those Mexican rendezvous things. I start undressing, and—thank God!—I got shorts under my pants.

We get into the pool and she's acting all sexy with me. She keeps saying all kinds of awfully romantic things to me in Spanish or whatever. All I understand is *te amo* and *si, señor.*

And then there's this loud-ass noise and the earth shakes or whatever, and the hotel goes up in flames. And she snatches my hand and dunks me underwater.

Anyway, the firefighters show up and everybody wants to know what happened.

The entire hotel has cleared out—and not *a single* soul was lost. Everybody is amazed.

Where the hell did everybody go?

I'm running around in my shorts with a million cameras celebrating the fact that I didn't die in the fire, and Ms. Garcia—with clothes on—is all smiles and giggles and handshakes.

Anyway, I end up going to sleep at some police station. But they treat me like royalty and—for the life of me—I can't figure out what the hell is going on. All I hear is this romantic Spanish all around, and I keep thinking every girl is reading Neruda to me and wants to suck my . . .

I'm as confused as a dementia patient off Aricept. A person who speaks English walks in and introduces himself as Chief Inspector Jose. (I swear everybody is either Jesus or Jose in Mexico.)

"Do you know why you're here?" he asks.

"No idea," I say.

"We had a tip last night. Somebody planted a bomb in the building," he says.

"How does that relate to me?" I ask, still confused.

"Agent Garcia had a brilliant idea. It's all really thanks to her—and you."

"Me?" I ask, confused.

"*Si, señor,*" he says. "You."

"But why me?"

"Well," he says. "You are a *leyenda* in these parts."

"A what?"

"A legend," he whispers.

I look around the room to make sure this isn't some kind of joke.

I touch myself. (Literally.)

Yup. I'm still here. Still alive. Still in this body.

Nope. It's not a dream.

"Señor," he says. "Agent Garcia had a wonderful idea. She thought, 'How can we get everybody out of the building *fast*?' And you know what she came up with? She came up with getting *you* out *first*."

At this point, I'm thinking this guy either ate several grams of magic mushrooms, or he's high off his rocker. None of it is making any sense.

"Oh, yes, *señor,*" he continues. "It was all about getting you out in time. And fast. In a hurry. So, we knew you like—" At this point he winks. "Our women," he says.

"So, you send a hot Mexican girl to seduce me?" I ask.

"Si, señor."

"And?"

"You came out of the building. And everybody followed."

"Huh?"

"The women were all spying on you."

"What?" I ask.

He pulls out a phone and shows me a video.

Lo and behold, in all the bushes and whatever, hundreds of women are hiding, all spying on me.

Yep.

Max McMillan about to have sex in the pool—and he's got a million eyes watching.

The next day, the headlines come out.

Oh, boy.

You might want to sit down for this.

"Max McMillan saves hundreds of lives out of burning building in Mexico City."

And, just like that, I became a superhero overnight.

Now you know why I hate so many things. All those voyeurs.

God, I hate cameras.

Anyhow, after all the stupid voyeur stuff at my house—the cameras, the bridesmaids, the groomsmen, whatever—we get in a limousine and the driver takes us to a place I can't really describe. I mean, if I describe it, it'll give away my location (and I'm tired of all the attention).

But, oh to hell with it, I'll just tell it like it is.

The driver takes us to Pier 33 and we board the ferry. I'm all dressed in a black suit with a pink tie, and my best man, Jack Gillman (soon-to-be world-renowned romance writer), is right next to me. Jane, his wife, is Jess's maid of honor—and she's looking about as good as the rest of us (the hell would I know how she did it?).

Star is wearing a pink dress with her back exposed, showing off a fresh butterfly tattoo. "Got it last week," she says, beaming. "Wanted the guys to know I'll give them more than just butterflies."

We giggle because she's hilarious. Star is.

Lucy is carrying a basket with rose petals in it and Jane keeps telling her to stop playing around with them.

"Save them for the ceremony!" Jane says to Lucy.

"But mommy! They're so pretty," Lucy replies.

Nathan is daydreaming about *Call of Duty*, but he is all right with holding a couple of rings in his hands. I don't even think he understands how much those rings are worth.

I swear she has no idea what the hell we're doing. Nobody does. Hell, it's *my* wedding day and even I don't know what I'm doing.

I came up with the craziest idea last night. I decided to scratch my First Wedding plans. Jess thought I was crazy. But, oh, to hell with it, I figured we had eleven more weddings to go. We could always do a planned wedding later.

I called up Jack last night.

"Hey," I tell him.

"Are you all right?" he asks. "It's the middle of the night, Max."

"Yeah, yeah," I say. "I got a small change of plans."

"Small?" he asks. "How small exactly?"

"Well, let me just come out and say it like it is: I'm thinking of changing the wedding to—"

He cuts me off.

"Change your wedding plans the day before the wedding?" He doesn't sound happy.

"Come on, Jack!" I say. "It's just a First Wedding. We can make the second one bigger and better if we screw up the first time 'round." I'm trying my best to convince him.

He sighs. "God. Max."

I can hear him rolling his eyes over the phone. I hear things like that, I promise you.

"Look," I tell him. "It's not that big of a deal. I want to surprise Jess."

"Surprise?"

"Yeah, you know, make this day memorable."

"Max, people don't surprise their fiancées on the day of the wedding."

"I know. That's why I'm doing it. It'll be a first."

I imagine him scratching his forehead or whatever. He's always doing that when he thinks I'm doing or saying something crazy.

I hear him scratching his head.

"Look," he mutters. "It's your day—so I won't interfere with that. But I will state my opinion on this matter. I think you are behaving in a very irrational manner. This—this just sounds bat-shit crazy, Max."

"I know," I say, "but tell me something: Have I ever done something that wasn't bat-shit crazy?"

He thinks for a moment. "Look, it's late. Let's just talk about this tomorrow."

"Tomorrow is the wedding, Jack," I say. "I have to talk about this *now*."

There's silence on the other end of the line.

"Well," he mutters. "What exactly are we talking about, Max? It looks like you've already made up your mind. You want to surprise Jess on her wedding day by *changing* the wedding day or plans (or whatever is going on in your crazy little head)."

"Yeah," I say. "That sounds about right. What a succinct summary on your part. Well done!"

He laughs. "Jeez, Max. You are nuts."

"But seriously: I'm a little nervous about it all."

And, honestly, I am. I'm nervous as a little toad sitting next to a boot that's about to crush it any minute. I feel exactly like that toad. Like, I'm about to have all my guts smeared all over some shitty concrete sidewalk.

I hear Jane coughing on the other end of the line. Maybe she's dry-heaving or vomiting or something.

"All right," I say. "I'm going to let you go take care of Jane."

"Thanks," he says. "Goodnight."

He hangs up the phone.

Jeez, what a piece of shit friend, I think. *What an asshole of a buddy.*

Here I am planning my first wedding and this guy just lets me go when I'm at my weakest point. He doesn't even care about me. I'm about to make the greatest and craziest decision in my life, like, ever—and he just tends to his wife, who's dying from cancer. What? Is she more important? How many more times is Max going to call you and say, "I'm getting married?" Like, zero times exactly. And this guy just hangs up and goes right back to taking care of his goddamn wife like he won't ever see her again. I swear people don't value their friends these days.

Have I ever told you about what I think about this "friend shit?" Well, let me tell you what I really think.

I have this theory: Everybody is fake. I'm not going to lie to you (asshole that I am): Everybody means *everybody*. And you know what that includes: me too. That's what I mean.

I'm not one of those assholes who isn't self-aware. I'm one of those guys who knows exactly where he stands. I know I'm not great. I'm barely above average. For God's sake, I've spent time in a high-security prison for killing a man. You don't have to tell me just how shitty of a person I am. I know. Deep down, I think I'm probably going to hell (if such a thing exists). I, literally, do not love my neighbors. *In fact, I hate my neighbors.* That old lady, I swear if old age doesn't kill her soon, I will. One of these days, she'll catch me in a bad mood, she'll run up to me and ask for an autograph, and I will—get this, I swear—push her so hard, she'll end up in the 1960s with three broken hips. I'm not even kidding you.

Look, at least you know that I'm an asshole. I come out and I say it. I don't even care to hide it. People respect me for that. They say things like, "Max McMillan he's—he's all right. He's an asshole but he's all right. He's honest, you know."

That's literally what they say about me. Of course, maybe they just say it because they are afraid of ending up as a nasty character in one of my novels. I don't know. I usually don't write people into my novels like that.

Anyway, back to talking about shit friends. I hate everybody. I swear I do. I hate my next-door neighbor. I hate the kids. I hate cats, dogs, ducks, turtles, ponds, lakes. I hate everything. The only thing I don't hate is ducks. But I might be contradicting myself. I like ducks. And don't you dare remind me of cancer—I fucking hate cancer.

I once saw a kitten. I guess I have a soft spot for kittens. And puppies. I love kittens and puppies. If you dare hurt a kitten or puppy, I swear I'll break your neck and throw you in a lake. I would do it and go grab a burger afterwards. And appear on *Good Morning, America!* later and talk about ethics and morality and shit. I swear I'm capable of evil things like that.

Damn, I hate moralists.

Chapter Eighteen

I swear I'm an awful writer.

In the last chapter, my hope was to describe my first wedding or whatever. Well, that didn't go as planned. I took a few detours. But, to be fair, weddings are really like that: They are pedantic and *detourful.* (Hey, look! I just coined a new word. Call me Noah Webster.)

I'll make another confession while I'm still in the mood: I am a vain human being. Allow me to explain my vanity.

All writers are vain and egoistical. Their sole wish is to eternalize their consciousness. At the end of the day, that is what every writer really wants. They want to be remembered. Oh, no—they don't only want to be remembered by you and you and you and you over there; they want to be remembered for a few thousand years.

It's not uncommon these days to hear the following in some backwater coffeeshop:

Curious Person: "What are you working on, Sir?"
Ambitious, Egoistical, Vain Author: "The next great American novel! Duh!"

You won't believe how many times I've heard that phrase "the next great American novel." Everyone is trying to out-write Fitzgerald's *Gatsby*.

Next time I walk into a Starbucks and some pudgy-faced fellow attempts to say something to me about "the next great American novel," I swear his face is going to need stitches. I'm having none of it.

I hate everyone. People are so vain these days. Everybody is into their cellphones and Instagram accounts. I can't even grab a coffee at Starbucks without having to deal with thirty girls lining up to take a selfie with me.

Everyone just wants to meet "the next great American author." I act like it's all right, but, as of late, I've been getting all depressed and cranky over it. Our culture is oversaturated with silly things like selfies and selfie-sticks. I don't even understand the explicit individualism that's on display. Every thirteen-year-old girl with access to the internet is on Instagram posting photos doing stupid shit like eating Cheerios for breakfast. "Oh, look at me! I need you to see this! Oh, looky here! I'm eating!"

Oh. My. God. Really?

"Well, Miss, I sure am glad you aren't starving!"

I mean, what the hell am I supposed to say to the kid?

"Oh, my God, those Cheerios look amazing?"

Hell no. I'm not saying that.

Who in their right mind wants to scroll through their feed and look at Cheerios in a damn bowl all day long?

I swear you must be an idiot to do that. And I am obviously aware everybody does that.

My agent called me the other day. You want to know what this loser told me? You might have to sit down for this.

"Hey, Max, we've got a problem," he says. He's all serious, as if he's about to relate something momentous like the Holocaust.

He continues: "It's your Instagram account."

He clears his throat and sounds nervous.

"Calm down, Daren. What's up with the Gram?" I ask.

"Oh, you're not going to like this," he says. "The publisher wants you to be more active on it. You know, post what you had for breakfast, lunch, dinner, snacks, that sort of thing."

I can tell he's not happy saying this. He knows my position.

"Oh, for God's sake!" I say. "Who the hell cares what I had for breakfast?"

"Well, Max, your fans seem to care."

"What fans?"

"Well, it looks like your numbers are tanking. You went from being the number one star on Instagram to—" There's a silence on the other end of the line. "Well, thank God, you're still number one, but still. Your numbers are tanking."

"What are my numbers?" I ask. I'm vain like that.

"Two trillion followers, Max."

"But there's only seven billion people on earth. How could I possibly have two trillion followers?"

I'm genuinely baffled by this.

"Look, Max, I'm not that great at math, you know. Four out of three people are bad at fractions. And I'm not a statistician, but maybe the numbers have to do with fake accounts . . ."

He sounds about as confused as my grandma on Oxycodone.

I have no idea why the hell people want to see what others are eating for dinner, especially when what they're eating is ordinary, boring, and yawn-inducing.

I mean, I used to use my Instagram account. I'd begin my morning by opening that dumb app. Then I'd begin scrolling. I'd scroll, scroll, scroll. I'd scroll through Frosted Flakes, Frosted Flakes in coconut milk, Frosted Flakes on the beach, Frosted Flakes in my bowl of cereal, Frosted Flakes on the table, Frosted Flakes in soy milk. After that, I'd put the phone down, take a little break, and resume looking through what everyone's had for breakfast. After a few hours of figuring out what everybody had for breakfast, it would be lunchtime, and the cycle would begin again.

Imagine how it would have looked in the olden days, say before they had the internet. Imagine, for example, our ancestors gathering around a fire and discussing what they ate that day.

Person One: "I had some beans with rice today. It was served on a warm plate made of clay."

Everyone claps.

Person Two: "Well, ladies and gentlemen, I had something amazing for dinner today. I had bread. Fresh, amazing bread. It was wonderful."

Everybody claps.

And they would go around the circle and everybody would talk about what they had eaten that day. And once the entire village was done talking about the food, the plate it was on, the color of the keys that lay next to the plate, et cetera, they would begin to discuss another meal, such as dinner.

Everybody claps, of course.

I don't know about you, but this just sounds plain silly to me.

To prove my point, I did something outrageous once.

"Okay. I'll use Instagram again. But on my own terms," I say to my agent.

I buy this silly video camera that has a light on it that is attached to a catheter. And I do something quite preposterous. I share it live on Instagram.

I eat a meal. I put this camera down my throat, swallow it or whatever, and walk around the house and do the chores.

Now, I must admit: It was rather unpleasant broadcasting the stomach contents to two trillion followers. But, as it were, that's what happened. I guess it became a trend.

My agent called me the next day, extremely excited.

"Max!" he yells into the phone. "I have great news for you."

"What?" I'm already annoyed.

"That thing you did with eating breakfast and then having the world watch you digest it was brilliant! Sheer brilliance! Everybody is talking about it."

"Really?" I ask. Now I'm terrified. (How stupid and preposterous can humans get?)

"Oh, yes! They lo—oved it!" He's gushing over it as if I landed on the Moon or something.

"Well, I'm glad it worked," I say.

"Oh, Max, but the publisher wants you to do it again. Three times a day. Broadcast your progress. Broadcast digesting breakfast, lunch, and dinner!"

He's so excited, you would think this guy just got laid or sucked off.

"What the hell are you talking about, Daren? You know that whole thing was a joke, right?"

"Oh, Max, you have no idea. This is great news. We've entered a new phase in human history. With that video you posted, now everybody wants to do it. You started a new trend! Now, we won't just get to see what others had for breakfast, we'll watch them digest it!"

I'm about to puke in my damn mouth.

"You gotta be kidding me, Daren," I exclaim, confused. "People aren't that—" I look for the right word— "stupid, are they?"

"Max, it's not about whether they are stupid. All we care about are numbers. If the numbers add up, you're a winner."

I swear people are . . . stupid.

I'm really not that bad a guy. (If you think about it.) I'm quite normal, actually (when it comes to social media and its uses).

You probably think I'm an inconsistent writer and thinker; that everything I say is loose and unconnected. Well, I have some news for you: you are partly correct. But only partly. I am returning to a subject I raised a few paragraphs ago that you, my friend, thought I forgot about (I have, in fact, not forgotten anything). Allow me to remind you of it, since I assume you in fact have forgotten it.

People are all fakes.

Let's talk about Instagram. That shit wasn't started until 2012 or something. And look at the crazy social expectations it has produced.

Half the people on it have absurd numbers of followers. I once bought a bunch of fake followers just to make myself feel faker (I don't know, but sometimes I'm so real I, too, need a little fake in my life). So, I spent twenty bucks buying something like twenty million followers. Next thing you know, the president of the United States was calling me. (He was an old man with dementia who had no idea how Instagram worked.)

"Max McMillan, this is Fred Mack speaking, president of the United States of America," he said.

"What do you want? I'm kinda busy right now, you know. I'm famous."

"So, I heard," he says. "That's why I'm calling you."

"Well," I say, rather exasperated. (At this point, the fake fame is getting to my head, so I'm feeling hella important.) "Tell me what it is you want."

"Sorry to bother you, Mr. McMillan," he continues, cautiously, "but I've been notified by our department about your social status."

"Have you, indeed!" I say, happy to be noticed by the most powerful man on Earth.

"You're rather famous now. Fox News and CNN all got notified of your rise to fame. You got something like nineteen million nine-hundred thousand and ninety-two followers in the span of twelve seconds. And you only created your account a few hours ago. Now, my question to you, kind Sir, is: How did you do it?"

I'm baffled by this. The president himself is calling me to talk about Instagram. I swear I'm living in The End Times and praying for Jesus' miraculous Second Return.

"Look," I tell him. (And it feels so good to be bossing around the president and offering him my expert advice.) "All you need to do is give me your login information. You know, the stuff you use to log in to your account. I will do all of this, for you and for our great country, for free. I swear, Mister President, you have my word on this. I will make you famous overnight."

The president is very happy about this. He says his password and shit right over the phone. I write it down and then say goodbye to him.

"I'll call you in a few hours—when you're hella famous, Sir."

"Okay, Mr. McMillan," he says, humbly. "Thank you so much. This is a great, great service you are doing for our country."

I log in to the Instagram app and—boom!—there it is on the top:

"Fred Mack, President of the United States of America."

So, it doesn't take a rocket scientist to find out what happened next. I'm the damn President. I'm literally the guy in charge of America. Max McFreaking President.

So, I throw twenty bucks at some dude out of India with a "click farm." He gets the president's numbers right up there with mine (but stops at nineteen million; I told the Indian kid to let me have "the upper hand" in this matter [I didn't want the president to get too arrogant and cocky with me]).

So, that's the story of how I became president for a day. (Except I'm really lying here because I still have that old dude's login information and make sure to write good reviews of my books before they drop.)

Here's a post I made last year. It was a picture of the president (Photoshopped and filtered, of course) holding a copy of my book. I wrote in the blurb: "Just got done reading the greatest book ever written, by one of our own living legends, the most-excellent Max McMillan. His novel *Wiped My Ass Then Took a Shit* effectively puts Steinbeck's *Grapes of Wrath* in the back seat. This book takes the wheel! Read it before it sells out (which I hear is going to happen in a few seconds!) God bless America, and God bless our great writer!"

That post was shared by six trillion "people." I ran the promotion on that post. Paid a guy something like an entire Benjamin to get us to that number. I mean, more people liked the post than had ever existed on Planet Earth.

The next day, the headlines read: "US president shared world-renowned writer, Max McMillan's book, and it got more likes than the total number of people who have ever existed on Earth: six trillion."

I swear people in America (and the world) are so stupid, they just don't get it. There aren't enough people in the damn *universe* to like that post that many times. I swear I want to shoot myself sometimes from how silly people are. No, my post wasn't liked by six trillion people. Those people are just bots. Hacks. Fake accounts.

Hell, if you think about it, *some of you are so fake, you might as well be bots.*

Call me Max McCrazy but—shit—I can see fake from twelve trillion miles away. If those miles were converted into likes, I swear, that's how many likes I'd get if I released an album. Of course, I'd win all the damn Grammys for it, too. (Everybody knows that you have to suck a few old white cocks to get a head-nod from the old dudes who pick and choose the "winners" [so-called].)

I'd suck those dudes' cocks in a heartbeat. I wouldn't even bat an eye. I'd just suck, suck, suck away. And—bam!—I'd collect the Grammys and take a piss on them the next day.

You think I'm kidding? I'm not even lying to you. There's no way in hell half of those albums that got Grammys will be remembered for more than ten years. Pick and choose from the following artists. Who do you think won a Grammy? Queen. Tupac. Snoop Dog. Janis Joplin. Guns N' Roses. Jimi Hendrix. Bob Marley.

Think really hard! Who do you think won a Grammy?

Seriously. Choose one or two.

Come on! You got this!

Answer: *none of them.*

I kid you not: I bet they didn't want an old white dude's cock in their mouth. That's why.

See, I'm different.

I don't care.

I'd rinse my mouth afterwards. That's what I would do. I'd suck it so fast like you wouldn't believe. I swear, people just need to learn how to suck a dick well. You do it well, and you could go places.

I'm the greatest writer and hack who has ever lived. I swear it.

Just last week, I had to do it. I logged into the president's account again and did the incredible. I posted a fake picture of him and wrote in the blurb: "Coming to Max McMillan's First Ever Wedding! Cannot wait to see him and his gorgeous bride-to-be."

I told you I was going to surprise my Jess.

Look, I have no idea what keeps you guys up at night, but I love me a good joke. And a good laugh.

The post was shared something like twelve trillion times (lots of bots, apparently, wanted to attend my wedding). The next day, the president calls me. He's senile and has dementia.

"Hey, I guess I'm invited to your wedding, right?" he asks, terrified I'll turn him down.

"Of course," I say. "You said it yourself yesterday."

"Yeah, I guess I did," he says. "Funny thing is: I don't recall doing it."

"Well, you are getting old," I say, politely.

"Yeah," he says. "It must be old age. Last night, I was going to . . . to take my wife for a roll in the hay, you know. Spent two hours looking for the Viagra. Then my wife bumped into me and was like, 'Freddy, your dick is as hard as moon-rock.' That's when I remembered: I had swallowed the entire container."

I laugh. "God, I hate old age."

He sighs.

"You're a good man, Max," he says.

"Thank you," I say.

"I'll see you tomorrow at the wedding."

So, that's how I got the president to go to my wedding. I faked his dumbass right into it. I swear people are stupid.

In any case, here I am. Day of the wedding—and *even I* don't know what I'm doing.

Jess is holding onto me. She's all smiles. She keeps kissing me repeatedly. God, I guess she really does love me, hack that I am.

I hug her and kiss the top of her head. I don't know why, but I love kissing the top of her head. She blushes. And so, I kiss her again.

These days, we're always kissing each other, acting like two lovebirds who have never kissed before.

She likes kissing a lot. I guess I do, too. It's weird. Kissing is. It's like: What the hell is it? Is it a form of cannibalism? Think about it: You put things in your mouth you want to consume, things you want to eat. I guess what I'm really trying to tell Jess today on our wedding day is: I want to eat you.

It's romantic, really.

I understand Hannibal Lecter. I really do. He was a misunderstood romantic. All he really wanted to do was kiss people. But I guess he took it a step further. See, we normal people, we stop at kissing. He just had to take it the whole nine yards. I guess I can see why people don't get him. He showed them who they all really were: goddamn cannibals. And they were afraid of themselves. So, they killed him. Anyways, that's my theory. I'm not saying it's correct, I'm just saying that's what I think.

God, I hate kissing. It's such a weird activity. Oh, well. The things we, men, do for women. It's insane. I swear it is. Kissing is.

Jess says to me, "Honey, is everything all right?"

"Yeah. Why?" I ask.

"You look lost in thought."

"Hmmm. Maybe. I was thinking about how we kiss a lot."

She kisses me. I guess she thinks I want to be cannibalized.

"You're so sweet," she says. "A guy that spends his days daydreaming about kissing."

She has no idea what the hell she's talking about. And I believe ignorance is bliss, so I don't tell her what's on my crazy mind.

"Where are we going, babe?" she asks.

"Alcatraz," I say. "We're getting on the ferry and taking a ride to Alcatraz."

"What's in Alcatraz, honey?" she asks, curious and surprised.

"The president."

Now she's really interested.

"The president is going to attend our wedding in Alcatraz?"

"Yes," I say. "Shhh. Don't ruin the surprise for everyone."

Jack and Jane are attending to their kids, so they don't hear any of it.

Star is distracted with some tall, dark, and handsome man with bright green eyes. I can tell he's really into her.

"It's a crazy thing I thought up," I say to Jess.

"Oohhh," Jess says. "I'm so excited."

She leans in and kisses me. Again.

Damn, I love cannibals.

Chapter Nineteen

There's a slight summer breeze blowing through the trees and shrubs. The plants and the greens and the sun all rustle with poetic fervor. It's a rather lovely day.

There is, however, no snow in this California.

Jess and I are standing under an ancient willow tree with white and pink balloons tied to it.

The massive prison looms behind us, with its melancholic greys and fading whites. Most of the buildings have these large glassless windows resembling eyes that began to stare sometime in the last century—and haven't stopped staring since.

The sun burns red in the blue California sky, a relentless beacon of hope and luster.

Everything is perfect. Everything is as I imagined it would be.

Our first wedding. And it is being held on "the Rock."

Alcatraz.

Most of the guests—and there are thousands of them—are entirely confused and bewildered by this spectacle. They all want an explanation. I can see it in their eyes.

Even my kindest of critics, Jack, is confused.

Right before the ceremony, he says to me, "Max, why are we on

Alcatraz? Is this some kind of joke?"

I say to him, "Have you read *The Fault in Our Stars* by John Green?"

He says, "No, I have not."

I say, "Well, in the novel, there's this sad kid dying from cancer. And he walks around with a cigarette in his mouth. He never lights it. He just walks around with it."

Jack is confused. "What do cigarettes, cancer, and weddings all have in common?"

"Look," I say, "it's a metaphor."

"A what?"

"A metaphor," I repeat. "It's all about what this island, this prison, represents."

"What does it represent?" he asks.

"The prison is a metaphor for marriage. It's about how marriage turns a man and a woman or whatever into an island. It's not a literal prison. But it is a kind of life sentence, if you catch my drift."

"Okay," he says. His eyes are sparkling now. He's getting it.

"In the novel, the kid walks around with a cigarette because it reminds him of cancer, death. It's about living life on the edge, not taking anything for granted. You can die any moment—and the unlit cigarette is a reminder of that."

"So, this prison wedding is all a great, big metaphor?" Jack asks.

"Yeah. It's a metaphor. Jess and I are partners." I point across the bay at nearby San Francisco. "Look at that city," I say. "That's society. It's out there. It has its own illusions, its own abilities, its own tasks. We used to be a part of it all. But today we are saying: no more. We aren't a part of it. Oh, we are, in some way, but now we are *something else*. We are a distinct culture, a separate island. To get to Us, you must swim across a bay in cold ocean waters. By the time you get here, you would have come to respect the ocean and the waters and the waves—and the beaches of this island would remind you of how great it is to be on land, to be in the presence of a great, married couple."

Jack laughs. "Now you really are a megalomaniac. A true idealist."

"I don't know, Jack," I say. "I think marriage is sacred."

"I can tell." He pulls out a cigarette and lights it. He blows smoke around and then looks at me. "You want one?" he asks. "This one's not a metaphor."

We both laugh, and I take one.

We smoke cigarettes and gaze at the bay.

"It's a wonderful day to get married, Max," he says. "And I'm glad you're joining the family. Glad that you are growing up, so to speak. I can see it now. There's a kind of transformation going on in you. Jess is making you a better person. She really is."

I cough.

I was never a smoker or a drinker.

I could never be what the papers said.

"Yeah, she is making me a better person. I feel it."

"You're no longer an asshole," he says. "I mean, you still are, but it's not as bad as it used to be. I remember the days when you were an arrogant piece of shit. I remember those days well."

"Yeah, the truth is: I still am. I just got better at hiding it."

"Max McMillan, the introspective genius?" Jack laughs. "What? You're going to come out as a moral philosopher next, pontificating on the subject of premarital sex and abortion?"

I laugh. "No, I'm never going to be a moralist. I think all moralists are frauds. Except for Cato. Cato wasn't a fraud."

"You have to make up your mind, Max." He points across the bay. "The world out there needs you—and they only need one of you. They have small minds. They cannot handle Max the Moral Philosopher and Max the Immoral Philanderer. They want you to pick and choose. Be one thing. Only one thing. Some little thing. They want it to be little because they are little—and they want to place you in their little heads in a little, teeny-tiny category. And they only have room for one thing. You must choose one thing. They cannot handle greatness or plurality or what-have-you. They only want one thing. Max McMillan—they only want to put you in a simple category, and leave you there, possibly, forever. But don't worry, pal, it's all just a metaphor."

He pats me on the shoulder and we both chuckle.

"Come on," I say. "We have to go. It's time. And I'm sure Jess is already looking for me."

We head back and the president himself officiates at the wedding. Dementia and all, it goes as planned.

We say our "I Dos" and everybody cheers and claps and drinks champagne. After the little quasi-religious ceremony, Jess and I shake hands with a thousand people. I meet her parents for the fourth time or so. They look happy. I guess my mother-in-law likes me. For now, of course. (We all know that phase never lasts.)

Afterwards, I make small talk with the president.

He says, "Why'd you choose Alcatraz of all places?"

I repeat what I said earlier to Jack.

He nods. "I don't get any of that, Max," he says. "None."

Adults are like that, I have learned. They never seem to get much of anything. It's like Saint-Exupery said in *The Little Prince*. You know, all adults are just a bunch of pricks who are good at forgetting.

They act like they were never children. I swear the older you get, the more lacking you become in wisdom. I'm feeling it myself already, too. It's like a fog coming over my mind. It's clouding up my vision and my thinking. I cannot think or talk the way I used to. I used to be intelligent. Now that I'm in my thirties, I'm basically halfway to stupid.

"Yeah," I mutter to the president. "It's not for everyone."

The president laughs. "It's all right, Max. I never was into philosophy or English writing. I've always liked mathematics more."

Inside, I laugh. The president is good at math? I swear this guy is some next-level crazy. He's as self-deluded as the rest of the fake world. Some of his Instagram posts have more likes than people in the universe. And he's telling me he's good with numbers. He can go kiss my—"

Jess interrupts my wonderful thoughts.

"Hi, Mr. President!" she exclaims.

The president likes her. It's obvious. Old, white men in power always like attractive, smart women. But I'm not worried either way. I have more followers on Instagram than he does.

Jess would be stupid to leave me for a man with only nineteen million followers. But maybe she's bad at math, too? I shrug the thought off. It's silly of me to think such things, especially on my wedding day.

Jess wraps her arms around me, and we make out. It's always like that with us these days. First, we hug—and then we kiss. Next thing you know, I get an erection in public. Jess always does silly things like that to me. It's like she's secretly trying to embarrass me.

They make small talk and I'm getting a little jealous, so I pull her out of the conversation.

"Hey, Jess," I say. "We forgot to say hello to Phil."

She gives me one of those stares. She knows we've already said hello to Phil.

"What was that all about?" she asks me afterwards.

"Look," I say, "I think the president was hitting on you."

She laughs.

I look at her as if she's crazy. "You know old men in power are hungry for a little bit of action."

"Oh, Max!" she laughs. "Don't be silly!"

I don't find any of it funny.

This one time, I was on a cruise with a few girls. (At the time, I was polyamorous or whatever.) And this prick runs into me.

He was one of those I-Love-You-Max-McMillan types. I could see if from a thousand miles away.

He says, "Oh. Ma. Gawd. I cannot believe it's you. Maxy. Maxy Mac!"

I hate it when people call me some childish thing, like Maxy Mac.

I'm about to punch this loser right on the nose when he whips out a book and my fist lands on it instead.

The prick hits the ground. He gets up and his nose is all bleeding and it's getting all the book's pages wet and red.

He starts crying. He's not even crying that I punched him in the nose. He's crying because that was the copy he's owned since he was a kid.

"Waw!" he cries. "That was the copy mommy gave me for my eleventh birthday. Waw!"

The book—*Loaded Diapers*—looks like it came out of a bleeding you-know-what. I mean, the thing almost looked like a baby just got delivered or something.

This prick comes back, and he's got blood and tears and whatever running down his cheeks, dripping all over the floor.

Everybody thinks the dude's an asshole. I have no idea why they think this, but they're all booing him. I'm not used to this. Hell, I was the one who initiated violent contact with this sore bastard.

I'm itching to go to jail or whatever. I have no idea, but that was on my bucket list. I wanted to do something bad so I could be badass Max. Like, I don't know, in those *Mad Max* movies. Hell, maybe I could have been called Mad Max, too.

Anyway, the point is: I really wanted to land my ass in prison so that I could come out and get even more pussy. I was already exhausted from all the slaying I was doing, but I heard prison makes men sound very attractive. I mean, every girl wants to be with a guy who will: (a) kill somebody for her; (b) spend a few years in prison writing her letters; (c) go all ham on her in bed like Al Capone. I don't know, but females fantasize about prison sex all the time. I learned that when I was on this cruise ship.

The girls I was with all wanted me to handcuff them and shit. They wanted me to carry a gun, smoke cigarettes, and wear a wife-beater. And when I'd bang them, these girls wanted me to dominate. I mean, they literally had to escape from my dick like those three dudes who escaped from Alcatraz. I swear. The girls were crazy.

And so, there I am punching this dude for no damn reason. And what's weird—and I learned this afterwards—the ship has nothing but girls on it. So, *they really* want to see Max McMillan win. (Not many dudes to intervene and stop the chaos.) So, instead of helping the gent up, like I naturally would, I just keep on punching him, and he just keeps on bleeding and saying things like, "Waw." And the girls keep cheering me on. I swear they do.

After he passes out, which happens rather quickly, I finally sit down from exhaustion. One of the girls from the crowd brings me a water and kisses me on the lips. I have this dude's blood all over me and the women are just going wild. They keep trying to kiss me.

I guess they think this was a fight over a girl. The next day, somebody releases a headline. I swear I'm not making this up. "Max McMillan defends three girls from potential rapist, man in custody."

Lo and behold, the cops find this guy had ketamine and Rohypnol in his pockets. I guess he really was trying to date rape somebody.

So, once again, my idiocy gets me headlined. For the millionth time, I am a hero. I don't even have to go to prison. After this event, especially after video footage is released of me fighting this guy, I stop dreaming about prison. Every girl after that event knows I am one hell of a fighter. (I never did tell them the guy was so drunk, he could barely stand. But, oh, to hell with it, I let people maintain their fantasies.)

But it's really that night on which I learn a great, great lesson. It's midnight on the ship, and I'm out taking a leak. Just minding my own business and pissing into the Atlantic. I'm about halfway through pissing when I notice an older gentleman standing in the moonlight, smoking a cigar. He's well-dressed and has a head full of beautiful white hair.

I put my dick back in my pants, zip it up to keep it from leaping out, and walk over to him. He just nods at me and says, "Good evening, fella."

I think, "Oh, why the hell not? I've got nothing to do. Might as well just spend a few minutes talking to this dude."

So, I tell him, "Good evening, sir."

We make some small talk.

He's apparently some sort of CEO of Something or Other. He's got lots of money and he's not afraid of making that abundantly clear.

After a few minutes of pointless banter, he asks me a strange question: "Those ladies you were with—they yours?"

I think, *That's a funny question. I mean, I don't own people. And slavery has been banned for a while now.*

So, I say, "I don't understand the question. I came with those girls, yes. But I don't own them. They're not mine."

He gives me a strange look and then pulls a bottle of whiskey from his suit pocket. It's a small container, one of those hundred-milliliter ones.

He takes a sip and then offers me one.

I think, "Oh, why the hell not? I'll drink." So, I take the bottle from him and take a sip. It's good shit. It really is. I take another sip.

We end up sipping on the whiskey and talking about boats and sailing and the north star.

Thirty minutes later, he says, "It's time for me to go."

I say, "Yeah, it's time for me to go, too." But when I say it, the words come out all slurry and shit. So, I sound like some drunk teenager from the Bronx.

At that point, I become aware of two things: (1) I am really, really drowsy; and (2) the drink had one of those roofies in it.

I collapse right there and watch the gentleman walk away like nothing happened. And as he walks away, I realize a third truth: (3) he's about to rape somebody.

The next day, when I finally do wake up, I don't remember much. The girls seem all right. But they do tell me a gentleman came over and they had a few drinks. I don't ask them any further questions. I figure if they were raped, and they don't know it, it's better that way.

I don't see the gentleman again during the trip. I figure that's for the better. Had I seen him, I probably would have killed him or something.

Anyway, that's why I don't trust rich and powerful old men. They are all potentially dangerous.

I stopped accepting drinks from strangers after that trip. I guess I became a little less romantic, you know. I accepted reality for what it was: a crock of crap. People weren't all good. Many were outright evil. And I never slept with those girls again. God only knows what that piece of shit gave them.

When the wedding is all wrapped up, I send everybody away. Jess and I go to some little hotel near the coast, where nobody knows we exist.

I'm exhausted, so I say, "Jess, I'm going to sleep."

She says, "Same."

And that's how our first wedding ends. We just fall asleep next to one another, tired as hell.

Damn, I hate weddings.

Chapter Twenty

The first few weeks after our first wedding go well. Jess is excited. She's planning our second wedding and it's sounding incredible. I have no idea what we're doing for it. She says it's a surprise. I won't lie to you, I love surprises.

One night, I make us hot chocolate and we crawl into bed and watch some sobby romance. Jess wipes her tears and she's acting like she's in love for the first time.

Something happens on the screen—the couple fights or whatever—and she turns to me and says, "Have you ever broken up with any girl? Like, where she broke *your* heart?"

"Yeah," I say, "I think I told you about it. Remember? It was the day before I proposed to you."

"Yes, I remember," she says. She pauses and thinks for a second. "But you never got vulnerable with me. Like, you said what you said, but I didn't feel much heart in it."

I frown. "Hmmm," I say. "Well, what do you want to know?"

"Well, tell me something heartbreaking. Make me cry or I don't know," she says.

"Cry? I don't know if I can do that. Remember? I promised never to make you cry."

She leans in and kisses me. "I know. But I'm *asking* you to."

I swear, women are weird. One second, she's happy-go-lucky; the next, she's asking me to make her cry.

"Okay," I say. "I'll get vulnerable with you."

She smiles. "Please do." She wraps her arms around me even tighter. I guess she really wants us to become "one" or whatever.

"All right," I begin. "There once was this girl—and you're not going to believe this story. I used to be a salesman, you know. Like, I sold cars at a Toyota dealership. So, one day, I see this gorgeous girl walk in. I'm with another customer. But I keep looking at her and one of my coworkers notices.

He comes up to me and says, "I can take over here—if you'd like." Then he winks at me.

So, I come up to her. She's this girl with wavy blonde hair and these large, blue eyes. I feel my pulse start to race and I get weak in the knees. You know, the standard mumbo-jumbo.

She looks at me and I swear I'm going to say something stupid or just stutter.

She says, "Hi. I'm looking for a car. Something affordable."

I say something intelligent, like, "Hi. My name is Max McMillan, and I will do my best to help you find an affordable car."

That's what I thought I said. Until I said what I said. And what I said was: absolute gibberish.

Literally. It was word salad that burst out of my mouth like uncontrolled diarrhea.

She starts to giggle and it's the cutest giggle in the world. You should have heard it. Anyway, her name is Laurie. It suits her well.

We walk around the lot and look at all kinds of cheap cars. Eventually, she settles on a Corolla. She drives off the lot and I stand there and watch her leave. I go back to my desk and sit.

My coworker comes up and says, "How did it go?"

"I didn't get her number," I gloomily reply.

He holds out a scarf and says, "She forgot this. Call her and tell her she could come by and pick it up or you could drop it off at her place."

I grab the scarf and immediately call her.

She picks up. "Hi. This is Laurie."

"Laurie, it's Max McMillan. You just bought the car here. Ummm, you left your scarf behind," I say.

"Oh, shoot!" she exclaims. "I'm sorry."

"Don't worry about it," I say. "I can drop it off at your place or you could come pick it up. Your place is along the way."

"Sure, you can drop it off here."

"What happens after that?" asks Jess.

"Well, I drop the scarf off and one thing leads to another. We end up going dancing. We dance at this small little bar that has this shitty singer-songwriter on stage. But, oh, to hell with it, he plays *Wonderful Tonight* by Eric Clapton, and I just waltz with her to that. It's a very elegant waltz, you know. And we start kissing and such. Before you know it, we're madly in love. Like, crazy in love."

"And then what happened?"

"We have a relationship. Date for a year or so. Then, one day, we fight. It's something stupid. I can't even remember what it's about. It's the only fight in our relationship. Just fighting about something silly, and she walks out on me. I spend a day or two thinking about it all—and I realize I have been wrong. So, I come to her house with flowers and shit. I bring some chalk, too. I write on the street below: *Laurie, I love you.*"

"Aww, that's so sweet," Jess murmurs.

"Then I knock on her door. A few minutes later, the cops show up."

"Oh, no, Max!"

"Yeah, the cops show up."

"I had written her this poem and love letter. Had it all written by hand. Thought I was going to win her back, you know. Anyway, I come there, and the cops show up. She never comes out or ever says anything. Just lets the cops take care of me. I talk to them. They say, 'Don't ever come back here again, or she'll get a restraining order on you.' So, I leave. I tear the poem and the letter up and throw the flowers away. It was one of the few times in my life when I was about to confess my love to a girl. And it ended badly. I mean, the cops showed up and that was that."

We sit in silence for a few seconds. Jess is thinking. "Is that why it takes you so long to say, I-Love-You?"

"Yeah," I say. "It's one of the reasons. You know, once bitten, twice shy, I suppose. I've never had any luck with saying I-Love-You. It's a disaster any time I say it. It's like abracadabra or something, a damn curse."

Jess laughs. "I'm glad nothing happened between us that was crazy."

"Not yet, at least," I say, softly.

"Oh, don't be so dark," she says. "It's still our honeymoon."

"Well, now you know why I'm crazy."

"True. I do."

"So, tell me about your crazy stories. You have any?"

"I have plenty," she replies.

"Go ahead," I say.

"One time, when I was twenty-two or twenty-three, I fell in love with this romantic. He promised me the moon, the stars, the sea (and everything in it). All kinds of pirate gold and wrecked ships and treasures. Little did I know what Bermuda Triangle I had sailed into!"

I laugh. "Bermuda Triangle, eh?"

"Yeah," she says. "He was a nice guy for about three months. And then everything went downhill after that. He became very demanding and abusive. Verbally abusive—at least at first. And if he didn't get his way, well, things would just escalate quickly from there. He was a passionate man. When he loved you, he loved you best. I mean, he loved me well. But when it was bad, it was bad. It was awful."

I nod. "Uh-huh. I'm sorry to hear that, babe." I place a soft kiss on her shoulder.

"Then one evening, he had a few drinks and decided to start chasing me around the house. I guess I broke up with him that night. Only he would have none of it. A week later, he sobered up all right. He came over to my house. Banged on the door. Demanded to be taken back. Apologized in this demanding way. I mean, he wasn't even apologizing so much as commanding me to take him back."

"He sounds crazy," I mutter.

"Yeah," she says. "That was the one time I really had to call the cops on a guy. I got a restraining order on him. He left me alone after that."

"He ever try to contact you again?" I ask.

"Yeah, years later. I ran into him at a gas station. He was with another woman, and it looked like they had a baby between them. He came up to me and apologized. Said he quit drinking, smoking, and said he began to see a psychologist. Apparently, it turned his life around for the better. They looked like a happy family."

"I'm happy he didn't become something worse. That's usually what happens. Relationships tend to bring out the best and the worst in us. Nothing people do 'for the sake of love' surprises me anymore."

"Yeah," she murmurs. "The things we do for love. It's crazy, isn't it?"

As she speaks, the night begins to settle all around us. It's getting dark out, and the moon is casting little rays of white onto Jess's face.

I look over at her and smile like I'm really in love.

"You look pretty," I whisper.

"What?" she asks, softly.

"It's the moonlight," I whisper. "It looks good on you."

"Does it?"

"Yeah," I say. "It really makes you shine. I don't know. Glow even."

She laughs quietly. "Crazy how we can talk about this kind of stuff now. In the moment, it's all so crazy. So hard, you know. And now it's like a big joke. The crushes we had, the heartbreaks—it's almost like none of them ever mattered."

"They really don't. We tend to forget so much. I don't remember my first kiss. I don't remember anything. I remember this one time that was romantic. It was back when I was nineteen. My dad bought this old 1977 Marlin. It was a ski-boat, I think. Anyway, half of the time, the thing wouldn't work. So, I took my first girlfriend out on the lake and the engine breaks down in the middle of it. And, get this, it starts to rain. Just starts pouring like one of those tropical-storm rains. I mean, we are wet the instant the rain hits the ground. So, I pull out the one paddle we kept on board for such occasions and paddle my ass off to shore. It takes us like an hour to get there. Anyway, by the time we get back, we're all wet and the towels I gave my girlfriend are all wet. It was quite funny, actually, now that I think about it."

"Can I ask you a serious question?"

"Sure," I say. "What's up?"

"Why did you marry me? I mean, really? Why me?"

"You want me to confess something to you?"

"Of course," she whispers.

"I was a virgin until I met you."

She doesn't believe me.

"Seriously?"

I nod. "I swear to God."

"How?"

"I don't know. It's weird, I guess."

"What is?"

"I just didn't want to have sex with anyone."

"But what about all of the stories and the books and the—the Reddits and whatever?" She's astounded.

I light a cigarette. "Look," I say, "I'm an interesting person. I do things a certain way. The way I do things isn't exactly . . . *normal.*"

I pause.

"Okay," she murmurs. "Go on." She sits up in bed and I can tell I got her attention.

"I guess I just did what I did for the hell of it. You know, I threw some big parties. Always had a lot of women over. But I never really wanted to be with any of them. At the time, I was obsessed with Ruth, you know. I was like Jay Gatsby. I couldn't let go of the past. I would eat a pussy out here and there. Finger a girl. Things of that nature. Get my dick sucked. But I never actually screwed anyone."

"And what about me?"

"I actually liked you."

"What did you like about me?"

"I don't know. You valued yourself."

"Well, I did—and do. But I'm pretty sure we slept together on our first or second night or something. It was pretty crazy."

"Well, that's what I call romance," I say.

She laughs.

"No, Max, seriously?" she says.

I blow some smoke. Mostly to look like I'm a cool dude on a movie set.

Then I inhale slowly. "Look," I say, "I'm being honest with you right now: I never slept with anyone other than you."

"But how? That makes no sense."

"The world is split up into a lot of little pieces, Jess. I'm Max McMillan. Everybody knows me as this playboy. I told you before: I bury the truth beneath a hurricane of words. I say things to deceive people, to hide from them. The more I talk, the less you know about me. It is only when I am silent that I am really myself."

"So, all of this—all of these parties people write about, all of these books about you screwing random people—these are all lies?"

"They're not lies. They're art."

"Art?"

"You want me to tell you how it all started, how my career was born?"

"Yes, of course. Tell me."

She's sitting up, her head perched on her neck, listening attentively. She knows this is a special moment. This is the moment when I am being vulnerable, dropping my guard, and telling her impossible things about myself, things I never thought I'd tell anyone, especially my wife.

"I was a nobody back then," I whisper, cigarette smoke carelessly leaving my lips. "I wrote a few books and some romantic poetry. Nothing crazy. No explicit content. No sex. Nothing of that nature. It was all tender stuff. Then I started to submit my work. I got hell for it. One editor took the time out of his day to tell me that all romantic poetry required subliminal or explicit violence. And my poetry was all lovey-dovey and tender and romantic. So, he told me, it would always get turned down unless I brought in some BDSM and choking and blood and guns and fists and shit. I also submitted *Snow in California*. An early unfinished draft. All of that got trashed. Everybody said I wouldn't be able to sell it. It was too clean. Too romantic. Too dreamy. Too conservative. Not enough sex. Not enough violence. Not enough filth. Not enough tragedy. So, I wrote a stupid book. And the rest is history. Everybody just assumed I was this huge hit, this massive liberal, this bastion of unhinged sexuality. But I wasn't. Privately, I was boring. I wasn't even getting laid."

"I still don't get it. I don't understand how you could fake so much."

"I never had to fake anything, Jess. The one time I stated in an interview that I wasn't really a playboy, they laughed in my face so hard and so long, I realized I should just play along with it. There was no use in arguing with idiots. And most people are idiots."

"So, you're telling me that I'm actually the only person in the world who knows you? Who *really* knows you?"

I finish the cigarette and put it out. "Yeah, you're the only girl in the world who knows me."

"Why didn't you tell me any of this stuff before?"

"Because you would have never believed me."

There's a moment of silence between us. I can hear Jess breathing, thinking.

"You're right. I wouldn't have," she says. "But I do now. It just sounds so crazy."

"I am crazy. I'm not even denying it at this point."

"So, all of those parties. All of those whores who claimed to have screwed you—all lies?"

"All of it."

"That's beautiful."

"Thank you."

"You've really . . . *played* the entire world."

"Yes, I have."

"Where did you get this idea from?"

"It's actually out in the open. Everybody knows him. I got it from Søren Kierkegaard."

"What did he say?"

"He said people can't tolerate the truth. They can't accept truth like they accept other things. For people to accept truth, it must be presented in a package of lies. People love lies. So, as long as truth is disguised as a lie, they'll accept it."

"Please explain," she whispers, tenderly.

"Look," I begin again. "I deceived people into the truth. I deceived you, for example. I lured you into my lair. You came of your own accord, thinking you were marrying a philanderer."

"I knew you weren't one. I just knew it."

"No, you knew. You're only saying that now because I told you. You thought I was this crazy dude—and you fell for him. But then you realized something: I'm not as crazy as they say I am. In fact, I may be the only sane person in the room."

"Max, that's exactly what I thought when I saw you. I didn't see you as the asshole everybody said you were. I saw you as a good person with idiosyncrasies."

"You were deceived into the truth. And now here we are. Together. As we should be."

She moves over and sits on top of me.

"I'm not wearing any panties," she whispers.

"I can feel that," I say.

"I kind of feel like making love to you," she says. "I mean, I want to make up for all of that lost time."

She places a finger between her legs and then runs it down my chest, all sexy and shit.

I chuckle. "There's no such thing as lost time, Jess. The only thing that is real is the present. Now is all we have—and even now is almost over."

She kisses me on the mouth. "Don't get too philosophical with me, Max McMillan. Or else."

"Or else what?"

"Or else I'll confess something to you, too."

"I like where this is going. Confess away," I say.

"You're only the second guy I ever made love to."

"I know."

"How?" she asks, surprised.

"Because you just told me."

She laughs. "You're crazy, Max McMillan. *And I love you.*"

She says it like she means it.

And I believe her.

"Aren't you doing something wrong?" I ask.

"What?" she whispers.

"Come on, you know my favorite position is reverse cowgirl."

"Oooh!" she exclaims. She turns around and I grab hold of her gorgeous ass.

"Ride me like I'm a damn virgin, Jess," I tell her.

And—oh boy! —does she ride.

Damn, I love losing my virginity. (A second time, of course.)

Chapter Twenty-One

The next day, I wake up and roll over.

My hand lands on Jess's bare and beautiful ass.

If I were still a virgin, I would probably cum just touching her ass. I swear to God there is nothing more beautiful in the world than Jess's ass. I can stare at it, kiss it, touch it, smack it, you get the picture.

Jess wakes up and looks at me.

"Last night was great," she mutters.

She's still sleepy.

"I know," I say. "I'm still *there*. Last night."

"You're crazy," she says.

She looks at me all serious.

"What?" I ask. "What is it?"

She sits up in bed and begins putting some underwear on. Her long hair falls along the small of her back. I want to reach out and touch it, but I don't dare to.

"It's crazy how it all works out," she says. "I mean, nobody knows anything. You think you know somebody, and you actually don't."

"Is this about last night?" I ask.

"Yeah," she says. "I've just been thinking about how funny this world is."

She turns and looks at me. I can't help but stare at her breasts.

My God, I'm an animal around her. She's incredible. Jess is.

She catches me staring and giggles.

"Anyways," she says with a smile. "It's crazy how the internet changed things."

"Yeah, isn't it? Like, now you can look at pictures of someone when they were twelve or see videos of them doing something in kindergarten. It's like nobody born today can ever escape their past. They can't—in a real, traditional sense—grow up. They will always have the videos out there on the web, on the cloud. Everything they've ever done is up there for the world to see. I mean, it's how I was able to become a celebrity. Thanks to the infinite and wise media."

"Yeah, and everybody thinks they know you."

"It's hard to escape what others think of you—when they number in the millions."

"Exactly!" she exclaims. "And you become just a pawn to them, a vessel who holds all of their dreams and fantasies in one place."

"Yep. And then you ask me why I can't be honest. I can't. Imagine if I went on national TV right now and made the following announcement: 'Hi, guys. I'm Max McMillan. Anyway, I have an announcement to make—I'm really not that cool. I don't slay pussy left and right. I don't actually kill people in my sleep. I'm really a boring person once you get to know me (nothing like my novels). So, yeah, just thought I'd let everyone know.'"

She laughs. "Nobody would believe you."

"Of course, they wouldn't. They'd say, 'Max, go home and get some sleep. You're obviously crazy.'"

Jess shakes her head. "What has the world come to? I mean, it's crazy how so much of the stuff on TV, on our phones, is just an outright lie, a big and beautiful deception."

"Just pixels and colors and outrageous things. That's all that sells these days. You know, I think one of these days, people will start to crave the boring, the mundane, the simple, the inelegant."

"What do you mean? Like, they won't want all this stuff that's crazy and exciting and out-of-this-world?"

"Yeah," I say. "You can only get so much of it before it becomes mundane, too. Like, it's only a matter of time when most of us will want something different—and this time, different will be smaller not bigger, quieter not louder, mundane not exciting, ordinary not extraordinary."

Jess leans in and kisses me. "I want you to be *my ordinary*."

I shrug. "We're all just regular human beings trying to make it in this crazy world where the pressure is to stand out, to be extraordinary. But even people like me, we get tired of shock value."

"Max McMillan tired of shocking the world?" Jess laughs. "That's the funniest thing I've heard in a long time."

"You ever hear about that one couple somewhere in the Middle East?" I ask Jess.

"There are a million couples in the Middle East, Max."

"Well, there's this story I heard. It's really crazy."

"Uh-huh," she mutters.

"So, there's this Middle Eastern couple that's, like, Jewish or Muslim. I don't know. But anyway. This couple is visited by some couple from America. And the Americans are sitting in this simple room that has all this basic furniture. Nothing special. Place looks like a basic dump. And the wife comes out and she's all dressed from head-to-toe in their traditional garb. And the husband is wearing his religious garb. So, this Middle Eastern couple is dressed like crazy. I mean, the Americans could hardly see their faces or skin color or what-have-you. And you know what the American couple said after dinner?"

"What?" she asks.

"They said the place was the sexiest place they had ever been to. Imagine what it was like in that simple and unadorned bedroom. It's like when the wife took off her clothes, the sexuality was so heavy in the air, you could literally reach out and stroke it."

"It makes sense," she mutters. "We're all so desensitized now. It takes more and more to get less and less. And in those cultures, you have less and less to get more and more. The less skin the men see, the more sex they have."

"Exactly," I whisper. "You know, Americans aren't even having sex these days. Have you read the latest research? Some people are in their forties and they're still virgins. I mean, nobody is having sex these days."

"Well, Max, they are having sex," Jess says. "But it's probably not any good."

"It's like those buildings on TV that keep blowing up. So much happening on-screen—and yet, nothing at all. It's all the shit we talk about. All the books and the movies and the music. And we talk, talk, talk. We talk so much about a whole lot of nothing. It's just all talk. None of those rappers are even getting laid. That's why they keep talking about it so much. They're creating their own reality. It's just CGI bullshit. I wouldn't be surprised if half of those rappers hadn't been laid in years. But they must rap about something—so they sell the world what it lacks but desires. That's how it works these days."

Jess yawns. "Max, let's stop solving the world's problems and grab some breakfast."

I get out of bed and begin putting clothes on.

Damn women these days.

I swear they're always ending conversations once they start to get good.

We grab breakfast at some run-of-the-mill breakfast joint. The morning starts off well enough, I guess. No crazy fans, no nothing. Jess orders pecan pancakes and dips them in honey. I watch her eat. It's a wonderful morning in southern ________________.

You thought I was going to tell you where I currently reside?

Not so fast.

The sun is out and there's that bright blue sky above. It's perfect.

And then I notice it. Out of the corner of my eye, I recognize that all-too-familiar look of absolute recognition. The waitress—or whoever she is—makes a beeline for our table.

Jess notices. I wink and she smiles. She puts her fork down, wipes her lips with a napkin, and looks at the quickly approaching girl.

I hesitate for a second, and in the second that I do the hesitating, she arrives.

"Mr. McMillan—" she begins.

Jess cuts her off. "He always gets that," she says. "But he's not the famous author."

The girl is flabbergasted. She was certain of it. I can see it in her eyes. She was certain that it was, indeed, me.

I politely nod and smile. I look at Jess and then at the girl. "Yes, I do get that quite often, don't I, Jess?"

The girl looks at Jess and then at me. She can't tell if we're crazy, stupid, or flat-out lying.

Jess nods. "He's always getting confused for Max McMillan." She reaches out and clasps my hand. "My husband is a famous man." She says it so honestly, the confused girl believes her.

"I'm sorry," she stutters. "I just thought—"

"Oh, it's perfectly fine," Jess says, waving a hand. "I'm sure it'll happen again. It's not the first nor the last time."

The girl takes a few steps back, then leaves.

I look at Jess.

"My God, you're an awfully good liar," I say.

"Why, thank you!" she murmurs.

"Shall we celebrate?" I ask.

"Celebrate the lying?"

"Why not?"

"Sure," she says.

I order us two mimosas.

I swear I'm quite the lightweight. I smell alcohol and immediately come down with a hangover.

We down our mimosas, and I glance at Jess.

"Geez," I say, "I feel like I'm already tipsy."

Jess laughs. "Have another one, babe," she says.

"All right."

I order another mimosa. I can feel the alcohol start to kick in. I swear I'm a lightweight.

Two mimosas later, and I can barely talk. I'm slurring my words and Jess is laughing her ass off.

She's crying tears and her face is as red from laughter as an orchard cherry. "Oh. My. God." she squeals. "I can't believe you're already drunk." She pulls out her phone and begins recording.

I swear women are crazy.

Next thing I know, I'm so drunk I step into another realm.

This one time, I got so drunk, I swear, I floated out of my body and murdered someone. I'll tell you the story when I'm sober. You won't believe any of it, of course, which just makes me want to tell it even more.

Oh, to hell with it, I'll tell it now, drunk and all.

I'm twenty-six years old (or something like that), and I'm on the rise with my fame. I get invited to this party in Atlanta.

"Not a big deal," Jack says. "Just a couple of friends hanging out on Lake Lanier."

So, I think, "Why the hell not?" I mean, I'm basically a somebody now, and people *want* to meet me.

We take a plane out to Atlanta and some friends pick the two of us up and take us to one of the marinas.

We get there and it's a day or two before the fourth of July. I mean, there are people everywhere. Most of the people are women—and they happen to be nude (or damn close to it). So, obviously, I'm in my element.

We start the morning off with some Jack Daniel's. Then we drink something Irish. Then we drink some beer. Hours go by. Then someone opens a jar of sangria. More hours go by. Next thing you know, I'm in my boxers, standing atop some makeshift stage, reading poetry to whoever would listen.

It's dark now. I mean, it's pitch-black. And this is the South. We're talking it's humid and warm and green and the entire sky around us is aglow with fireflies and birds chirping and grasshoppers buzzing. It's quite the experience.

So, I'm drunk off my rocker and I'm reading all this cute, romantic poetry. I see Jack making his way towards me. He's stumbling, sucking on a bottle of Corona. He's got this fire in his eyes.

He pushes me off the "stage" and starts to recite something off the top of his head. This guy, I swear he's a genius.

He's got everybody's attention.

The entire universe seems to be listening.

Naturally, I get jealous. I want to punch this guy in the face for stealing all my thunder and wonder and glory.

I make my way back to the "stage" and try to push him off it. I want to "grab the mic," so to speak.

Jack pushes me. I push him. We push each other—and end up in the water.

I'm swimming and he's swimming. The crowd above—still dry on boats—is laughing.

Jack looks over at me and says, "Man, you really did a number on me up there."

"Yeah, you did too," I reply.

"What'd I do?" he asks.

"You recited a better poem, Jack!"

He laughs. "At least they were listening."

I swear friends these days are nothing but thunder-thieves.

I never did murder anyone that night, but it sure did cross my mind. (But that was all before I met Jess and stopped being a total asshole.)

Jess looks at me. She shakes her head. "Are you lost in La-La Land again, Mister?"

I nod. "Jess, I don't feel so well," I tell her.

"You want to go home?"

"Well, let's go see Jack and Jane. Maybe the kids will make me feel better."

"Okay," Jess says.

We leave a massive tip and drive to Jack and Jane's place.

I walk in and get knocked over immediately.

"Uncle Max!" Lucy screams.

"What?" I ask.

I take the sweet thing in my arms and kiss her cheeks right off.

"Can you fix it?" she asks.

"Fix what, darling?"

She's getting all serious now and it's very evident.

Jessica is making conversation in the kitchen with Jane. Jack is sitting reading a newspaper. They don't pay any attention to us.

Lucy looks up at me with those large eyes of hers and whispers, "I know mommy is dying."

And for a second, the asshole part of me disappears—so much so that it's almost like it never existed in the first place.

I pull her close and hold her for a second. I don't know what to say.

Out of the corner of my eye, I see Jane eyeing me with suspicion. It's as if she knows I'm stealing secrets right from under her nose.

Women are like that. They are emotionally more intelligent than men. A man will never know if his wife is plotting to murder him. A woman? Always. She's always ahead of the game. That's why women get away with murder. They do a better job at it. All *known* serial killers are male. That's because they all get *caught*. Most serial killers are women. I'm not even kidding you. I'll tell you about serial killers when the time is right.

My thoughts return to little Lucy.

"Mommy will be okay," I reassure her.

She wipes a tear. "No," she insists. "She's going to go up there."

She points at the ceiling. "Heaven," she whispers.

"Yeah," I tell her. "Heaven."

"I'll see mommy every night," she sniffles. "Daddy promises she'll come every night."

"Uh-huh," I murmur.

God, I don't feel like being an asshole—but shit—your mommy is going to die. She's basically dead already.

I want to tell her something true, something sad. But I don't. Kids make adults do strange things. We create lies to make them feel better. But kids are emotionally intelligent, too. In fact, I'd argue that kids are smarter than females. I'd go so far as to say most serial killers are children. They're so damn good at it, we have yet to catch one.

Sometimes I wonder if Lucy is a serial killer. If she is, I have to say: more props to you, kiddo, you're doing a damn good job.

I hold her like that and start crying. Kids make you do strange things. I swear I'm a horrible crier. You don't ever want to see me cry. It's a freaking waterpark on my face.

Damn, I hate cancer.

We cry like that, Lucy and I, and I swear I start feeling better.

Jane, who stops eyeing me with suspicion, comes over. She wraps her arms around the both of us. Then Jess comes over and wiggles her way into my arms. And Jack drops his newspaper and comes over. He's all teary-eyed and none of us have a clue how to deal with children who are crying.

Nathan hears the emotional turmoil and walks into the room. He comes to us, too. We're all standing there like a bunch of morons, crying our eyes out.

I swear it's a shitshow whenever there's cancer involved.

Jane begins to speak. "Lucy," she whispers. She breaks down and starts to cry even more. She can't get any words out.

What the hell do you tell a four-year-old? Life ain't a theme park. It's a hellhole full of all kinds of nasty people plotting to legally murder you—with words, knives, Twitter posts, Instagram shit, and Facebook pokes. I swear people sending you Facebook pokes want you buried in a cemetery.

I know I swear a lot. It's been an issue ever since I started talking about cancer with Lucy. I can't say a word without resorting to Fuck-This and Fuck-That.

I don't even have enough fucks left in me to say Fuck some days. I swear if I die, I'm writing "Fuck" on my tombstone.

So, we're crying, and I tell you: This asshole part of me goes to this stupid-ass story that once happened when I hired an assassin to kill me. I did it for one simple reason: fun. I wanted to see if anyone out there was smart enough to kill me. I swear I'm the smartest guy in the room. No way in hell can a man be this smart. It's like my IQ goes from 79 to a solid 80.

When there's a cute girl around, I am always running a solid 80. You don't even want to meet me when I'm in my zone. It's like I'm Einstein creating new gravities and pulling entire universes right out of my—

We finally stop crying and Jane manages to say something articulate. She says, "I love you, Lucy."

And I swear it's like one of those Hallelujah-moments. Heebuz Jeebuz comes down and shines His little light on us hopeless sinners trying to make the world a better place, one cancer-victory at a time.

Jess says something beautiful, too.

She says, "I love you, Lucy."

I swear I never heard more beautiful words.

It makes me wonder sometimes. What a beautiful world it would be if only assholes like me could keep their mouths shut. If only we didn't talk or think or whatever.

Imagine if all we did was stand around, hug one another like hippies, and whisper sweet I-Love-Yous into the ears of children. Kids would grow up all right. They'd even stop being serial killers. We'd see those killing rates tank like the Titanic. I imagine people being all lovey-dovey and madly in love.

All the kids adults mess up by never telling them, "I Love You." All those kids would disappear. We wouldn't have crazy kids running around shooting up schools like they do now. We wouldn't have all the violence. I think we could make the Kingdom of Heaven come right down with a single I-Love-You said at an appropriate moment.

Hell, I'm not even a Christian but I think the Kingdom of Heaven isn't a place you go to. It's a place you come from.

But you go and tell those religious pricks a truth like that and they'll send your ass so far into hell, you'll begin to think you are Satan himself.

Anyway, I got so caught up on my soapbox, I forgot to tell you about the assassin I hired this one time. But it's getting late and I'm aching to have an existential discussion with Lucy and Nathan and Jess and Jane and Jack. I just want to get all this off my chest. I'm sure Jane wants to get some shit off hers as well.

We sit down in the living room and huddle close.

Jess is wrapped up in my arms, and Lucy is holding Jane with one arm and holding onto my thumb with another.

It's a touching moment—even for an asshole like me.

"Do you know what happens to people who have cancer?" Jane asks Lucy.

Lucy looks at me and then at Jane. She's not sure why the adults are being so serious. Maybe she thinks life is a kind of video game; a place where people get second chances.

"It's a bad, bad monster," Lucy says. "A monster that grows inside you until it pops out."

"Yeah," I whisper. "And we're going to make sure we pop that monster right out."

Jane looks at me. She, too, wishes this were true.

But we're adults—and we know better. Life is mostly shit with a few beautiful moments thrown in. And most of us choose to live for those few and fleeting instants.

"Lucy," Jane begins. "It's not always the case that the monster loses. Sometimes the monster wins."

Lucy stares at her mother. You can tell she's processing the information, but in a strange, childlike way.

"But Uncle Max said he'd make the monster pop and go away!" she insists. "Uncle Max can do anything. He can do anything, mommy. I know he can."

Jane looks over at me. She shakes her head softly.

"Sometimes the monster wins, Lucy-honey," she says.

Lucy refuses to believe it. She's in complete denial.

"No." She shakes her head. "Uncle Max," she stutters. "Uncle Max can fix anything."

She looks at me. She looks at me dead in the eyes. "Right?" she asks.

How do you respond to a question like that?

I take her little hand and press it to my lips. "Right," I say. "I can fix anything, even monsters."

She smiles. It's one of those rare smiles. A smile that says, "Everything will be all right. In the face of monsters and cancers and hurricanes, everything will be all right." Only kids have those kinds of smiles.

Adults aren't ever as good as children. Most grow up to be assholes like me. And most of them have forgotten how to smile.

A while later, I go upstairs and hang out with Jack. He lights a cigar and puffs on it.

"It's not going well," he confesses. "Not going well at all."

"The book?" I ask.

"Yes," he says. "Can't do it with all of the things going on in this household."

He looks beat. Tired. Exhausted. Cancer has taken a toll on him.

"You should just spend time with Jane and the kids," I say.

He blows smoke out of his mouth.

"Can't," he says. "I'm losing my mind."

I nod in silence.

He continues. "Max, you have no idea what it's like. No idea."

"Uh-huh," I mutter.

Of course, I have no idea what it's like. No clue. I can't even begin to fathom how shitty it must be for him watching his beloved wife die like that.

"You never think it's going to happen to you," he whispers. "Not in any real sense of that word. I mean, you think—of course—but it's all just intellectual head-knowledge. It's not stuff that hits your heart. It's all theoretical and detached. But when it hits you—it's everything but that."

"You can't ever prepare for it, Jack," I say. "You can't."

"Yeah," he says. "There's no way to. It comes at you in waves. One second, I feel like I'm doing all right. I tell myself, 'You have to be brave. For the kids.'"

"For the kids," I repeat.

He's lost.

His gaze, out there.

"Yeah," he says. "I keep telling myself, 'For the kids.' It's like a mantra now. One second, I'm fine. I'm okay. I'm breathing. The next, I'm on the floor bawling. And I don't want Jane seeing me like that. It hurts her too much. She needs to think—you know, she needs to think that I am strong. That I'm a man. That I can do this. That the kids will be okay when she's gone."

"Keep pretending it's all right, I guess," I say. "Isn't that what the world wants from us? Another fake emotion."

"It's not fake, Max," he whispers. "I just have no tears left to cry, you know?"

He smiles. It's a strange smile. "You know, those clichés are true. You just run out of tears. You don't have anything left in you."

He turns and looks at me. "I don't even know the last time I slept. It must have been ages. I don't know anymore. Ask me. Ask me when I slept."

"When have you slept, Jack?" I ask.

"I don't know," he says. He shrugs. "I don't know, Max."

"You want some drugs?" I ask.

He waves a hand. "No," he says. "You know I don't like taking anything."

"Have you been drinking?"

"A little."

"What's a little, Jack?" I ask, softly.

"A fifth a day."

"So, you're an alcoholic then, Jack?"

He shrugs. "Maybe," he mutters. "But I don't want to be," he adds.

Alcoholics that don't want to be alcoholics. That's a first.

I look at him with pity. I don't even know how much pity I have left in me. I swear it's a pity-party in here. Every time I come here, it's a pity-party. I feel so selfish for thinking it, but I guess the asshole part of me is allowed to think such asshole thoughts.

"Well," he mutters. "You got anything to say?"

"Don't drink?"

We both laugh.

"Isn't that a solution?" he mutters.

"I don't know, Jack."

We sit in silence.

"I have an idea," I whisper.

He turns and looks at me. "Uh-huh," he says. "What is it?"

"What if I made something happen?"

"Like what?"

"What if I helped make you a success overnight?"

"What will it matter?" he asks. "I'm losing her anyhow."

"You'll lose her, Jack. I know. We both know."

He starts to sob softly.

"I'm such an asshole," I whisper and then look away.

"Come on," I say after a second, "what if I'm able to pull some strings? She needs to know her kids will be taken care of. She needs to know you won't fall apart after she—"

I don't dare say the word out loud.

"Yeah," he says, quietly. "What do you have in mind?"

"Oh, it's crazy, Jack," I whisper. "It's crazy. It'll change the world. It'll ruin my life."

I start laughing out loud. I'm laughing my ass off and Jack is looking at me all crazy.

"You okay?" his face seems to ask.

"You're crazy," he says. "Bat-shit crazy. You know that?"

I keep laughing.

"My God, Jack!" I exclaim. "This is wonderful."

"What is?" he asks, confused.

"My God, Jack!" I say. "I think I have found the solution."

"What solution?" he asks.

I stand up and kiss him on the forehead. "I have to go, Jack," I say. "But I will call you when it's all done."

"What's all done, Max? Max?" he calls after me.

But I leave him sitting there, pondering the greatest trick ever conceived in the history of literature.

I swear I'm the smartest guy who's ever lived. I should have been born a female.

Damn, I love Jack.

Chapter Twenty-Two

Occasionally, I tell Jess stupid stories at bedtime.

I don't tell her everything because if I did, she'd divorce me in a heartbeat.

Tonight, I felt like telling her about my assassin experience. I've been talking about it for so long, it's about time I told it.

"Jess?" I say.

"Uh-huh," she mutters. She's half-asleep, and I'm kind of happy that's the case.

"You want to know something crazy?"

"Everything about you is crazy," she whispers.

"I've got a confession to make," I whisper. "Want to hear it?"

I feel like a twelve-year-old kid talking on the phone with his girlfriend while the parents sleep in the room next door.

"Sure," she mutters. I'm certain she's about to fall asleep any second.

"Well," I begin, "one time I hired an assassin."

She turns over and looks at me. It's dark, but I can see the white of her eyes.

"Say what?" she asks.

I can tell I have her attention.

"I once hired an assassin," I whisper.

"Why are you whispering?" she asks.

"Because it's crazy," I say.

"Go on," she says. "I'm listening."

She kisses me on the forehead.

"Okay," I say, "so, this one time, I wanted to kill myself. And I thought, 'Why do it myself when I could pay someone to do it for me?' So, I hired an assassin."

"Uh-huh," she mutters.

I swear women these days don't believe anything their husbands tell them.

"So, I call up the assassin. I find him on the dark web, you know. I say, 'Hey, I need to kill somebody. How much?' He says, 'Ten thousand dollars.' And he says it as if it's a lot of money. I laugh. He says, 'Why are you laughing?' I say, 'Because that's cheap.' He says, 'What? You want me to charge you more? I could charge you more!' I say, 'Look, buddy-boy, I just need to hire your best assassin. The best assassin in the whole, entire goddamn world.' And I'm saying this in my most serious voice. He says, 'Twenty thousand and it'll be the best assassin in the world. It'll be some straight-up John Wick shit.' I say, 'Okay.' I give him a description of the person I want killed. I email him my photo and my address and shit. Anyway, I pay him in Bitcoin. So, we set a date when I am scheduled to be killed. Are you still listening?"

"Uh-huh," Jess mutters.

But I swear she's lying.

"Okay, so, I hire this assassin to kill me. I'm like that *Home Alone* kid getting all ready and stuff. You know, it wasn't even this house now that I think about it. It was the other one. I swear the old place was bigger than this one. That's probably why the assassin never killed me. He never stood a chance. I mean, he got lost in the damn place twelve seconds in. You still listening?"

Jess moves her arm and repositions herself. "Yeah," she mutters. "Keep talking."

I swear she's sleeping—but, oh, to hell with it, sometimes I like to hear myself talk, so I just keep talking as if I have an audience of ten thousand or something.

"I get all ready and shit. It's midnight when the little assassin shows up. I got all kinds of radars and cameras and hounds on the property. I have laser detectors. I got the entire place wired up like it's a whorehouse and I'm pimping the hottest you-know-what the world has ever seen. Anyway, the little prick shows up on my property right around midnight. I get notifications on my phone, you know. I see he's wearing a mask and black suit and tie. He's one of those guys, you know. Hell, I'm laughing my ass off in the attic. I'm not even dressed for the occasion. Only thing I'm wearing is underwear—and it's camouflage for kicks and giggles. I see him on my phone. He's scaling the fence. I'm pretty sure he's an ex-Marine or something. But—what the hell does it matter? —ain't no little Marine going to wipe out a world-renowned writer that fast.

"Next thing you know, the hounds are on him like he's a piece of ass. He shoots one; shoots the other. He's a pretty good shot. I panic but only for a second. I mean, I'd never even seen anybody with a gun before, much less firing one.

"Now I'm getting worried. I thought hiring an assassin was a damn good idea. Sounded funny at the time. But here I was about to get shot. And that wasn't so funny.

"I'll be honest, baby. I got the urge to call the damn dude. I mean,

I wanted to call the assassination off. I was nervous as a young girl going on a date for the first time with a star football player. I'm sweating up a storm, cursing like a sailor.

"So, I pick up my phone and call that strange number. The dude picks up on the tenth ring. I'm sweating bullets. I can tell I woke him up. 'What?!' he yells into the phone. 'Quiet down, buddy-boy,' I say. 'I'm in a pickle,' I say. 'What's a pickle?' the dude asks. 'Oh, I just hired an assassin. But it's the wrong dude I sent you.' He hesitates. I can tell he's pissed. 'What dude did you send us?' 'Max McMillan,' I tell him. I hear a long pause on the other end of the line. 'Max freaking McMillan?! Are you out of your mind!' He's yelling so loudly, I swear the old lady on the Moon is waking up from it. 'Max freaking McMillan!' he keeps yelling. 'What the hell is wrong with you?!' He's so angry, I feel like he's going to kill me over the phone. 'Look,' I tell him, 'I am Max McMillan and I hired an assassin to kill me. As a joke, of course.' The guy can hardly believe what I'm saying. He's cursing like a sailor. I can hear him using an inhaler or whatever. He's angry.

"After a minute or so, he finally settles down. He puts me on hold and he's calling the assassin. Problem is, after numerous attempts, he can't get hold of him. 'I guess the world is going to lose you, Max McMillan,' he says with a strange sadness in his voice. 'I guess it is,' I say. I'm honestly a little bummed that things must end this way. I can hear the door being opened. Not literally hear it but my little alarm buzzer thing on my phone is going off. Anyway, I prepare to die. And I think: What have I done with my life? And I think about that some more.

"Like, what have I actually done with my life? Hasn't most of it been for pleasing others and making sure I get enough smiles thrown my way? Hasn't most of it been a kind of ruse? It has been what one might call 'a life well-lived.' Er, that came out wrong. More like: 'A life well-faked.' I guess that could go on my tombstone, you know? Jess? You there?"

I can tell she's sleeping now. That's the way it is with wives. The moment you start to say something interesting, they fall asleep. Then they wake up and say things like, "Oh, but you never listen to me and you never tell me how you feel."

And I'm going like, "Oh, really? I don't talk to you? Wow. Really? And here I thought I was the most talkative, most emotional man on the planet. A damn excellent husband."

Yeah, that's me. (At least in my humble opinion.)

Anyway, I stop telling Jess the story. There's no point in telling it. She's busy dreaming about our second wedding. Crazy girl that she is.

So, I'm sitting there in my underwear. It's the middle of the night. And I can hear the guy walking around the house. Next thing you know, I hear the assassin-guy brewing tea. I'm appalled by his actions! Tea?! He's supposed to be doing his damn job shooting me and here he is in my kitchen making tea. I get so fed up with that, I jump right up and head downstairs. Nobody messes with my tea like that.

I walk into the dark kitchen and I swear the prick is sitting there like a sitting duck. I look at him and he looks at me. There's just enough starlight dropping into the house for the both of us to know we are human beings. That's it. He keeps looking at me and I keep looking at him. And he's sitting there steeping his teabag. I pull out a chair and sit next to him. I have no idea what happened to me, but crazy stupid Max McMillan isn't scared shitless anymore.

"So—" he says.

His voice is almost girlish. In fact, it sounds so weird for a guy his size that I burst out laughing. This guy, this huge six-foot-six monster, talks like a twelve-year-old girl.

He's not happy with my laugh. But I sense something is off. He wants to laugh, but he can't. A second later, I realize he's choking.

I get behind him and start performing the Heimlich maneuver.

A minute later, I'm on the ground next to him, out of breath.

He turns his head and looks at me. "Thanks," he mutters.

I laugh. It's his damn voice. It's funny as hell.

He shrugs and smiles. "I don't talk before I kill. I kill and then I talk."

I laugh again. I can't help myself. I almost want to ask him to say something just so that I can laugh at it.

He smiles.

"Hey," I say, "you've got a nice smile."

He keeps smiling. He's looking at me like a kid who just met his hero. His eyes are shining.

I call it "the shine." It makes sense to me, you know. I like calling things by what they do. The noun is the verb. The shine is when a person recognizes me as their hero. It doesn't happen often, but when it does, boy, is it wonderful.

"You're Max," he finally blurts out. "Max McMillan."

"Yep," I say. "It is I."

He reaches out and touches his forehead. "My God, who wants you dead?"

His mind is racing. He's very confused.

Finally, after a few moments of hard thinking, he says: "It must be an old girlfriend. Am I right?"

I shake my head. "Nope."

He begins to think again. He looks over at me. "You want yourself dead?" he asks.

"How'd you know?" I reply, genuinely surprised that he figured it out.

"You talk about this happening," he says. "In one of your books."

Wait. What?

"I had a character do this in one of my novels?" I ask.

"Yeah," he says, "I think it was called *I Hired an Assassin to Kill Me and Laughed.*"

"Shit," I mutter. "You're right."

"You're starting to become like one of your characters," he says. "You might need to take a break. You're losing it, Max."

"I swear that's the smartest thing I've ever heard anyone say," I reply. "By the way, what's your name?"

"Liam," he says.

"Liam?" I ask. "Liam Neeson? Like, the guy in all of the movies?"

"Yeah," he says.

"Liam, why is your voice so weird?"

"Oh," he says in his regular voice, "I was just trolling you. You know, I didn't want you to recognize me."

"Wait, you're actually an assassin in real life?"

"Yeah," he says. "How do you think I got the acting job?"

"How?"

"I assassinated all of my competitors."

I burst out laughing.

"My God," I say, "that's hilarious."

He chuckles. "I think it's pretty funny, too."

I get up and turn the lights on. Liam gets up after me.

"Let's celebrate," I say.

I grab some scotch and pour us both a glass.

We drink, and I toast. "May our sons have wealthy fathers, and our daughters have beautiful mothers."

Liam laughs at my toast. "I've never heard that one before," he says. "But it's funny."

So, we spend the night talking about assassinations and kill techniques and such. Once we're done talking, I sign a couple of copies of my books and hand them to him. He signs a few movie posters for me, and we call it good.

It's a stupid story, I know. I know because I was there. But I will say this: Liam Neeson did change my life. When I was up there in that attic thinking about my inevitable death-by-assassination, I came to a solid conclusion: Life is awesome.

What I mean is: It's not all bad. There are some good moments scattered here and there. And, as a matter of fact, most of my life has been rather wonderful. I've had a good time. I really have. It's been mostly fun and games for me. I can't blame myself. I'm an asshole.

And assholes can be wonderful humans if you let them be.

I swear it. Look at me. I'm all right.

Anyway, I will let you know about my idea for Jack. It's basically what this entire novel is about. I told you that I'm a hack, right? And I told you this would be a story about me falling from grace, right? Well, it's all going to shit in the next chapter.

I saved the worst for last.

I wanted you to fall in love with me, you know. That's why I wrote all that good stuff about myself in the first few chapters. I wanted to build rapport with the reader, make myself out to be tolerable, even likable.

You know, be honest with me. When you go on dates, you too put your "best foot forward." Don't lie to me. You can't out-lie the greatest liar on Earth. I'm an expert in deception. And even I know that we all present ourselves—*initially*—in a positive light. That's why I put some good stuff into the story. I put some love in, romance, whatever. I put it all in so that you could like me as a character. And now you're about to cry because this might be the greatest book you've ever read. And you never thought Max McMillan was capable of writing anything this good or this emotional. You thought Max was a fraud, a shell of a human. And you were wrong.

But . . . but now I'm going to be very, very honest with you.

(Are you even ready for this? You sure?)

I swear you won't believe what happens next.

I swear it. You never saw this one coming.

Damn, I hate cancer.

Chapter Twenty-Three

I call my sister, Star.

It's three or four in the morning, and I'm being an ass for doing it. But, oh, to hell with it! Sometimes older brothers must drive sisters crazy.

"Hey," she mutters in that raspy-sleepy voice of hers. "What the hell is wrong with you calling me at this hour?"

She's upset, and she should be. I would be too if I were her. But I'm not. So, I'm not upset.

"I needed to talk to someone," I whisper.

The line goes quiet.

"Okay," she says.

I can hear her getting out of bed, sitting up on the edge, putting on her slippers.

"I want to ask you something," I say, slowly.

"Right now?" she asks.

I can tell she's listening. We've known each other all our lives. It comes with the territory. I can sense things, even over the phone. She's listening alright.

"Yeah, yeah. It's a . . . it's important we talk right now."

"Go ahead," she says.

"I have this bad feeling, you know. I've become famous for all the wrong reasons. I've become too rich, too fast, and . . . and I don't know if I like it anymore."

She sighs. "You've helped a lot of people, Max," she says. "Most of them don't know it was you. You're not a sob story. I'm your sister. I know what you do behind closed doors. I know it because I'm the one sending millions to charity on your behalf. You can't fool me."

"It has nothing to do with the millions . . ." I retort. "It's more the . . . the fact that I have it too good. I don't know if I deserve any of it at this point. Not with Jack being what he is. And you know Jane is dying from cancer, right? And there's got to be something we can do about it. There's *got* to be something . . ."

"Oh, Maxy pants," she says. "I'm so sorry about Jane. I really am. But you need to stop doing this to yourself. You . . . you can't blame yourself for everything. That's not the way cancer works. It just . . . it just doesn't work like that. Some people get it, and some people don't. It's a coin toss. You know this. You've done more than enough for people. And they still hate you. And that's sadder than anything I've ever seen. That's what kills *me*."

"I don't know, Star," I whisper. "I don't know if that's right. I don't know if this is just a movie set and all this stuff that's been handed me is going to go back to the warehouse the moment the cameras stop rolling. And while the cameras are rolling, I just want to do something good while I still can."

"What are you talking about, Max?" she asks, exasperated. "You've done a shit ton of good."

"Really?" I ask. "You really think so?"

"Yes. That's a fact. You're one of the most generous writers ever. That's not an exaggeration."

"But . . . how did *that* happen?"

"You make a shit ton of money, Max. And you don't spend all of it. You spend very little of it, actually."

"I do?"

I'm baffled. This is news to me.

"Yes, Max. You are pretty stinking rich, my dude."

I'm blown away by this. I knew I was giving away some money, but not anywhere near the levels Star is talking about.

"So, like, how much are we talking?" I ask, quietly. (I'm pathetic like that.)

Now I want a number to know how much kinder I am than everybody else. Like, suppose Stephen King donates $10 million a year and I'm doing $11 million. Now that would make me feel better about myself.

"The numbers don't matter," Star replies. "What matters is you're helping lots of people, including Jack's family."

"Damn," I whisper. "Maybe I'm not as bad as I thought."

"Not at all."

"Huh."

"Huh yourself," she says.

"So, you think I do a lot of good for this world?"

"More than most."

"Huh." I pause to think. "Even with the personality?"

"That's what pays the bills in the first place."

"So, you're not lying when you say I'm not that bad a guy, right?"

"I'm your sister, not that grandma fan of yours across the street. I wouldn't lie to you. Can I go back to sleep now?"

"Uh-huh," I mutter and then hang up.

I'm blown away by all this news. I knew I was rich. That much was obvious. But I didn't know I was as generous as they said I was. I thought people were just making stuff up about the donations. But, oh, to hell with it, maybe the idiots got one thing right.

Damn, I hate idiots.

Chapter Twenty-Four

So, we've come to the end.

The final chapter.

If I'm being honest, I'm writing this with tears in my eyes. I'm not even lying. I'm crying right now.

It's weird how you could fall in love with yourself by writing about yourself.

Anyway, I know I'm an egomaniacal-something—whatever they call those people. But one thing I am not: a totally depraved person. I don't agree with that theologian John Calvin. I really don't.

I mean, I get it: People are awful and evil and depraved. But, come on, all of us? Really? (I'm not even talking about myself here. I'm just talking about people in general. I mean, I've seen people who are better than Jesus or God or Martha Stewart. I've seen plenty of good people in my life. I can list all kinds of people who aren't depraved.)

Jess. She's not depraved. Lucy. She's not depraved. Even Jack and Jane. I think both are pretty good people. And, of course, there's Star; she's a darling.

Hell, there wouldn't be a damn novel if it weren't for them. All these wonderful people! So many of them.

So, here's my confession: I'm going to do something horrific.

It's a tragedy, really.

And I have no idea why I'm telling you all this at the end.

Now that you've fallen in love with me, it'll hurt like hell. But life is a bitch—and surprises do happen.

No, I'm not going to kill myself or whatever.

Don't worry.

I'm not even going to do anything that qualifies as Max McMillan crazy.

Hell, I'm going to stop talking and just tell it like it is—

(Insert a few long pauses and spaces here to indicate a lot of time has elapsed.)

"Hey," I say. I'm on the phone with a publisher. It's a big publisher. Biggest one in the world.

Yeah, this one is Max-McMillan huge.

"Hey," my editor says. (I would say his name, but I forgot it.)

"Yo!" I say.

"Yes?" he asks. "Strange to hear you calling me this late in the day."

"Yeah, whatever," I mutter.

"Go ahead," he says. "What's up?"

"Look," I tell him. "I've got a new book I want you to publish. It's going to be a surprise release."

"You've been working on something, Max?" he asks, his voice all serious.

"Yeah, yeah," I mutter. "I'm always working on something. You know that."

"Sure, sure," he says. I can hear excitement in his voice.

God, I don't like doing this. It feels unethical.

I'm sure Jack is going to hate me for this.

"I'm curious," he says after a long pause. "What's the title of the book?"

God, I hate doing this. I really do.

I swear I'm such a hack.

I look over at the manuscript I stole from Jack's room. It's a huge, fat manuscript. I run my hands over its smooth pages. Jack put a lot of work into this. He really did.

"*The Final Romance*," I finally manage.

It comes out all weird and shit. My mouth knows I'm lying.

"What?" my editor asks on the other line. "I couldn't hear you. What'd you say?"

"*The Final Romance*," I say again. "*The Final Romance* is the title."

Silence.

I can hear him taking a deep breath.

"Max," he says, "that sounds epic."

"It is," I say. "It's very epic. It's my best work yet."

"When can you send over the manuscript?"

"I'll fly there and hand it to you personally."

"It's not typed?"

"No," I say, "I wrote this one on a typewriter."

I'm such a damn good liar. I swear everybody believes me when I say something outrageous.

Max McMillan wrote *The Final Romance*? The hell he did!

"All right. When should I expect you?"

"Give me a few hours. I'll get my stuff together and fly over there."

"Okay," he says.

We say goodbye to one another and hang up. I look over the

manuscript lying on my table. I can hear Jess taking a shower in the other room.

"Jess," I yell out.

After a second, she turns off the water.

"What?" she asks.

"I'm going to meet with my publishers," I yell. "Going to be back tomorrow."

"Okay," she replies.

Sheesh, that was easy. Usually, women don't let you go out of town on such short notice. But Jess is great. She really is the best. I have no idea how she married a hack like me.

I pack my stuff and grab the manuscript. I'm such an asshole, I don't even hesitate. It's like this comes second-nature to me—being a hack and all, you know.

Jess is probably planning our second wedding and such. She has no idea what's coming. But, oh, to hell with it, I know I *need* to do this.

A few hours later, I'm sitting with my publishers and editors and agents and all that.

I present them with a copy of my new novel.

"This isn't standard procedure," I announce. "No, I want this novel to drop in two weeks. It needs to be a surprise summer hit."

"We've never done anything like it before," some old, white dude says. He's wearing a grey suit and a pink bowtie. He's a relic. A walking fossil.

My agent interrupts him. "Sir, I don't mean any disrespect, but almost everything we do with Mr. McMillan is a first. I mean—"

I nod, approving people who approve me.

The old, white dude thinks for a second.

"I suppose you are correct," he says. "I suppose we can publish a book in two weeks."

"Will it need much editing?" someone asks.

My agent looks at me. My editor does, too. They're both staring at me like I'm some poor speller or writer or something.

I shrug. "It's the best yet," I say. "I think it's damn near perfect the way it is."

"All right," everyone mutters in unison.

The old, white dude speaks up again. "Let's get to work, everyone." He looks around the room at all of us as if we are his minions. "We have a lot of work to do."

I leave the meeting in relatively good spirits.

Hell, I'm going to have a new novel out in a few weeks.

Once it drops, oh, the storm and ruckus it'll cause!

How will I ever look at Jack again? Or Lucy? Well, they'll finally realize how depraved I really am.

Shit, none of them saw it coming. (Let's be honest: *Neither did you.*)

I swear I'm the best damn hack who ever lived.

In fact, I might just buy myself another Corvette. A real one. One that I don't rent and pretend to own.

I head to a nearby Chevy dealer.

I walk up to the front desk and am—almost immediately—recognized for the great writer I am.

"Max McMillan!" a man no more than twenty says. He's excited. "What can I do for you?"

"I want a new Corvette," I say. "One of those Z06s."

"Any color in particular?" he asks. He leads the way, and I follow him.

"I want something that makes a girl drop her panties."

The young man laughs. "I've got just the color for you!"

He walks up to a cherry-red Vette. I look at it and immediately get horny. I swear Vettes make me horny.

I nod. "I want it," I say.

"All right!" the young man says. "It's yours."

Instead of flying back home, I drive my new Vette. It's one of those 7-speed manuals. Driving it is like driving Pharaoh's chariot or something. I mean, one second, you're a nobody; the next, you're liberating people out of Egypt like you're goddamn Moses. People follow people who drive Vettes. I swear they do.

I come home late. I park the Vette in the garage and go into the house. I walk in quietly. I find Jess sleeping on the couch. She probably fell asleep waiting for me. Poor thing.

I come over and look at her. She looks beautiful from here. I mean, she's always beautiful. But—right now—I can tell she's *more than pretty*. She's sleeping quietly—and she looks so good when she sleeps. It's like she's some goddess that floated down from one of the heavens and decided to settle for a small nap on my couch. Damn, the woman is gorgeous.

I get on my knees and look at her. I can't help but stare at her. I want to kiss her. I have this primordial urge to kiss her. I guess I get emotional sometimes. It's like a wave of emotions comes over me and all I want to do is kiss, kiss, kiss.

I give in. I tilt my head and kiss her cheek. She's got these soft cheeks. Did I ever tell you about them? They're cute and puffy. I don't know how to describe them. I just know they are the softest and cutest things in the world. I almost love her cheeks as much as I love her breasts.

She stirs. I stop kissing her and just breathe. I don't want to wake her. She's a doll—and dolls deserve to sleep. I have no idea where my tenderness comes from. Maybe it's my grandma. Maybe my grandfather. I don't know. Now that I think about it, both of my grandparents were damn good. I have no qualms with either of them. You know, my grandfather was a romantic. Did I ever tell you that? I guess you can say that stuff is inheritable. It's like a disease. Romantics are interesting creatures. I speak as one. I don't even know what the word means—but I believe I am an expert.

One time, when I was six or seven, my grandfather told me a story. I'll never forget it. It was about how he met my grandmother. He was nineteen and she was sixteen (or something like that). They were on the beach, and he saw her from out of the corner of his eye. He says she was the most gorgeous girl he had ever seen. And—you know what? —I swear he was right. He showed me some old pictures, and I swear it wasn't my grandmother in the pictures. It had to have been some model. Anyway, he saw her dancing and he stared and drooled and such. Then he grew a pair and walked over. It was dark, and the stars were shining above, and the fire was burning below. He danced the tango with her. And it really wasn't what my grandfather said about the moment that struck me; it was what my grandmother said that really did me in. You know what she said? She said, "When he took me in his arms, I knew in them I would be loved forever."

She danced with him that night—and they haven't stopped dancing since.

You see, I find that rather romantic. Call me crazy, but every great romance requires faith—faith in its ability to survive the eternal. My grandfather and my grandmother both had faith. They just believed it was going to happen to them. And you know what? It did.

I think Jess and I are like that. We have faith. Lots of it. Hell, I'm a hack. There's no way in hell anyone could love me. But you should see the way Jess looks at me sometimes. It's as if she sees me for all that I intend to be. It's like she sees something in me nobody else does. And she makes me want to be a better person. She really does.

I kiss her one last time and head upstairs. I need to shower. In two weeks, I'm going to have a lot of explaining to do. I don't know how I'm going to do it, but I guess I'll think about that stuff when it comes. In life, I've learned that it's best not to think about some things. It's better to just let them come when they come and think about them then. Overthinking something does not always lead to better results. Most people who think too much get little to nothing done. I stopped thinking a long time ago. Hell, look at me. I'm basically a machine in terms of what I produce. When I die, they'll probably say I was the greatest writer who ever lived. Of course, that's not going to happen. I mean, shit, you really have no idea what's coming, do you?

Damn, I hate writers.

The Final, Final Chapter

Two weeks later, the phone rings.

It's *The New York Times.*

I've never heard one of their reporters this ecstatic.

"Max McMillan?! You there? Hey, it's Eric with the *Times.*"

I can tell this guy is going to write one of those glowing reviews.

"Yes, this is he," I say.

"Max, I'm going to come out and say what everyone is saying: this new novel you released, this thing—it's beyond amazing. It's the best thing I've ever read in my entire life. It's gorgeous. I mean, it's not even a book. I think it's a kind of experience. It's like having an orgasm for the first time. Max? Max, you still there?"

I'm silent on the other end of the line. I mean, I thought they would like *The Final Romance.* But this much? I didn't think so. Even I didn't see that coming.

"Yeah, I'm still here."

"Max, this novel is going to win the Pulitzer, you know." He's talking so fast, he's out of breath. "I wouldn't be surprised if you win the Nobel. I'm going to come out and say it: I will make sure this book wins a Nobel. If it doesn't, I am certain people will take to the streets."

Sheesh, really? Nobel Prize? I really didn't see that coming.

"Max, you're a friggin' genius—a genius!"

"Thanks," I mutter.

He has no idea what I just got myself into.

Damn, I'm officially a plagiarist.

Jess walks into the living room and sits next to me. She can tell something is up.

"Who is it?" she mouths.

"*The New York Times*," I mouth back.

"Oh," she says. She gives me a thumbs-up. She has no idea.

"You still there?" the reporter asks.

"Yeah," I say.

"You have time for an interview?"

"Sure."

"Can we do the interview in person?"

"Yeah, I can do that."

We arrange a time. He wants to meet me at some Starbucks in half an hour. I agree to it. Hell, I just want to drive my new Vette wherever.

I get off the phone and tell Jess I'm going to meet with a journalist.

She still has no idea her husband dropped a new novel. I kiss her on the mouth and leave.

A few minutes later, I'm sitting with coffee in hand talking about the origins of the book.

"So, when did you decide to change your writing style?"

I think for a second. I never even read the damn thing. I have no idea what's in it. I read a sentence or two when Jack called that one time. Maybe I read a paragraph. But really? I have no idea what the hell it's about.

I decide to do a totally Max McMillan thing: I begin to pull shit right out of my ass.

"Look," I say, "the idea for the book came to me when I got married to Jess. She inspired me so much, I just couldn't help but write a book about it."

The journalist, whose name is Max also, examines me closely. He's playing with a pen in hand. He's nodding every time I speak. He's very intense.

I take a sip from my coffee while he writes something on his notepad.

"If I may ask: What is it that drew you to Jess? And in what way did she inspire the novel? To be honest, there's this scene that really stood out to me. It's on page six-hundred five. Where Kiara stabs Faber and then begins to cry immediately after. Was that scene inspired by anything real?"

Kiara? Who the hell is Kiara? And, holy crap, Jack wrote a novel with more than two-hundred fifty pages? What in the actual . . . ?

"Look," I say. "Kiara is a romantic." (I always say something is romantic when I don't know what the hell it is.)

"A romantic?" he asks. "Interesting. I never saw it that way." He scribbles on his notepad again.

"Yes, a romantic. She wants what she can't have. She desires it so much, she's willing to kill for it."

He nods. "Oh, I see." He takes the pen and bites it. "So, what exactly does she want that she can't have? Because in the novel, she is pursued wholeheartedly by Faber. And it seemed clear—at least to me—that their love was mutual. Passionate, even."

"It's like the subconscious," I say. I have no idea what the hell he's talking about, but I'm so damn good at lying, it's insane.

"Subconscious? Interesting that you say that. Very interesting."

"It's like when you do something but have no idea why you do it. The body is an expression of the subconscious. When she grabs that knife and stabs Faber, it is her subconscious that is in total control. And what the subconscious represents here is a desire for the thing-it-desires and a desire for that very thing to die. It's a strange place to be. But this is where humans find themselves: They are almost always ambivalent about their own actions."

He nods. "Fascinating," he mumbles. "Absolutely brilliant." He thinks for a second. "So, in your own authorial opinion, Kiara is ambivalent about her love towards Faber?"

"Kiara is an interesting character. She's very certain about her uncertainties."

Notice how I'm speaking in absolute nonsensical terms. I'm using words like "ambivalent" and "subconscious." And notice how I'm contradicting myself. One second, I say Kiara is certain; the next, she's uncertain. I'm just so good at creating gibberish, it's crazy. And most people are so damn ready to eat my shit up, I don't even have to make sense to make sense.

"Interesting," he repeats. "Very interesting."

No duh. I'm interesting. If you haven't noticed that, what the hell *can* you notice, you dimwit? I'm the most interesting person who has ever walked Earth. I'm having an interview with the *New York Times* about a book I didn't write—much less read—and it's going well.

I swear people are all half-wits.

"And Faber, he is a man. He's very masculine. He's aggressive by nature," I say.

"In the novel, Mr. McMillan, he came across as very effeminate. At least to me."

Of course, he did, you dim-wit. Of course, he did.

Well, how the hell do I get out of this mess?

"Look," I say, "the entire novel is written from a post-Kierkegaardian perspective."

"A what?" he asks.

"In my reading of Kierkegaard, at least as it relates to a human's ability to relate to truth, I think he was right in that he wanted people to be aware of one simple truth: People, in general don't like truth. We don't like reality as it is. So, we create myths and fables and stories to delight ourselves with. These myths and fables are what get people into the truth by means of fanciful deception."

"What do you mean exactly?"

"I mean that people can come to truth only on their own. And since most people are plagued by original sin, they cannot help but come to truth by means of sinning. So, in the novel, I create all kinds of sins. And what attracts people to the novel are those very sins. And then I pull a surprise on them. I say: Surprise, bitch! You thought this is what was happening, but this is really what's happening."

"Excuse me, Mr. McMillan, but I am still a little confused."

"Go ahead," I say. "Ask away."

You moron.

"So, you think people, who, you say, are plagued by original sin, are drawn to sin and not truth. And since that is the case, your novel reels people in by feeding them sin. But then you reveal truths within those sins. Is that correct?"

I'm honestly surprised. This dimwit got it right on his first try.

Shit, I'm going to start calling you Einstein.

"That's exactly right!" I exclaim. "The novel is about deception. It is about luring people into the truth by means of deception. When you think Kiara is stabbing Faber, she's really in love with him. It's all a façade, a metaphor of sorts."

The interviewer nods. "That's fascinating, Mr. McMillan. I must be honest with you: There's more to this novel than meets the eye. I may have to go home and re-read it."

No duh you're going to go home and re-read it, Einstein.

"Thank you for your time," he says.

"You're very welcome," I say.

We shake hands, hug, and we're done.

I watch him leave.

I shake my head.

The guy has no idea what bombshell I'm dropping tomorrow.

I leave Starbucks and head back home. I'm sure Jess is angry with me. She must be. I mean, hell, I'm a hack—and she's about to find out.

I come home and walk into the kitchen.

Jess is on the phone.

She doesn't look too happy.

She hangs up when she sees me.

"What's going on, Max?" she asks.

She's confused, sad, horrified. The look on her face is one of utter shock; as if I had cheated on her.

I sit down and exhale. "It's crazy, actually," I begin. "Crazy."

She sits down across from me.

"How could you do that to Jack? I just got off the phone with them. Publish a novel behind his back? Steal his work? What kind of man are you, Max?"

The world is a crazy place. It really is. One second, you're on top of the world, doing the right thing; the next, you're pimping out your own daughters without even batting an eye. It's a bad place to be. I know because I've been there.

"I just got this idea," I whisper. "It's a good idea, Jess."

"What's good about stealing someone else's work?"

"It's not like that, Jess. Not at all."

"Well, what is it then? I need to know. You need to tell me."

"Okay," I tell her. "I'll start from the beginning."

Damn, I hate beginnings.

The Reorientation

Part Three

The Actual Final Chapter (No, Really)

I'm a damn liar, you know.

I told you the previous chapter was the final chapter (along with the one before that). And that I was crying and shit.

Well, I lied.

I wasn't really crying—and it wasn't even the final chapter.

I don't know if you trust me anymore, but I promise you this is the last chapter.

I'm getting all sentimental writing it.

You should really see me now. I swear I'm crying.

I hate explaining myself. And when I must, I start crying. I'm like that little kid who cries every time his mom asks him to explain what trouble he has gotten into. I swear I am.

So, you probably think I confessed to Jess; that I told her how I'm a hack and blah blah blah. Well, I did. A little. I told her what went down. It's quite the story. You might need to sit down for this one.

One last time.

I'll be honest because I decided I should be.

The cameras are rolling now. I'm on national TV.

"So, Max McMillan, you have an announcement to make, right?"

"I do," I say. I'm looking right at the camera.

"Your latest novel—the critically acclaimed *The Final Romance*—is actually plagiarized."

"Yes," I say without hesitation. "It's completely and totally plagiarized."

The interviewer is stunned.

She's silent.

A hush comes over the already-hushed audience. Utter shock is seen on their faces, even grief.

She knew this was coming, but to hear the words out of my mouth means something else. It means this is no Max McMillan joke. It means that I am finally what I knew all along: a hack.

The world now knows, too.

I have been found out.

I have been placed on the proverbial, biblical scales and found wanting.

"What made you want to come out and confess? What prompted that?"

"I'm going to be honest," I say. "For once."

She's listening. I can tell because she's looking directly at me. Her toes are pointed in my direction, and she's leaning in close.

"We want honesty," she whispers. "Total honesty."

"Can I tell you a story?" I ask.

"Sure, tell us a story, Max," she whispers. "It better be true!" she adds.

We both chuckle.

I clear my throat.

"Look," I start to say, "this story begins a few years ago. Like, years and years ago. It begins with my good friend, Jack Gillman, author of *The Final Romance*."

"Sorry to interrupt but you're saying that Jack . . ."

"Jack Gillman," I say.

" . . . That Jack Gillman is the author?"

"Yes," I say. "Jack is."

She nods. "Okay," she says slowly.

"So, a few years ago, after a few successful novels, I realized that my good friend wasn't getting the attention he deserved," I explain. "And he's a proud son-of-a-gun. I mean, he's proud. He wouldn't let me help him. Not much, at least. He couldn't get any book published. Ever. So, there I was, writing junk and selling hundreds of millions of copies. And I have this friend—who is much better than me—not selling squat. I felt bad for him, and he knew that. Then his wife got cancer. And you must know this: I fucking hate cancer."

She laughs. "We all do, Max. We all hate cancer."

"Yeah, but not like me," I say. "I *really* hate cancer. So, I try to get his work published, but nobody would listen to me. They all think it's hogwash. Those idiot critics! I mean, you should have seen the reviews. Awful, awful reviews. And one night, I get this brilliant idea: What if I, Max McMillan, published *The Final Romance* under my name? The moment the idea came, I knew I had to do it. But I also knew Jack wouldn't let me. So, I decided I would just steal the damn thing. So, I stole it. Broke into his house one night and stole it right from under his nose. I'm that good. You should see me at night. I'm a ninja."

"Max McMillan a ninja?" She laughs.

The crowd follows suit. It looks like they're warming up to me.

"Anyway, Jack has these two little kids, you know. They're lovely kids. And I just wanted to help them out. And I knew if the book was published, it would make his wife happy and proud. And she needed some of that. You know, she's got cancer. It's an awful disease."

"Let me get this straight: You published this book to help a person with cancer?"

"I guess you could say that," I mutter. "It was the least I could do."

She's stunned. The crowd is stunned. Everybody is stunned.

The next day, the news articles and the blogs and all the stations are talking about Jack Gillman as if he were a national hero.

You know how many copies the book sold in a single week? North of thirty million.

I swear people had no idea what kind of crazy crap I was capable of. I told you: You had no idea this was coming. None whatsoever. I'm so damn good. I really am.

Anyway, I become a hero of sorts as well. I mean, they say nice things about me in the papers. Even the old lady, the one who used to chase me around, still chases me around. Even the kids. I feel like they treat me better. It's as if I became a holy saint or something. People don't even ask for autographs anymore. They just stare at me. It's interesting, really. I don't know if I'll ever get used to it. I mean, people are weird.

Jess is doing great. She about had a heart attack once I told her what I was up to. I think she loves me more for it. But that's Jess for you—she's always looking to find something to love in everyone.

You probably want to know what happened to Jack and Jane. Well, Jane is still alive. It's true. The last time I saw her, she was out gardening. Her hair is all grown out now. She looks pretty good. She seems healthy. Jack is famous now, you know. I mean, he's more famous than me. He made a few billion dollars and started a cancer foundation. He spends a lot of his time helping people. I'm happy for them. I really am.

We see each other once a day, usually for breakfast.

I finally got around to reading his book, *The Final Romance.*

I swear I cried reading it. It was the best book I had ever read in my entire life. It was so damn good, I re-read it three times in a single week. I never did that before. I guess there's always a first.

Some major Hollywood film studio called me recently. They want to make a movie about my life. I didn't know they still cared about me. But life is like that: always pulling punches and giving you weird surprises. Anyway, I told them I would think about it. I'm starting to get old and such. Life does that to you. You stop caring about fame and people and whatever. I have some good friends, you know. Jack and Jane. And Jess is a friend, too. Weird how we are married, and I truly like her. And Star. (She's getting married, but I'll have to save that romance for another book.)

Lucy is growing up fast. She's been reading a lot of books and I think she's going to be a writer when she grows up. I love her so much, I think I'm dedicating this book to her.

Nathan is all right, I guess. He's all nerdy and stuff. I think he plays too many video games in his spare time, but that's kids for you these days.

The kids came over to see us a few days ago and you should have seen them around Jess. (Did I tell you she's pregnant? Isn't that crazy? I swear life is weird.) Lucy helps her with the dishes and Nathan carries all the groceries in for her. Hell, at least he's a gentleman. I swear that's better than being a druggie.

Sometimes I sit with Jess, and we wonder what it'd be like to finish having all those weddings we once planned. I think we quit on the second or third one. (Jess got tired of planning them; it was too much work.)

I'm about to publish a new book. Did I tell you? It's a lot different than anything I've ever written. There's not going to be any sex in it or cursing or drinking or anything crazy. Just two people in love with one another living in a tiny house out in the woods. It's about small things. Nothing big ever happens in this one. Just small things. You know, a fawn walking across a lawn in one scene; a husband opening a car door for his beloved wife in another. Nothing special, but I like it. Jack read the book. He thinks it's my best work. I don't know what's good anymore—and, to be honest, I stopped caring. But if Jack Gillman likes a book—well, it'll sell a million copies. All he needs to do is write a blurb for it. If he does that, I just might become famous again.

In my spare time, I've been listening to this new album that recently came out. It's probably not going to win any awards or anything, but I think it's pretty good. It's called I ONLY HAVE A HUNDRED YEARS TO LOVE YOU. Anyway, I've been playing it on the record player for a few days now and really like one of the songs, "Black Sky, White Moon." You should look it up on Spotify. I swear it's not bad at all.

Did I ever tell you about the one time I almost broke a leg when I played hopscotch with the kids? It's a crazy story. One of these days, I'll have to tell you. Right now, I must return to doing some things around the house. Jess likes it when I help her. I prefer to do laundry and she prefers to vacuum.

Anyway, I don't really know how to end things.

I feel like if you'd let me, I would just keep on talking. But sometimes it's good to just shut up and listen to the kids playing outside. Lately, I've been doing a lot of that.

Just listening.

I learned a few things while listening. I learned that other people are interesting, too. In fact, I bet one of the kids out there is going to grow up and become president. I do wish it's a Her for once. Girls need a chance. (Maybe it'll be my daughter. Who knows? And wouldn't that be crazy? President Marianna McMillan.)

These days, I'm not much of an asshole. I love the kids, and I even like the old lady. I'd go so far as to say I love everybody.

But there is one thing I'll always hate.

And that's cancer.

Damn, I fucking hate cancer.

THE END

Things You Can Do to Help Stop Cancer

Please donate money to cancer research foundations, such as the Children's Cancer Research Fund. In addition to this, you can also spend more time with loved ones, friends, family, et cetera, who have been diagnosed with cancer. We always tend to think we have more time than we really do. (Even when you know you don't have time.) When my mom was diagnosed with cancer, we knew we had little time. We thought it was a few weeks. It ended up being a few hours. You have less time than you think.

If you enjoyed this book, please leave a review on Amazon and/or Goodreads. Thank you for reading my work, and I do hope you enjoyed it.

Acknowledgments

I have a lot of people to thank. Unlike Max McMillan, I love more than five. It's not much more, but it's more. One of my close friends read this manuscript many, many times. In fact, if it's a weekend, he might be reading it now. He read the first draft in one sitting, called me up two hours later, and told me it was my greatest work to date. I disagreed. It's been a few years and I've returned to the manuscript to expand it, edit out some of the vulgarity, and clean up the foul language. If you think this version is foul, you should have read the original. It was much, much worse. So, this is to William McLaughlin. He read it more than anybody else and loved it more than anybody else. If this book were a girl, he would date her. So, thank you, Will, for supporting me while I wrote this thing. Another person who read this thing and enjoyed it was Andrei Semenov. I'm grateful for our friendship. Michael Waitz edited this book several times. He suggested I cut out the foul language almost entirely and get rid of some of the more explicit scenes. I didn't argue with him. The book has very few f-bombs and such. I cut the scenes and refused to bat an eye. So, if you enjoyed this version of the novel, it's thanks to Mike. Otherwise, it would have been closer to a porno. Seriously. I'm grateful for my friends in Seattle who supported me while I wrote this thing. I was going through a rough patch, and this book was written to distract me from my pain. Here's to you, Oleg Solovey, Pavel Krutskikh, Brandon Vaara, Yuriy Stasyuk, and Roman Kondratyuk. I'd also like to thank my entire family for being supportive throughout the entire process. I love you. The character, Star, is based on an amalgamation of all my five sisters. (Yes, I was raised with five.) Cheers to you, girls! The inspiration for Jess came from a girl I met in Seattle in the spring of 2018. She was a ray of sunshine—and still is! I'm grateful that people like you exist, Ginger. I mean it. Finally, I'd like to thank my parents for raising me into the man that I am. I'm grateful to Mom for teaching me how to be an ethical person, and to Dad for teaching me everything I know about comedy and humor. The interest in philosophy, theology, and ethics I inherited from Mom; the comedy, the artsy writing stuff I inherited from Dad. Without them there would be no Me. I miss you two every day. If I forgot anyone, please forgive me. My brain is fried from all the editing. Honestly. And to anyone who has made it this far, thank you. Thank you for reading and supporting my work.

About the Author

Moses Yuriyvich Mikheyev is a Russian-American novelist who studied theology and philosophy at Whitworth University before obtaining his graduate degree in theological studies from Emory University. He is the author of numerous novels, including *Vanishing Bodies, This Time Next Summer*, and the children's book *Olivia & The Gentleman from Outer Space*. He is also an alternative rock musician. His debut album *I Only Have a Hundred Years to Love You* was released in 2023. He lives and loves in Los Angeles.

Made in the USA
Coppell, TX
03 March 2023